Resistance

—Bloodlines, Book 3—

K. LARSEN

Edited, Produced, and Published by
Writer's Edge Publishing
© 2014 by K. Larsen.
All rights reserved.

Other Books by K. Larsen

30 Days
Committed (Sequel to 30 Days)

Saving Caroline
Dating Delaney

Tug of War (Bloodlines, Book 1)
Objective (Bloodlines, Book 2)
Resistance (Bloodlines, Book 3)

ACKNOWLEDGEMENTS

First, to Emma, Emma, Sherry, Reagan, Marisa, Renee, Yaya and Tara. You know who you are. You are my sun! You make my life so much fuller just for knowing you. Thank you for all your encouragement and feedback. Resistance would not be what it is without you all. Truly. You help me in ways you will never fully understand!

I always need to thank my family. My daughter. My husband. My parents (all of them). My sister her husband. My friends. I have so many amazing people in my life. I'm truly blessed.

Resistance, crap. It gave me nothing BUT resistance while writing it. I don't know why. I don't much care why. It took longer to accomplish but I got there. I hope you fall in love with Sawyer. I hope you understand Pepper (better than before). I hope you get the "feels" from this book.

There are so many blogs who support me: Short and Sassy, Ana's Attic, SMI, I'll Be Reading, Book Quarry, Beg Me for Beta, Talk Books, This Redhead Loves Books, I Heart Books, For the Love of Books, I Love Bookie Nookie, Talk Books, the list seems endless to me. I've missed many. I know that. It's not that you aren't important to me, it's just that I can barely keep all the names and faces straight! I appreciate your pimping and love SO SO SO much. It's made such an amazing difference in my experience as an author. People, if you don't follow blogs—what are you waiting for?! They are awesome!

As always, you can find me on Spotify. All my books have playlists. Check them out! Feel free to stalk me—let me clarify—feel free to stalk me on social media. Please—I love you and thanks for reading my books—but don't show up at my door unannounced, it's just creepy. I love hearing from you all. Messages, emails, tweets, or posts. It brightens my day!

Okay, what are you waiting for?! Go jump into Sawyer!

Prologue

I'm crawling in my skin. Always. It never ceases. I've had this feeling for the last sixteen months. Time has done little thus far to mend me. People keep promising that time heals all wounds. Bullshit. I call *bullshit*. I intend to kick the "I have a penchant for wounded women" addiction. Relationships are a death sentence. Casual dating is my new m.o. Love is a four-letter word.

Love is not blind – it's blind*ness*. I didn't want to see. I *don't* want to see. I chose to ignore all the signs, and there were plenty. I was in denial. I pretended that Clara and I were more than we were. I knew it was wrong, but I buried that feeling way down deep, flat-out refusing to let it bubble to the surface where I'd have to deal with it—where *we'd* have to deal with it.

I'd tear out my insides if I could go back and change it. I don't want that statement to be true, but it is.

I didn't give her room to breathe. I never gave her the chance to come to *me*, to want me. I gave her what I wanted to give and convinced myself that it was exactly what *we both* wanted and needed. It wasn't.

Our arrangement had been simple. We slept together if and when we wanted to. We were always best friends first and we were to raise Allie together with love. Four years into it, did people assume we were married? Yes. Did people assume I was Allie's father? Sure. Did I love every second of that? Most definitely.

We met when Allie was four. It fizzled out fast but I stuck around as a friend because we got along so well and we'd been a threesome ever since. I'm all Allie knows of a dad.

The problem is, real women don't *need* you, they *want* you. Clara always needed me. I knew that. I liked it; hell, I loved it. I thought it would be enough to keep her attached to me, but it wasn't. She put my heart in a blender and watched it spin around until it was a pureed mess. I'd love to blame her entirely, but when shit hit the fan and she told me she never asked for my love outside of our arrangement, she was right. She never did and I never listened.

She was upfront, honest, and clear with me from the start. I tried to change that subtly over time, to embed myself into her life so wholly that eventually she would want to submit to me entirely. My game got sloppy, I grew complacent. I used my dating life to try and piss her off and make her jealous. Sometimes, depending on the woman, it worked. Mostly she held up her end of our deal and knew that we'd agreed to be able to date, therefore never bringing it up.

My weakness was that I let myself care too much. It was all a well-played game between the two of us. A balancing act with no safety net. Games that never developed into more than they were meant to eventually played themselves out.

Stupid

I watched her put the car in park and stare ahead blankly. It was just after one. Allie would be home from school in two hours or so. My motorcycle was parked in the driveway, she knew I was home. She exited the car, heading into the house. I was on the couch, head in my hands, doubled over. I know she was with him. I felt it in my gut.

"Hi," she called softly. The house was a disaster: dirty clothes strewn all over the floor, take-out containers littered the coffee table, and the entryway was covered in shoes. I knew she was probably disgusted at the sight. I snapped my head up, feeling more pissed than I had ever been.

"Were you with him?" I barked at her.

"Yes," she mumbled.

"Does he know?"

"Yes."

"How could you, Clara?" I shouted, pushing to my feet.

"Sawyer, we both knew this was coming. I don't love you like that." Her voice wavered ever so slightly.

"Really, Clara? That's the line you're going to use?" I snorted. "I've given you five years of my life. I've raised Allie, loved her, loved you! Does he even know you? Does he know Allie hates tomatoes or how to braid her hair? Does he know you hate mushrooms or how you take your coffee? Does he?!" I shouted. Her bottom lip started to tremble and her eyes welled with tears.

"That's not fair. He deserves the chance to learn all those things," she cried out. "I don't love you like him." Her words made me stumble a step backward. I felt them like she'd physically slapped me. "Sawyer, please...let me go," she pleaded.

I stalked to where she stood and pounded my hands on the wall at either side of her head, trapping her.

"Let you go?" I snarled. "I've supported you. I've loved you, I've cared for you and been there for everything. I've given up so much to just to stand by your side," I hissed.

"I never asked you to do that," she snapped.

"You never asked me?!" I shouted, offended. "Tell me, Clara, does he know you like it rough?" I growled and leaned into her face. "Does he know how much you like to be dominated and thrown around?" My hands slid up her arms, hooking Clara's jaw tightly. "Does he do it better than I do?" I whispered, seething.

"Stop," she cried.

"Stop?" I barked back. "Why? You never stopped for a second to think about me. Or Allie for that matter! Who the fuck takes off for a week and leaves her kid?!" She recoiled from me. "You're a liar and a bitch." I released her face and punched a hole in the wall next to her head before storming upstairs to my room.

"Sawyer..." she called as she stepped into my room.

"You're right," I answered.

"Huh?"

"You never asked me. I just gave and gave, hoping that you'd return my feelings," I said. How could this happen? I'd been so sure to entwine our lives together. I'd thought we'd had it all.

She knocked lightly on the door. I glanced at her briefly as she crawled onto the bed with me, staring up at the ceiling.

"I'm so sorry. I never expected this," she murmured. My hand found hers and grabbed it, holding on tightly. I just needed to feel her. Truth be told, I'd believed her. I knew she didn't plan all this to happen. It just did.

"What are we going to do?" I asked dejectedly.

"I can move out..." she started.

"No!" I cut her off. "You and Allie stay in the house. Please don't uproot her because of me."

"Where will you go?" she asked quietly.

"I'll find a place to rent."

"What about Bloodlines?" she hedged.

"We'll figure out a way to work together, all right? I just need some time," I lied. "You and Allie will always be my girls," I mumbled. Clara sobbed again.

"Sawyer, I don't want you out of our lives...I just want to be friends and free to fall in love."

"We'll get there. Consider yourself free," I muttered, rolling off the bed. "I'm going for a ride. We need to tell Allie tonight," I clipped, walking out, leaving Clara a bumbling idiot curled up on my bed. I wanted to hold her. I wanted to soothe her. Yet, I couldn't. She didn't fucking want that from me. I punched a hole in the drywall on my way out the door. My frustration was better taken out on that than her.

I was careless and stupid.

Clara is many things, but she's not an asshole, contrary to what most think. She's a straight shooter. Calls it like she sees it, a take-action kinda gal. She loves fiercely and wholly, even when she's not *in* love with you. If she loves you, you get all of her for better or worse.

All things I love about her.

Clara makes mistakes and people view her actions as self-centered, but they don't understand how she works. She's not a selfish woman. She's bold. Takes no prisoners. Driven. She gives back in so many ways.

People look at her and judge; they don't see or maybe they choose to overlook all the things she does from the heart. Her friends and family and their personal well-being come first. Her two jobs follow next. She's committed, blunt to a fault, and owns her flaws. It's refreshing, really. Her past was so much worse than even I knew—and I knew most of it—but when the parts I didn't know came out, so much came to light, for me at least. But by then it was too late for us. There was a void so endlessly deep, a chasm so impossibly wide between us there was no bridging it.

She loves Allie fiercely. She is a wonderful mom. I admire that about her. Sure, she's made mistakes—we both have—but she's never claimed she hasn't. When the school told her the chorus program was being cut, she volunteered to continue teaching the kids for free. Bloodlines thrives as a business because she puts her heart and soul into it. Even from a distance she's loyal to Marg and Amanda, staying in touch, talking often, putting in the effort to make sure they all stay connected. She's thoughtful and kind and funny. Maybe that's why being without her hurts so much or maybe it's just that after years of living together and pretending I feel empty not coming home to my family—the family I built up to more than it was. The one I should have realized was slipping away.

Dominic Napoli, Clara's now fiancé, swooped in and threw us all off balance. I can't say that had the situation been reversed I would have handled it any differently than she did. It was confusing. Where did we draw the line? How do you give up someone that has been an intimate part of your life without giving them up completely? How do you tell what's right and wrong? Can we maintain our family still for Allie? When you never talk about the hard stuff together, how can you expect the other to just know what's in your head? Bottom line, you can't. It was a clusterfuck to say the least. We've found some semblance of peace now. We're just rearranging. We both knew dating other people could lead to wanting to make it permanent with someone else, but I guess I just never thought Clara would be the one to settle down. She was always so restless, a free spirit. Being a two-household family is shitty and hard but I'm supposed to accept that and move on.

"Supposed to" being the key phrase.

I haven't figured the "moving on" part out quite yet. The heart wants what it wants, right? Or maybe the mind wants what it wants *for* the heart. All of those scenarios are bullshit, though. It's about being in control. Clara went for the gold. She carved out the happiness she needed, wanted.

Now it's my turn.

Chapter 1

I adjust myself a little to the left to go deeper.

"Please. I need this," she whines. Good Lord, this woman is going to kill me. I push in deeper, making slow, deliberate circles. Her skin is like silk, it feels so good. I stifle a groan and continue on. One hand grips her shoulder firmly and the other where her shoulder meets her neck.

Heaven. It's one of my favorite spots on her.

"Ohhh, shit, Sawyer, don't stop," Clara moans and breathes heavily.

As if.

"Yeah?" I grunt out. It takes all of my effort to control my breathing.

"Yeah, that's good. Don't. Stop." Her breaths come in short puffs of air as I stroke long and deep into her. I have no intention of stopping until it releases. I move a wisp of electric blue hair out of the way gently and watch as goose bumps break out across her skin. She's radiant today. I've never seen her more stunning than she is right now, even with her face scrunched up with tension. This is going to be the hardest day of my life. "Yes! That's it! Right there!" she moans. I shake the thought away and continue my plight. I never could say no to her anyways. I push harder and deeper until she lets out a feral-sounding groan and lets her body relax completely. I smile at myself for a job well done as her head hangs limply.

"Thanks for working that knot out, Sawyer, I wouldn't have made it ten feet with a neck cramp like that." She works her neck back and forth and rolls her shoulders, testing my work.

"Ready?!" Allie squeaks, pushing the door open. I'm thankful for the distraction. This day sucks. "WOW! Mum, you look awesome!" Allie squeals. The two of them are stunning. My girls.

"Most beautiful bride there ever was," I say sincerely, watching Clara's face in the mirror. Pure joy and excitement billow off her in gusts. You'd have to be dead not to feel it emanating from her, she's glowing. I wish it was me who made her look like that, feel like that, but it's not and I've accepted that...kind of.

No. That's a lie. I haven't. Maybe a little, but not completely.

She motions for Allie to come to her, which she does, and then turns to me with Allie under her arm.

"Family hug?" The look in her eyes should kill me. Stop my heart from beating. It's of pure love, but not the kind of love I want from her; this kind of love screams family, friendship, but nothing more. I swallow the lump in my throat.

Gutted.

This hurts.

I don't have to be here. I willingly agreed to attend today, and more than that, to walk her down the aisle. I am such a sucker. I lift my arms and spread them wide, plastering a smile on my face. When my two favorite girls wrap their arms around me tightly I do the same and hold them as close as possible to me, relishing in the feeling.

A perfect moment.

Clara pulls away first. Then Allie. And just like that my perfect moment is gone.

Allie beams up at me.

"You look pretty dashing," she compliments, grinning a wide, toothy grin. I wonder briefly when her face will finally fit her adult teeth now that she has them all.

"Dashing huh?" I arch an eyebrow, smile back at her, and tuck a loose strand of hair behind her ear.

She pulls the soft curl back out and makes a face at me.

"Sawyer. It's supposed to be there," she scolds, exasperated as only an eleven-year-old girl can be.

"We should go. It's time," Clara directs, wringing her hands together. Her skin looks creamy, almost giving off an aura of peace, like when the sun hits it first thing in the morning. I nod my head and watch as Allie bounces with excitement towards the door. I can't help but notice the exposed skin of Clara's shoulders and back. The dress drops down open to the small of her back, leaving it all exposed.

Her tattoo—my tattoo—is proudly on display.

My name is written permanently in the veins of the butterfly. I suck in a wheezy breath through my nose and follow Clara out. Allie is standing up ahead with Marg and Amanda when Clara stops short, causing me to shuffle my feet to avoid stepping on the short train.

"What the..." I grind out. She places both palms on my chest and stares up at me, tears welling in her eyes. Suddenly she's terrified. This woman will never stop surprising me with her instantaneous mood swings.

"I'm not good enough. What the hell am I doing?" she breathes, staring at me wildly. She looks like she's going to bolt.

My moment. This is my chance.

She blinks twice at me, waiting. I run my hands up and down her arms softly. Silky goodness. I take a deep breath and speak.

"Clara, you love him. He is crazy about you. You can do marriage." I grimace at my own words.

So much for my chance.

Sucker.

She tucks herself tightly against me and I wrap my arms around her, careful not to screw up her hair or dress. She sucks in a few steadying breaths and I take the time to do the same.

"What the hell would I do without you?" she sniffles.

I've asked myself that, like a fool, many times, but it seems as though she does just fine without me. Steeling myself, I stand her up straight and turn her around. With a swat to the ass, she's moving in the right direction again.

Toxic.

This whole day is poison to my soul.

I'll be lucky if I don't cry like a little bitch, drink myself into a stupor, and vomit all over the reception hall.

Really lucky.

"Sawyer, handsome as ever," Marg says with a smile and winks at me. Amanda gives me a sad smile and a head nod. Is it that obvious? I've done everything possible to get over Clara. To move on. Problem is, nothing seems to work. Sixteen months ago, when Dominic Napoli proposed to Clara and she accepted, I'd known my life with her was over. No hope left. Needless to say, it's been a long sixteen months. Sure, I'd put myself out there after I moved out and tried to date. Nothing seems to stick, or no one seems to stick I guess.

Death.

This must be what death feels like.

A tug at my hand breaks me from my depressing thoughts. Allie's wide smile beams up at me. She tugs again on my hand so I lean down to her level.

"You know I love you forever, right?" she says gently. Her eyes swell with pure adoration and loyalty.

Impaled.

It's like the kid can see through my soul.

Dammit.

"Allie, I'm fine," I promise her. "And yes, I know that you love me forever. The feeling's mutual, kiddo." She worries too much about me, for me. At eleven years old, she shouldn't bear that burden.

She kisses my cheek and turns around as the a cappella group starts singing *"Unchained Melody."* I watch as Allie makes her way down the aisle just as practiced. Dominic stands tall at the other end grinning from ear to ear in an entirely too expensive tuxedo.

Asshole.

I grind my teeth as Marg starts her descent and I feel like I'm losing air. It's happening. When Marg is halfway down Amanda starts walking and I take my place at Clara's elbow and wait. I'm going to suffocate. Her skin is warm and comforting in its familiarity but cruel and punishing in the reality of the situation. I should be standing where Dom stands. I should be walking down an aisle with her— just on the way out. I nudge her when it's our time to go because she's stuck staring at Dominic. Our first step changes everything. The singers in the balcony break out into their rendition of *"No Diggity."*

Surprise. Not the scheduled music selection.

Dread clenches my insides, twisting me up. I need this day to end.

Clara stops dead center in the aisle, wide-eyed, and spins around to the balcony. I mimic her movements. Her mouth gapes open and her eyes sparkle as she realizes this is indeed planned. Dominic and Allie grin like Cheshire Cats fifteen feet from us. A romantic surprise. Clara's chorus kids appear in the balcony and join the a cappella group. Everyone in the church is standing and clapping now. Good God. Why? This romantic gesture is going to throw me over the edge. All I want to do right now, in the moment, is lean down and take her lips to mine. To kiss her amid the fantastic music and have everyone else fade away.

The song morphs seamlessly into *"Faithfully"* and I know, right this second, that I was never good enough for her. Pain squeezes my chest, making it hard to breathe. I could have never given this to her.

I never would have thought to do it, I never would have thought she'd want it.

It hurts.

Knowing that truth hurts.

Finally the group mixes the song into Clara's favorite, *"Since You've Asked."* She's trembling on my arm now. It's the kind of tremble you *want* a woman to feel. I squeeze my eyes shut and grit my teeth to keep the smile on my face.

For her. I smile for her.

I will not be the one to ruin this day.

Her day.

I squeeze her elbow gently and nod my head to keep going. She follows suit and we walk. We reach the end of the aisle and I detach myself from her with a soft, lingering kiss on the temple and hand her to Dominic. He shakes my hand and smiles gently at me.

He's not stupid.

He knows.

I take my seat in the front pew on the bride's side and watch the whole Goddamned shit show happen.

I'm breathing.

"I do," she whispers breathily. For a split second I imagine that she is looking at me the way she's gazing at Dominic. With intimacy. I shake my head and focus instead on her long, inky lashes.

I'm not breathing.

"I do," he states with grandeur.

Mr. and Mrs. announced.

Everything seems so cut-and-dried.

So final now.

We're in the limo on the way to the reception. Clara has no family outside of Allie and myself...well that's a lie, but it's true, too. She has no contact with her mother and I don't blame her. So I'm it. The bride's pictures will be me, Allie, Clara, and Dominic. I slap on a smile and do my best to just make it through the next hour. Why do brides need so many damn pictures anyways?

Torture.

"You okay?" Marg asks, sliding up to me while Clara and Dom are posed in various positions. I watch as they smile at each other and kiss. It's a lover's kiss. An intimate kiss. One that screams, "we're having a conversation without words."

"Nope," I clip.

"Sawyer," she starts, angling her head up to look at me.

"Please don't. I already feel like a big enough vagina today." I stuff my hands in my tuxedo pockets and stare at my feet silently.

"You're a good man. The best, actually. Try to enjoy yourself," she mumbles before leaving me alone.

"Sawyerrrrrrr!" Allie shrieks, running full tilt at me. I crouch down, arms spread wide, and catch her as she leaps into my arms. Picking her up, I spin us around until I feel sick. Her peals of laughter make my heart feel lighter for the moment. She's the most amazing eleven year old I've ever encountered and I'm nothing but lucky to be her surrogate father. I hear the shutter click of a camera and realize that Clara directed the photographer to capture me and Allie's impromptu moment. Well at least there's one picture I'll enjoy.

I'll never give her up.

I smile at her beautiful youthful, face, happy she's still here with us. I almost lost my mind after the accident. The car that hit her was going too fast and the driver wasn't paying attention. Allie didn't stand a chance even though she was on her bicycle on the sidewalk. As if that hadn't been bad enough—seeing her mangled and bruised—we had to endure waiting for a kidney transplant afterward. The damage done internally from the accident had led to a kidney transplant and a slew of other messes. Namely her real father emerging for the first time ever. At least he disappeared as fast as he'd shown up. It had all worked out in the end but the mess that ensued during the ordeal was enough to drive a man insane.

Clara.

The sight of her glowing with love and happiness makes my heart constrict. I wanted to be that man. For a while I was.

Sorta.

Our life was perfect. Our family, albeit unconventional, was perfect.

Then he happened.

Dominic Napoli stole her heart. He stole her away from me. It happened in slow motion. I could feel the distance between us growing. I could see where it would all end up, yet still I stayed and took it.

I held out hope. I wanted her to pick me.

Pick me.

Did I tell her that?

No.

Not really.

Not until it was too late.

I should have fought for her from the beginning. I should have noticed and taken it as my cue to step up my game. To woo her, or whatever that shit's called. I should have done *something*.

I didn't.

Women don't want status quo and that's what I gave her. Then again, some people won't love you no matter what you do. Comfort, familiarity, and security were never what she truly needed. I knew that. I knew how to work around it, even. She got restless, I wrangled her in. That was our game. I knew what I was doing.

I should have altered my game.

I didn't.

Too late now.

The flashes blind the happy couple over and over until I can see in Clara's face that she's had enough.

She rocks up on her toes and whispers something to Dom who then grins and promptly lets the photographer know that they are done. He should have seen that in her face like I did. He should know her that well.

He should.

I do.

Therein lies the problem.

The reception is amazing. I want to hate it, I really do, but Clara planned it and we're so alike in music choices and style that I can't find it in me. My foot's been tapping the entire time I've been sitting at my table. All our favorite songs play softly in the background. I'm lost in the moment. Lost in thoughts. Just lost.

Amanda kicks me under the table and nods her head. I grunt and snap out of it, eyeing her wildly until I realize what's going on. It's toast time. Standing, I lift my glass to the Bride and Groom's table. Clara sits perched on Dom's lap, lost in the moment. It looks good on her.

Radiance.

Happiness.

Bliss.

She's all of those things right now.

The room is quiet. So quiet. I breathe deeply and start before I lose my nerve.

"Ladies and gentlemen, as 'father' of the bride I have the pleasure of making the first speech." I smirk right on cue, sure to bear my dimples to all the single ladies. "I have been given lots and lots of advice on what or what not to say, such as keep it short, no smutty jokes, try and remember...names...et cetera. However, it is been over six years since I was allowed to say anything without being disagreed with, laughed at, or ignored, so this is too good an opportunity to miss. At the end of the day it is my speech and I can say what I like." Clara's eyes narrow in on me. Her brown to my blue eyes holding each other, waiting. I drag a hand through my shaggy dirty blonde hair. I know she's worried.

She shouldn't be.

"Thank you all for coming to help celebrate this very special day. As I look around the room I realize how many friends Dom and Clara have and I hope that you all have a wonderful afternoon and evening. Today I must admit that I am the proudest man in the world to have accompanied Clara down the aisle. I think that you will all agree that she looked stunning." I stop and wait for the requisite head nods. "This is where I am supposed to say a few embarrassing things about her when she was younger but she works with me and she probably knows more gossip about me than I know about her, so I have called a truce. Suffice it to say that I am very proud of how she looks today and the woman she's become and am delighted that she has found someone who she obviously loves and cares so much for."

Now we get to the tricky part of the speech.

"According to the Internet's idiots' guide to wedding speeches, this is where I am supposed to give advice on the subject of marriage. Many would probably say that I am probably not the best person to do this. Perhaps the only thing I know about marriage is that it's the time when you stop painting the town and start painting walls and ceilings. But I've never been married, so what do I really know?

"I know that falling in love's not hard, yet staying in love is." I pause and stare directly into her eyes. "Anyway, you two don't need my advice. The only thing I would say is that you must choose the right partner for the right reason and I think that they both have done this."

I suppose that after five years of living with her I ought to be able to manage something a bit more constructive.

"Dom, just remember these three words: *all, just, and only.* You will hear them time and again, like, 'all you need to do is, it *only* costs so much, and it will *just* take five minutes.'

"These are all gross understatements, but as a great philosopher or comedian said, 'women are to be loved and not understood.' Mind you, helping around the house is not a bad idea. I know from crime statistics that there has never been a case of a wife shooting her husband while he was doing the dishes." Everyone chuckles right on cue.

"Marriage is the meeting of two minds, of two hearts, and of two souls. It is clear that Dom and Clara are a perfect example of this." I pause and raise my glass higher. "May they be blessed with happiness that grows and with love that lasts and a peaceful life together." I bring the glass to my lips and chug everything in it.

Clapping. So much clapping. It hurts my ears.

Clara rounds the table, heading right for me, and slams into me with such force that I'm now seated again. Her arms wind around my neck as she strangles me. I can feel warm, wet tears at my neck.

It breaks me.

"Beautiful, Mr. Pokey, just beautiful," she mutters softly into my ear. I cringe at the old term of endearment for my dick. Mr. Pokey retreats into himself. I pat her back gently and she unlatches herself from me.

"Go back before Dominic kills me with his glare," I grumble. Her head whips around to look at him and she chuckles.

"It's good for him," she quips before kissing my cheek and sauntering back to his lap.

His lap.

Not mine.

After the speeches have been made, the food's been eaten, and the cake's been cut, the party takes off. Music blares, the dance floor throbs, and I stand at the bar drowning myself in gin.

"What's got you in such a snit?" Amanda says as she wobbles to a halt next to me. Clara's two best friends are the shit. I love Marg and Amanda but Amanda always seems to want in my pants. Not that she doesn't stand a chance, I just don't seem to be into anyone at this point. It's too bad, because Amanda is smokin' hot. I'm grumpy, though, and her presence irritates me at the moment.

"Really?" I bark. I sense immediately that my response was a little over the top and try to soften my face but I'm so wasted I'm not sure if it's working or not. I probably just look like a stroke victim.

"Sorry, Sawyer. It's tough, I get it, but it's been like two years since you two've been together or lived together, you know? It's time to move on, mend, heal, whatever you want to call it." She waves a hand sloppily in the air.

"Wanna fuck?" I blurt. Where did that come from? Her eyes widen with surprise.

"Holy shit. YES!" she squeals. I can't help but chuckle. She's subtly been hinting that she wants to get in my pants for the last six months. I'm ready to leave and she was the first opportunity that presented itself.

Women.

"Let's get outta here. The bike's out back." Her eyes widen with excitement and sloppy lust.

"Are you good to drive?" she asks hesitantly. I can almost see her mentally kicking herself for distracting me and possibly ruining her chance at tonight.

"You staying here?" I ask. She nods her head vigorously up and down.

"Lead the way, princess."

She grins wide and starts for the lobby. I follow Amanda out of the reception hall but glance back one last time at Clara. Her eyes find mine and for the first time all day they don't shine with bliss. It's only a split second but regret, sadness, hurt, even, is directed at me while she watches me walk out with her best friend.

Clara decimated my heart.

I swing my head around and watch as Amanda's pert little ass sways drunkenly in front of me.

I'll do anything to forget for a couple hours, to block out my twisted obsession with Clara.

Anything.

Chapter 2

DEATH BY HEART EXPLOSION

I've lost her.

Two little words shot deep into my heart and decimated any hope I'd held onto: "I do." That was the moment it was really final. Completely over. I've been drunk most every day since the wedding. It seems to help. I like feeling nothing. It's a nice change for me.

Fourteen days. Fourteen days since the wedding. Fourteen days they've been away on the honeymoon. They came home last night.

I only know this because Allie called at 11:00 p.m. when they landed, squealing about snorkeling, zip-lining, and other fantastic adventures they'd had in Fiji. *Good for fucking them.* That's the last thought I have before a knock at the front door startles me from my thinking.

I open the door wearing the same jeans I'd been wearing the night before, but with a black t-shirt and an unsnapped, faded denim shirt over it. I haven't even shaved. Clara's warm brown eyes and tight little body assault my vision. It almost hurts to look at her. I was getting close to being able to not remember her.

"How long since you've eaten a full meal or had a few hours of sleep? Have you walked by a mirror lately?" Clara prods, looking shocked at my appearance as she pushes through the entry. I scrub my stubbly jaw with one hand and cock an eyebrow at her.

"Sorry, but visions of you on your honeymoon getting fucked senseless interfered with my ability to function," I snap. Oh sweet baby Jesus, why did I say that out loud? It's like I'm forever missing the filter needed to speak to her lately. She sinks onto the plaid camelback sofa, looking embarrassed and pissed off, straight down to the roots of her hair.

I'm an asshole. A bonafide shithead.

"Fuck you, Sawyer," she spits, glaring at me.

"I'm sorry." I sigh deeply and collapse on the couch next to her. I scratch at my scalp and try to think of a decent apology. That was uncalled for. It's been long enough that I should be moving on now. *Should.*

"Allie wants to see you, like, NOW, but I had a feeling you might not be in the best shape to accept eleven-year-old visitors. And thanks a lot by the way for Amanda," she snaps at me, changing the subject. For that I'm grateful.

"What about Amanda?" I close my eyes and rest my head on the back of the sofa.

"WHAT ABOUT AMANDA?!" she shrieks at me. I scrunch my face up and plug my ears. The lungs on that woman could kill a small town and make babies two counties over wake up and cry. It's torture.

"Clara, please, you're making my eardrums bleed," I groan, cringing. She swats my hands away from my ears, looking like pure evil.

"I've been fielding texts from her the entire vacation! *THAT'S* what! Of all the people you could've screwed, why her?! I mean, not just screwed, but you called out my *NAME*? Sawyer, really?" she yells and throws her arms up in the air in dramatic flair and slaps her palms down on her thighs.

Fuck.

Amanda.

I'd almost managed to rid myself of that memory. Colossal screw-up on my end. Never have one-night stands with people you know or with friends of people you know. Stranger danger does not apply to the one-night-stand scenario.

"I don't have a good excuse," I admit sheepishly. The truth will set you free. *Right*?

"Well tell *her* that, not me! I didn't need to know any of the details of your goddamned night together," she huffs, irritated.

"I think it's best we just have no contact," I say flippantly.

"Yeah," she snorts. "I gathered that from her whining about you not taking her calls or texting her back," she drones on sarcastically. Can't she just cut me some slack?

"What? I was wasted, in a bad place mentally, and fucked your friend. It happened. Deal," I snarl. She stares at me for an ungodly amount of time, her face twisted up in a scowl, before standing and kicking a pizza box on the floor. It slides two feet before hitting a pile of sneakers near the door. God, I love her mad face. Sick.

I'm sick in the head.

"Pick up the house, shower, and get dressed, Allie will be over in three hours," she buzzes, thoroughly irked. It makes me want to smash a plate over her head and fuck her at the same time. My emotions for her always sway from one extreme to the other. Never a happy, contented medium. She slams the door behind her, leaving me grumpy and irritable. I grind my palms into my eyes and get started cleaning up because one thing that will never wane is my overwhelming drive to be the best father Allie will ever have. Clara's right about that, I need to at least make it appear that I'm pulled together and ready for her to spend the night.

For all the hurt I feel over Clara and I, it still amazes me that in an impossibly hard situation she was able to be true to herself. She did what she needed to, to carve out her own slice of happiness. That's more than I can say.

Chapter 3

ROAD NAMES

Five months ago, just after Clara asked me to walk her down the aisle, I'd felt that since I was in the throes of a midlife crisis, I deserved to do something impulsive. For most people, it seems, that means getting a tattoo, or having a threesome, or buying a new sports car, but I own a tattoo shop, have a motorcycle, and have no leads on how to obtain a threesome. Okay, well, I'm probably capable of securing a threesome, but really, it seemed like a moot point. My impulse move needed to be big. I needed something that would stay in my life permanently.

Epic.

I joined Mayhem Motorcycle Club, or rather, I prospected. Motorcycles have always been a passion for me. I've always owned one and I've always craved being out on one over driving some fancy sports car. At fourteen I had my first bike, a 90cc Honda Trail. It was black and chrome with a side pipe and high ground clearance. By sixteen I had gone through two other bikes, a CB 160cc Honda and then a CB 305. In the 12th grade the Honda was traded in for a 650 Triumph. Just before I met Clara I bought myself a Harley Softail Fat Boy and I've never looked back. My bike, outside of Allie, is my baby. To many, riding a motorcycle is an acquired taste, but to others it's just in the blood. It is a lifestyle. Many don't, won't, and can't understand that.

I don't buy a bike only to burn it up racing it on the streets and then trade it away for another. A motorcycle to me is almost a sacred thing. I ride to bring things back into focus. My bike has a soul. It is almost a living, breathing being, an entity of its own. I need it to stay sane. Like Clara, I can be restless in life and the bike takes that feeling away for me. Plus, chicks dig it and of course Allie *loves* bike rides with me.

To become a member in the MC it takes about a year of prospecting, but that really didn't seem like a problem to me. It keeps me busy, out of the house, and I've managed to meet some pretty interesting new friends, Hoot and Carmine being two of them. I really like Hoot, he's...well, a hoot. Always smiling and down for a good time or a long ride. He's a bit younger than me, maybe mid-twenties but we get along really well. Carmine is a little shady but I try not to judge someone without getting to know them really well first. Carmine is always down for a party which is fun, but he's a little rougher than the rest of the club. Sometimes I wonder why Beau, the president, took him on instead of telling him to find a 1% club. Carmine seems to think that taking the less-legal way around things is the right way.

The prospecting period shows Mayhem if I'm willing to ride on the hottest days of the year or the coldest days of the year, and it proves how committed I'll be to the club. They wanna know how respectful I am and if I'll stay loyal. It also gives them time to show all us newbies about the MC culture and teach protocol.

Clara had yelled and pitched a royal fit when I'd told her, stating that those kinds of people were not to be around Allie. I had to nicely explain to her that this was not Sons of Anarchy. This was not a 1% club. Mayhem is a legit MC. They don't participate in illegal activities. She seemed to relax a bit after that. It helps that because of my profession I've now commissioned all the club tattoos.

Clara was all for that, considering that with one year of membership you're allowed to get a certain tatt, at five years another, and at ten years more club-related tattoos, but most of us have lots of non-club tatts and are always getting more work done. Once a few of the guys came in and Clara got to meet them and know some of them she really loosened up about the entire ordeal. Not that I need her permission, but for Allie's sake and the sake of ease, it helps. I've even been comfortable bringing Allie to some of the more family-oriented gatherings. There are a couple other girls her age that she seems to get along with well. It's actually nice to get out and do social things together instead of hiding out in the house the entire weekend. My need for Clara seems to dissipate more and more each day, thanks to Mayhem and Allie.

"Sawyer?" Allie calls out over the blare of the music as she approaches me.

"What's up, Alliecat?" I say and tussle her dark chocolate colored hair and she shies back from me a step. Her glower is almost identical to her mother's. It's uncanny and endearing simultaneously.

"Uh, how come no one has names here?" she asks, cocking her head to the left. I can't suppress my chuckle, which clearly doesn't please her.

"Most of the guys go by nicknames that they got when they were prospects like me," I explain.

"Um, okay, but what motorcycle dude wants to be called *kitten*?" she inquires.

"None," I answer as we both start laughing. "But love, we don't get to pick our nicknames so it kinda doesn't matter if you like it or not. If it sticks, it's yours."

"Kinda like Alliecat?" she huffs. Now that she's eleven she's expressed clear disdain over the decade-long term of endearment Clara and I use for her.

"Right. Just like that." I smile down at her. God, she's stunning. I am not looking forward to boys showing interest in her any time soon. Not. At. All.

"Well, what's your nickname?" she asks, scooting under my arm. I wrap my arm around her shoulders and squeeze her tightly to me. She has the ability to make my world feel at peace when she's tucked into my side. I love that about her. "Don't have one yet, kiddo, but I'm sure I'll get one," I say while taking her perfect face in. Pride ripples through me just looking at the kid. She turned out so damned awesome. I love this kid.

"If I have ideas, who should I tell them to?" she quips back at me. I chuckle and shake my head at her. No way. The kid might only be eleven but she's decades above her level and I can only imagine what "ideas" she might have.

"You tell my dad," a tween boy a few feet away pipes up. Allie slides her eyes to him and blushes deeply before pushing her face into my stomach. Every protective nerve in my body fires off warning messages.

"Who's that dude? Do I need to talk to him?" I lean down and whisper to her while I hold her to me tightly.

"Sawyer!" she squawks at me, looking up, horrified. "He's no one!" She pulls away from me and skips over to her friend Lisha without another glance. I will never understand girls. Never.

"I'm Danny." The boy steps over to me, hand outstretched. I look him up and down. If he thinks he is getting anywhere near Allie, I'm going to have to throw down. Yes, I'm willing to beat a kid senseless. I take it and give it a firm shake that says, "I don't care if you're twelve or sixty, I will not hesitate to beat your ass if you mess with my girl." "Sawyer," I answer rather shortly.

"I know, my dad says you're one of the good prospects." He gives a head nod and drops his hand.

"Who's your dad?" I ask.

"Beau," he answers. Well color me shocked, the president of the MC has a son. I had no idea. He's a cool guy but tight-lipped about his personal life.

"Danny buggin you?" Beau says, slapping me on the shoulder as he appears out of nowhere.

"Not me, but I gotta say," I say as I look directly into Danny's eyes, "keep your mitts off my Allie." Danny's eyes bug out slightly but he regains his composure quickly. Laughter rumbles out of Beau.

"I think they're both a little too young for all that, no?" Beau asks lightly.

"I think I'm going to go find Neal." Danny looks down and shuffles his feet before taking off.

"He's a good kid, but twelve is an awkward year," Beau says and chuckles.

"Allie's only eleven and *really* innocent," I say, stressing my words.

"I wouldn't worry about it. Everyone has crushes at this age." He chuckles at my overbearing nature.

"Nope. Allie doesn't. My Alliecat will most certainly never have a crush on anyone until she's twenty," I state, horrified at the thought of my little girl fantasizing about a boy. They don't do that at eleven, right? Shit, what was I doing at eleven? No. Nope. No crushing at eleven.

"Damn, bro, you got a lot to learn. Fatherin' a girl isn't easy, but you better learn to loosen the reins before she just slips out of the harness to get away from you." He smiles big before slapping my shoulder again and walking off to talk to more people. Allie, dating?

Kill.

Me.

Now.

Over my dead body will she be dressing herself, wearing makeup, or flirting with boys anytime in the near future. Shaking myself from that train of thought—or more accurately, the anxiety train—I head over to the prospect table to hang out with Carmine and Hoot. Carmine and I are the only prospects who don't have nicknames yet. Not that I'm complaining. Generally nicknames come from something that happens during your prospecting year that sticks out, or a funny story. There's a brother named "Hardware" because during his prospecting he broke his leg in so many places he had to have rods and screws put in. There's another brother named "Free Fall" because he jumped a fence at night not realizing the other side was a twenty-five-foot drop. I'm not really looking forward to what my nickname will be.

What I *am* looking forward to is my prospecting time coming to an end. Don't get me wrong, I love it and everyone has to put their time in, but when you're a prospect, you're a nobody. You have no say. You have no vote. If you are asked to do something within the limits of the club bylaws then it needs to be done.

I clean bikes or watch the bikes when the rest of the MC is out. I even fetch drinks and food. I've driven to pick up brothers who were broken down, and prospects are designated drivers when we're needed to be. Often when the old ladies have a ladies' night we're asked to attend to watch over them. A peon. A tiny little shit on the bottom of a boot being tested endlessly. I wanted to go from life crisis to badass overnight but it didn't exactly happen that way.

It's a brotherhood and we're being tested on how badly we want to be a part of that. Many prospects fail to make it. Some problems the club has had are members failing to be committed, whether it is from being lazy or that they just don't have the time needed to be in the MC.

This lifestyle isn't for everyone; it can beat you down, the constant going, especially as a prospect, since you're expected to be everywhere and do everything. Owning the shop with Clara and having certain days free each week, being single, and the fact that this club is based in Christiansburg, Virginia, only twenty minutes from Blacksburg, makes my time prospecting a lot easier than some of the others. I don't have to worry about the nine-to-five, full-time job deal. I can arrange and rearrange my time at the shop with Clara and my time with Allie.

"Sawyer," Allie starts, tugging on my sleeve. I set my beer down to focus on her.

"Why do you call your dad by his name?" Lisha interrupts. Allie spins around, hands on hips, to face her friend.

"Because I can." The amount of sass that was in that simple statement should knock Lisha flat on her ass.

"Allie," I growl in warning. We've been through this many times before.

"I know!" she says and throws a hand up to stop me. "Be polite," she says, irritated.

"Lisha, I'm going to hang out with my *dad* for a while, okay?" Oh sweet Jesus, this is like watching a miniature catfight. Lisha looks confused and pouts before walking away.

"Allie, that was kinda harsh," I scold.

"I don't like explaining to people our business," she chirps at me defiantly. Ever since the truth came out two years ago about her real father, she's been extremely protective of me and our relationship. I've tried explaining that it's okay. Just because we learned about Daniel and Senator Hollingsworth doesn't mean that our relationship will change.

I've been raising her and I'm never going to stop. Her feelings only amplified when Dominic and Clara moved in together. Allie might be a child, but she's fierce when she loves and I'm lucky that she loves me.

"I'm aware, but we've talked about this, remember? It's okay to explain to people that I'm your dad but not your biological one. No one is going to judge you for that," I offer.

"Don't care," she clips, "people should just mind their own business, *Dad*."

If this is eleven, I am not looking forward to sixteen or twenty or anything until thirty, when women generally come back to reality and act sane.

"Hey, don't get sassy with me. I'm the one you're all possessive about." I shake my head at her and grin before poking her side. She squeals and leaps away from me before coming back and sitting on my knee.

"Okay. Sorry. I was just coming over because Lisha says girls can't be in this club. That's stupid and sounds like a lie," she states. God, I love this child. Honest and speaks her mind. Bows down to just about no one. Makes me so proud.

"Actually, Lish is right. It's an all-male club. The history is that MC stood for Male Club, but changed to Motorcycle Club over the years because some clubs do let women join, just not this one."

"That's bullshit," she huffs. Carmine and Hoot both snort and snicker at her words.

"Allie..." I groan and roll my eyes.

"I know, no swearing. Be nice, polite, no cuss words, get good grades...yada yada," she preaches flippantly.

"Keep it up and I'm telling your mom," I groan.

"Ugh, please don't. Seriously, she's all...less...sassy since we moved in with Dom. He makes her more ladylike," she pouts.

I can't help it—she's right, of course, but the way in which she chose to word it is dead-on. My ribs constrict as I try to hold back my laughter. It sorta hurts.

"None of that matters, you are still expected to act like a lady. A sassy lady, but a *lady*," I stress, narrowing my eyes at her.

"Whatever," she scowls. I squeeze her to me and hold tight for a moment before letting her back up to go find her friends.

This kid is going to give me an ulcer. I need to get out more. I need to dive back into the dating scene. Maybe.

Chapter 4

Five Months Later

The bar is quickly filling up. I glance around and spot a seat at the bar. One lone stool. I have a rare night alone and nothing going on at the MC. Allie has been going through a spurt where she wants to spend weeknights at my place because it's closer to school. Not that I mind, but everyone needs down time once in a while. It's been a while since I've gotten laid and I just can't seem to make myself mix business with pleasure at Mayhem. There are plenty of girls there who want to be someone's ol' lady, but they've all been around the block a little too much for my taste. The MC is something I do for me, not something I do to get pussy.

"This seat taken?" I ask the long, black flowing hair next to me. It's shiny and I bet it's soft. I kinda want to touch it. She turns her head just slightly so she can make out my face. Her eyes are a warm brown with flecks of light gold in them. They accentuate her olive skin. She might do for the evening but I'm in a shit mood and really don't feel like chatting all that much, so maybe not.

Clara and I had a rough time coexisting at the shop today. Things have been tense since they returned from their honeymoon. I don't know what's up but I'm sure it'll all come out soon enough with the way she's been brooding and picking fights with me. The black-haired chick's lips make this perfect little unintentional pout that takes my mind off my wandering thoughts.

Hot.

I watch her gaze flit to my left hand hanging limply at my side. No ring to be found. She smirks, just barely, but I caught it.

Flirt.

"Nope," she answers and turns back to her drink. I slide onto the stool next to her and flag down the bartender to order. Stealing a glance, I notice a tattoo peeking out of her t-shirt sleeve and I wonder who did it and how much more of her it covers. It's only natural to wonder. There aren't many shops outside of mine and Clara's. We know all the local tattoo artists around. The bartender slides my beer to me with a nod and heads down to the other end to attend to more people. I stare into my beer, feeling tired and run-down. Everything's been such a clusterfuck the last year and the wedding was just the icing on the cake. With the tension going on at the shop between me and Clara, and Kylie calling me non-stop wanting to go out, I've been in a funk, mood-wise.

She's gone.

Really gone.

Married with a ring on her finger for six months now.

I stupidly held out some small nugget of hope that we still had a chance but I handed that chance, literally, to Dominic when I gave her away that day. I'm not hung up on Clara, I'm really not.

Fuck. My. Life.

"Play a game with me," prompts the black-haired beauty's sultry voice as she turns to me. I don't bother slapping a smile on my face; social graces can suck it. I turn to her slowly, being snapped out of my pity party, and let my gaze openly roam her body. She's the kind of girl who has curves in all the right places, just enough chest and hips that you can hold onto. She looks young. I bet she tastes sweet. I wonder if she'll be enough to make me forget Clara for a night.

"Fine. I'll bite," I say with a grin, but it doesn't reach my eyes, I can feel how fake it is. She doesn't seem to notice, though. Maybe she's subpar, intelligence-wise. Somehow I find that many of the really attractive women out there are a little lacking in the brains department. Maybe it's because they never had to try. Their looks did all the work for them.

"Truth or lie?" she asks. A small scar at the bridge of her nose crinkles. I want to know how she got it.

Stumped.

Did I mishear her?

I'm not sure what that means.

"I don't know?" I ask quizzically. She throws her head backwards and laughs loudly. It's a guttural laugh. Her eyes look like they hold the secret to life as she laughs. It's incredibly sexy. She shifts her body so that her knees face my body.

She's invested now.

I know body language.

"I'll give you a topic after you choose truth or lie. Then you have to tell a truth or a lie about the topic, as you picked."

"Ahh, okay. Lie," I retort, slightly uneasily. I'm not sure this game is going to end well. I watch her with fascination as she thinks of a topic. It's almost like you can see her thoughts moving around in her head. She's really quite beautiful. Her skin is olive colored and blemish free. Her hair hangs in very long, thick sheets down her back and she looks fit. Pouting mouth, neck like a swan, just natural beauty. A little too old, I think, to be a VTech student, but maybe she's here for grad work.

"Kids," she states, leaning back slightly and looking smug.

She's waiting on me.

"Kids? Okay. The lie," I start. "You will feel nothing but joy and love. It will feel like the most gratifying thing you've ever done. You will be rewarded for any hardships you face while raising them with a grateful, loving, wonderful child by the end. It's all sunshine and puppy dogs," I finish.

She snickers before taking a sip of her drink. Her lips wrap around the edge of the glass in the most seductive way. It's like a train wreck—I can't tear my eyes away.

Want.

Lust. My dick twitches as I watch her. Yeah. She'll do.

"Did I do it right?" I croak, trying to drag my mind out of the gutter. She seems so indifferent to me, to this whole thing she suggested. She's all business. It's throwing my game off.

"Oh yes, well, really, I don't know, I don't have children so maybe the lie is truth or the truth is a lie."

Her no-bullshit response is telling, but only to a point. I like talking to her and I'm going to take a chance and throw her game back at her.

"Truth or lie?" I quip with a wink. Her nose wrinkles up with surprise. That tiny scar disappears with the movement.

I like it.

"Topic first," she answers, fingering her glass with slender fingers.

"That's like cheating," I say and chuckle. She shrugs and remains silent. "Fine. A one-night stand." Her lips twitch for a moment and she studies my face intently. She's not shy.

Desire.

It's in her eyes.

"Lie, then." She cocks her head to the side and studies my face some more. It makes me squirm internally. Bringing a hand to her mouth, she traces her pouty bottom lip with her fingers and closes her eyes. Her finger drops to her collarbone. "It starts with us, here. You like what you see. We flirt intelligently over drinks for a bit before I excuse myself for the restroom. When I come out you're waiting for me. Your hand grabs the back of my neck and pulls me to you. Our lips collide. Soft. Silky. Exploratory. Perfection." She sucks in a deep breath and slowly lets it out. Her voice is low but clear.

I'm hot.

It's really so hot in here.

"Taking me by the hand, you lead me out of the bar and take me home. We're not even through the threshold when you tear your shirt off, followed by mine. You, of course, look photoshopped with your six pack of rippling abdominals and I have a Victoria's Secret model body. You lean down, firmly holding me. Your tongue traces trails from my neck down and over my breasts. It's divine, actually. Slowly tasting me. My nipples are hard little nubs. Savoring me. Making me burn from the inside out. I wrap my arms around you and jump up. I love the feel of your hands digging into my ass and your erection pressing into my crotch as you walk us to the bedroom, never breaking our kiss." Her voice is calm, confident, and sultry.

This girl will kill me.

I know it.

I can sense it.

She's a death wish.

I want her.

Here.

Now.

On the bar top, I don't care who sees.

Her chest heaves as she speaks, her breasts pushing up and out against her tight cotton t-shirt. Her full lips, moving as she speaks, are captivating. I can't tear my eyes from her mouth. She breaks the tense silence, continuing, "You toss me on the bed and yank my pants off with a growl. I'm wet. So wet. For you. I tremble with need for you. I tell you to touch me. I tell you I need you to touch me, to taste me, and so you do. Your hands explore every last centimeter of my skin, setting me on fire. Your tongue follows suit. When your mouth reaches my pussy I squirm and wiggle and beg you for more. I'm a mess of pleasure by the time your rock hard co..."

"I get it," I interrupt, feeling like I'm about to explode. There is no way my face isn't fifty shades of crimson right now.

She smirks and leans forward. "The truth is a cold shower."

"Oh? Now I want to know what the other answer would have been." And I do. Her brashness, her brain, it's like everything she says is calculated.

Intense.

I need more.

Desperately.

"I'll tell you on one condition," she says and smiles coyly.

"Uh. All right, shoot."

"You take me home after." Shock courses through me.

That's the only thing I feel. Don't get me wrong, one-night stands are about all I'm good for these days, but usually I have to work for them a little more than this. It makes me wonder, actually. She's gorgeous. She doesn't need to be so upfront. Why no chase?

Do I care?

Nope. No, I do not.

Hot, young piece of ass sitting in front of me will do just fine. I can already imagine her panties dropping to her knees for me.

"Deal," I say and shrug. I am the motherfucking king of the world right now.

"One-night stand, the truth." She clears her throat and pauses, thinking. "It's terrible. We flirt, but it's strained. We awkwardly make our way out of here. You don't know whether or not to hold my hand or kiss me. You want to, but you aren't sure that's how the situation works. We fumble through undressing, unsure of our abilities in the sack now that it's go time. I have scars and you probably have some weird mole or beer gut that's well hidden under clothes. Bodies slapping, sweat beading, strange sounds produced by two bodies that don't know each other. It's dirty and not sexy at all really. The orgasms are mediocre at best because you don't know my body and I don't know yours. We don't have the history that lovers do, the time spent learning all the likes and dislikes. You'll move over me and I'll make noises and pretend it's the best ever, and quite frankly, you'll do the same because you feel the same. Men aren't so different from women in that regard. You'll finish and we'll pretend to really want to do it again or even talk to each other again and the best part of the night will end up being the relief you feel when I'm gone. The pretense will be over and you can finally just lay back and relax," she finishes, sounding slightly bored.

She's not mad.

She's not being sarcastic.

This bitch is being completely honest and it's the most attractive speech I've heard in a long time. Her soft porn account got my dick twitching, I won't lie, but she just called it out and owned it.

I fucking love that.

"Let's go have the worst night of sex ever then, yeah?" I chuckle and stand. I toss a fifty onto the counter to cover her drink as well as mine and stare at her expectantly. Her eyes narrow slightly in a way that makes me wonder if I've done something wrong. "How'd you get here?" she asks.

"I walked," I answer, realizing that I walked from the shop. But we can't walk to my house, it's too far. Maybe the back room at the shop wouldn't be so bad after all.

"I live in the next town over, so I can drive us." She waits, the cutest face of irritation shadowing her features. It's as if she's put out, having to deal with this at all. It's comical, really. Maybe I should just take her in the bathroom quickly and be done with it.

"Better idea, princess," I rumble. "There's a hotel close to here. I'll pay. Let's go there."

Her hand rakes through her long, black hair as she glares at me. Uh-oh.

"Don't call me that. Ever. A hotel is fine," she clips, shrugging on her hoodie. Note to self: Pet names are not appreciated.

"Name, then? I should probably know what to scream out in our moment of awkward pleasure." She smiles at me. It's a real smile this time. Toothy and white and stunning. She has dimples that I want to kiss at either side of her mouth.

"Ma...Pepper. You?" she asks.

A fake name, perhaps?

Do I really care?

No. Maybe. Her coffee-colored eyes bore into mine. She blows a single strand of black hair from her face.

No, definitely no. I do not care.

"Sawyer," I answer. She sidles up to me coyly and wraps an arm around my waist. Her body fits well with mine. She's taller than Clara.

Shit.

No.

No comparisons.

Not tonight.

Her head rests just in the crook of my arm. "I think you're decent so I'll give you one tip: I like oral." I'm shocked by her bluntness and boldness but I silently thank her for the tip because I find myself actually wanting to please her. I think I want to prove her wrong. I want her truth and her lie to be swapped, if only for a night. I lead her to the door and hook her elbow with mine as we head a block up and to the right towards the Hilton.

We walk in silence. It doesn't feel awkward, though. She seems completely at home in her silence. It puts me at ease. I don't want to ruin the moment by saying something dumb. I don't know her at all but I want her all the more because of that.

Then a thought slams into me.

A simple kiss.

It can make or break two people, really. Just before the hotel, I pipe up, "We should probably kiss first." I tug her to a stop. She stares at me quizzically.

Her bottom lip is sucked between her teeth as she stares up at me.

Sexy.

"What if I don't want to kiss at all?" she retorts finally. She's all sass. It makes me hard. So hard. Who is this chick?

"I'd say you're lying." I tangle my fingers in her hair.

Soft.

Like cashmere.

Honeysuckle perfume wafts from her in small puffs. It's a great smell on her. Her hands grip my arms with strength and she looks wide-eyed but still playful. She's taunting me. Lowering my head, I lick her bottom lip before drawing it out.

Heat.

Shit.

I didn't expect to feel a connection. I work my lips over hers, our tongues mingling. My dick is painfully hard.

From a kiss.

I'm a sucker.

S.U.C.K.E.R.

But her lips are divine. I'm not going to stop. I drop one hand from her hair down to the small of her back and pull her tightly to me. I need more. I want to feel more. Her fingers stroke the back of my neck at my hairline. She nips my bottom lip before smoothing it with her tongue. She plays with my lip ring, tugging on it playfully, and I groan.

She's fire.

Her hips press into mine. I pull back.

"Let's check in," I all but pant. Her face is flushed with color and her eyes look dazed and confused.

Good.

Mission accomplished.

She nods her response and looks away. Her face drops ever so slightly. Distance, a gaping chasm of it, forms between us. She's withdrawing. I do it all the time. Put up the protective barrier. Fight feelings. Well, good for her. I can't wait to make her come. I can't wait to hear my name screamed from her lips. Fuck sloppy and disappointing. I'm not rushing this tonight. We will both get what we want, how we want.

Chapter 5

USED

The room is quiet as we enter. Just our breathing can be heard. Unsteady breaths. I'm nervous. She's different somehow. I just can't figure out why. I watch as she walks to the TV and clicks it on.

"I have rules," she states simply. I don't answer. I don't think she really wants an answer. I wait. "No chitchat. No snuggling after. Don't bother trying to pretend to make love to me. This is fucking. Got it?" She turns, hands on hips, and waits with her head cocked to the side.

"Yes," I huff.

She's bossy. I like it.

She flicks through the TV channels until settling on one of the music stations.

Electronic. Interesting. Turning to me, her hands skim the hem of her shirt and with a quick motion it's tugged off. Her bra goes next, followed by her pants. Her eyes never leave mine. It's as if she's sizing me up, taking stock of my reaction.

Control, I realize. She needs it.

It's very apparent in her movements, her demeanor. Just panties. Plain white cotton panties. Somehow I've never seen anything more attractive. Her body is toned and muscled. A faint scar mars the skin at her waist on her right. A longer, jagged one near her belly button. I want to touch them. Kiss them. She faces me in nothing but those damn cotton panties.

Hot.

Her lips move almost imperceptibly. I squint to focus on them better. It looks like she's counting. I advance on her slowly. I'm worried that if I move too quickly she might just vanish into a cloud of smoke. Her body language screams dominance, confident control, rage, even. But her eyes, her eyes scream with sorrow and defiance. The two emotions clash, making it hard to read her. I can see what she *thinks* she needs and I know what I'm going to give her instead.

"Kneel," I state gruffly, my decision made. Her eyes widen before narrowing. I run a fingertip from her shoulder to her hip along her ribs. "Kneel," I repeat firmly. She flashes me a fairly bitchy smile but complies. I grab a pillow from the bed and place it between her legs. Fully dressed still, I lay my head on the pillow between her legs as she kneels over me. Her expression is of wonder. I move my hand up her inner thigh to the heat between her legs. Pushing her panties aside, my fingers slip inside of her. I watch her face as a soft groan leaves her lips. I pump my fingers deeper then withdraw them slowly. She watches curiously.

I like that.

She's already so wet. Hooking my thumbs on either side of the plain cotton panties, I pull, ripping them from the elastic waistband. I push the ruined material up her waist further, out of the way. I wrap my hands up and over her thighs and pull her down onto my mouth. Breath hisses from her as I lick the length of her slowly but firmly. Her hands rest atop mine, supporting her while kneeling. She tastes sweeter than I thought. I lap at her leisurely, focusing on every crevice and fold.

She's strong.

Her thighs contract, pushing upward but I keep her pressed firmly to my mouth until she starts to wriggle and buck.

Nip. Suck. Lick. Repeat. God, I love the clit.

She's grinding my face so hard that I think I might suffocate. But hell, what a way to go. I release one thigh and spread her wide with two fingers.

Sucking her clit hard, I swirl my tongue around the bundle of nerves. She gasps and grinds down on my mouth, scraping herself along my teeth lightly. With a drawn-out shudder she finishes in my mouth. I lap at her center slowly while she comes down from her high, her muscles slack and useless.

"Fuck..." she hisses between pants.

"On your back," I command. She thinks that was my A-game, but she's about to get a lot more. She narrows her eyes at me.

"I prefer to be on top." Her voice is firm and assertive.

"Get your pert little ass on your back. Now," I growl as she stands. Pushing down the ripped panties from her waist, she steps out of them as I sit up. She drops to her knees and pushes my chest hard.

"My turn." Her hands run down my torso, stopping at my belt buckle. Her fingers work swiftly and before I have time to form a thought she's tugging my pants down around my ankles. Not that I don't want that perfect pout wrapped around my dick, but now's not the time. I sit up, snake an arm around her waist, and roll, securing her under me. Her tattoo sweeps up colorfully just over the top of her shoulder. I want to lick it. I want to trace it in its entirety with my tongue. I want to see the rest of it. All I know is that there are gorgeous blossoms so far.

"On your back I said," I rumble, dipping my head to her neck and kissing.

She stills under me.

Meeting her gaze, I notice she looks like she's mentally checking out on me. "Eyes," I bark and her eyes snap to mine and come into focus. Her hands lift my shirt up and over my head. Her brown eyes have the strangest flecks of gold in them. They're intoxicating. Her fingers feel like feathers torturing me as they explore every ridge and valley of my abdomen. A single nail traces the outline of the tattoo on my stomach. Her lips toy with my nipple piercings, making it hard for me to form a rational thought. Reaching back toward my ankles, I fish around my pocket for a condom and quickly put it on. Lifting her left leg up and back so that her knee rests near her head, I tease her entrance slowly until her lips part and the faintest sound escapes.

"More," she whispers.

If she wants more, she'll get more. I thrust in fast and hard and draw out again slowly before pushing in deep again. Her eyes roll back and close and she adjusts herself to my rhythm. She's tight and wet and gorgeous as she writhes underneath me. "More. I need more," she pleads, her voice small. More I can do. I move her right thigh to match the left and pin her down, my forearms on the backs of her thighs, and increase my pace.

Harder.

Deeper.

Shit yes.

Her legs push up against me as she angles her hips to take me deeper. A groan, or more likely a grunt, leaves me as I near the edge. She's so brazen with her needs, her wants. I haven't been this turned on in a long time. Her hands come up between her legs and wrap around my neck tightly. I'm done for as she grips me, just teetering on the edge. I slam into her as she finds her release with a low, feral-sounding groan. Her body relaxes as her pussy convulses around my dick, milking it. I push in a few more times before I come. She arches up and kisses me hard as I withdraw from her. She drops her legs to the floor, unfolding herself from me.

"I lied," she blurts out, still flushed.

"About?"

"One-night stands." She grins, standing. Scooping up her pants, she inserts one leg, then the other, and tugs them up. Her tatt starts at her buttocks, twisting up her back. The gnarly trunk of a Magnolia tree spans into twisted branches. The work looks familiar. The colors are bright, the detail immaculate. Miller, perhaps? If Clara or I had done it, surely I'd remember her. It had to take a week at least. I want a closer look but she's moving too much. She buttons her pants.

Commando. I watch from the floor as she finds her bra, clasps it, and pulls her shirt back on. She's leaving.

She's really going to bail.

I pull my boxers and jeans back up from my ankles, realizing I never even got my boots off, and buckle myself up.

"That was really fantastic." She picks up her bag and turns to me. "I...I appreciate it." She stumbles over her words. Her face registers determination, but something more, too. Regret maybe?

I can't believe this chick.

There is no way in hell that she's just bailing. I mean, women don't do that. It's just...wrong.

She's broken. I slap my hand to my forehead and drag it roughly down my face. How did I not notice before? She's so broken. It wafts off her in thick, foggy sheets masked in honeysuckle and beauty. I take three easy strides and fold her into my arms snuggly. Her whole body tenses. Rigid. She looks up to me, startled, but stays still. I stare into her haunting eyes and wish that whatever was missing from her life I could provide. But I can't.

"That was amazing." I lean down, tangling my hands in her long, silky hair and kiss her passionately. She instantly kisses me back, relaxing in my arms. Lips gliding over lips. Tongues dancing together.

There's fire in it.

The kiss is wicked.

I want more.

There is more here.

I haven't felt more in a long time.

She tugs my lip ring again with her teeth and I pull back and look at her. She looks taken aback and flustered. "I want your number," I state, caressing her cheek with my thumb. "No..." she replies, hesitantly looking anywhere but my face. I'm about to argue with her when she pulls out of my grip, opens the hotel room door, and steps out.

Just. Like. That.

She didn't even look back.

That's the thought I have as the door clicks shut. What in the fuck just happened? I know she got off. I know she got off twice. It was damn hot and our bodies clicked. How the hell did I just get played? I tug on my shirt, check the room for anything that may have fallen out of my pockets, and head out, slamming the door behind me. Like a fool, I keep my eyes peeled for her down the long corridor and through the lobby just in case she comes back for me.

As I exit the hotel an older Harley cruises by at quite a clip. The engine rumbles as the tires grip the pavement.

Damn.

I love an old Harley. The way they sound, the power they give off, the feel of it vibrating between your legs as the wind whips around you. Shaking my head, I make the walk two blocks to the shop where my bike is parked. I climb on to my very own Harley and start her up. At least *she'll* still be around in the morning when I wake up.

Chapter 6

PUSH AND PULL

Julieanne is face down on my table, her porcelain skin smooth and soft, perfect for the reverse cityscape I'm doing. She has Rome from mid-spine up across her back already. Now we're doing a mirror image under it that looks like it's underwater. It's very intricate and very cool. Pepper's soft skin under my fingers infiltrates my mind as I touch Julieanne's back. What the fuck. I can't seem to shake that night from my brain. Pepper. Damn. Just. Damn. I zero in on the work I'm doing and try to focus.

"Tell me what's happening with you," Julieanne says above the sound of the gun.

"Not much. Just Mayhem stuff and Allie," I reply.

"Come on, there must be more than that. Seeing anyone?" she purrs. I suck in a breath and raise my eyes to Clara. She doesn't meet my gaze but I know she's listening. She's been cleaning her station up for the day for the last thirty minutes. It usually only takes her fifteen.

"Nope. Just enjoying life," I respond blandly.

"Wanna grab a drink sometime?" Julieanne asks, a twinge of hopefulness in her voice. My mind wanders to Pepper again and our one-night stand. I haven't seen her around since then and it irks me. I'm curious about her. If I'm honest, she's occupied plenty of my thoughts over the last month. I tasted the merest sample of her, but I want more. So much more. I want to indulge. Something about her, even after the way she left abruptly, captured my attention. Her body is a constant source of spank bank material these days.

"I'm not really up for dating," I share.

"It's just a drink, Sawyer, not a marriage proposal," Julieanne huffs.

"I'm out," Clara calls from her station, giving me a chance to dodge Julieanne's response. "Don't forget you have a two o'clock appointment tomorrow for Hoot. I'm on for Carmine's at three but it looks like that's it for tomorrow."

"Great."

"Oh, Allie wants to stay with you tonight. You cool with that?" Clara asks.

"Yeah, I promised her we'd hit Adventure World," I say and chuckle.

"You? Skating?" Clara bursts out laughing. Julieanne follows suit and I have to stop my progress on her latest tattoo until she steadies her breath.

"Hey, what the kid wants, the kid gets," I state.

"You spoil her," Clara says with a grin. She brushes a bright pink chunk of hair over her shoulder.

"Yup."

"All right, well...see you later then. I'll drop her after chorus practice," she informs me while waving her goodbye to Julieanne and me.

"All righty."

I resume my work on Julieanne and try to dodge her feeble attempts at getting me to agree to a drink with her. All the while I can't seem to get Pepper's seductive pout out of my brain. I should give Julieanne a go. Really, I should. She's pretty. She's nice. I've known her a couple years now and she's never shown any sign of being crazy. But, I don't feel anything around her. No pull. No attraction. Nothing. She's just...there.

At four I close up the shop and stop at the MC to make sure nothing's needed of me before I head home and wait for Allie.

"Bro, you *need* to hook me up with that fine piece of ass," Carmine pleads as I show him the pictures of the piece I was working on for Julieanne today. His face looks greedy as he drools over the pictures. He looks slightly ghoulish. He's slender with sharp features, shiny dark hair, and dark eyes. Like Gollum with hair.

"She's single," I say and instantly regret it. Why did I tell him that? Julieanne is too good for him.

"What are you waiting for?!" he scoffs.

"I'm not sure you're good enough for her." I laugh. "She's a nice girl."

"I can be nice," Carmine drops sarcastically.

"Right," I answer. Carmine, although fun to hang with, is a little harder than the rest of us. I'm not really sure what's different about him, but something just makes me a little hesitant around him. He's always disappearing to take calls that no one seems to know about. Or he's taking care of "family" stuff, yet he doesn't have a wife, kids, or family in the area. No one else seems to overthink his rough-around-the-edges character but to me, he seems a little off. Like he's waiting for the right moment to pounce. At what, I don't know.

"Give her my number and let her decide," he says, lifting his chin at me.

"Maybe," I offer noncommittally. Footsteps echo down the hall from the back of the clubhouse and Beau appears to the left of the bar with a smile on his face. He's the kind of man you want to be like. He almost always has a grin on his face and keeps business and pleasure separate in his life. It seems to work for him.

"What's up?" he calls out as he approaches Carmine and me.

"Finished work and thought I'd see if anything needed doing here before the kid gets home," I offer.

"You have that *kid* a lot for not being her dad," he returns, not in a scolding way, but more out of curiosity.

"That kid is mine. I am her dad. Blood isn't everything," I respond firmly.

"Good answer," he says with a head nod. "Carmine, what about you?"

"No kids and I'm here for whatever." His response is snarky and cold. Why does he set off red flags for me?

"Good enough. Boys, I'm out. My boy's got a game tonight. Sawyer, I need another bit of work done to my sleeve. You got any time open in the next week or so?" he asks.

"For you, sure. Just lemme know," I tell him. My pocket vibrates as I push off the stool at the bar. I tug my phone out of my pocket and grimace at the screen. Kylie. Swiping the screen, her text appears.

"If you stop by, I'll make it worth your while."

I roll my eyes, momentarily wondering why I ever thought she was worth dating. She thinks she's being seductive and coy but it only comes across as trashy. If Carmine asked me to set him up with her, I would say yes. They seem like a much better match. Ever since Clara and I ended things, Kylie has been like cum after a blow job. Sticky in all the places you don't want. I ignore her as much as possible but there are times she hunts me down and almost refuses no for an answer. I should have known that she'd pursue me thinking I was finally free of Clara. I glance up at Carmine and smile.

"I have a number for you," I say.

"Lay it on me, bro." He grins widely. I text him Kylie's number before heading home. There, maybe he will have more luck with her than I did.

What the hell was I thinking? Adventure World Skating Rink is packed with tweens and slightly older little shits. Pop music blares through crappy speakers that crackle and pop and the constant sound of arcade machines dispensing coins is enough to make my ears bleed. Allie tugs on my hand, bringing me out of my mental fog.

"The lobby isn't really that cool," she says sarcastically. I realize as soon as we stepped into the lobby I just stopped moving. I try to unwrinkle my face and smile at her.

"Right. Where to?" I ask, hoping I sound excited instead of horrified. Allie has been begging me to take her here ever since one of her friends had a birthday party here. I thought after hearing about it that it'd be a fun night out for us. Now I'm regretting my decision greatly. This is every parent's hell. Loud. Crowded. Sensory overload. I stifle my groan and let Allie lead me to the front counter where my wallet will no doubt be raped and pillaged of whatever's in it.

I'm lost in a sea of dancing neon lights, blaring music, and small children squealing while moving at light speed when I crash into Allie's back, sending her off balance.

"Hey!" I squawk at her. She turns to face me, looking irritated, her eyebrow arched and expectantly waiting. She looks just like her mother. Dark hair, golden skin and a glower that can bring a man to his knees. I look past her to see that we're at the counter. Every single atom of oxygen leaves my body at that moment. The black-haired stunner sitting behind the counter raises one eyebrow at me and smirks. I forget all the complaining I was just thinking about and suddenly relish the kid at my side who forced me to come here. The gorgeous, raven-haired girl's chocolate eyes are fixated on mine and I feel like I'm living in a dream state after thinking about her so much. Pepper.

"So? What size?" she asks, looking amused and perplexed.

"What?" I ask, confused. So much for playing it cool.

"Skate size. What size are you?" she explains. Her eyes flit over Allie and light up with recognition. What is happening?

"Sawyer. What the heck. Why are you being so weird?" Allie complains. I look down to her and stare blankly. Pull it together, man. This is your chance.

"Uh, thirteen," I respond. Allie looks between me and Pepper curiously.

"You look familiar," Allie states bluntly to her.

"You do too," Pepper responds, nodding.

"My mom did your tattoo," Allie says with certainty after a beat.

"Yes. And you had a crush on a kid named...Adam," Pepper says.

"WHAT?!" I cry out. Allie turns sixty shades of pink and Pepper laughs as she turns around and grabs two pairs of skates before setting them on the counter.

"Sorry, I didn't mean to rat you out," Pepper says sincerely to Allie.

"Uh. Yeah. Well. I don't like him anymore, so..." Allie says, struggling with her speech. I look at Allie and narrow my eyes. We don't keep secrets. Or at least, I didn't think we did. I'm going to have to drill the kid now to get information. Crushing on boys is NOT cool. I really hope I just conveyed all that with my look.

"Thirty-two dollars," Pepper states, boring a hole through my head with her eyes. Damn, those eyes. Her yellow work t-shirt is baggy and hides all her perfect curves, but I know what lurks underneath and it has me way outside my element. Her jeans hug her legs and she's wearing little makeup. It makes her look younger than the night we met. Her hair is loosely tied up in a bun yet she couldn't possibly be any prettier somehow.

"Sawyer!" Allie's little voice distracts me from my train of thought.

"What?" I ask, confused. Allie looks at me, also confused, then to Pepper, and then back to me. Her eyes bug out and then the world ends.

"You *like* her!" she squeaks happily. Pepper's gaze is cool and smug as she watches me drown in my attempt to quell the situation.

"Allie. That's...uh...rude," I sputter. Allie grabs my wallet from my hand and turns to Pepper.

"Here," she says, fishing out some money. "I think he likes you and...you should like him back because he's really great."

Pepper's jaw drops as she takes the money and she makes the most adorable choking sound.

"Wow. You're a real spitfire, aren't you?" she asks Allie.

"My mom says I'm full of sass." Allie preens, thinking it's a compliment. Pepper laughs and I find myself unable to rip my eyes from her or form a complete thought. I want to do dirty things to her. Scratch that, I need to do dirty things to her. I shake my thoughts from my brain and focus on the facts. Allie. I'm here with a kid. I don't know jack shit about Pepper, not really. She's great as a fantasy but...reality is a bitch and she's probably bad news.

"Have fun," Pepper says, handing my change to Allie. I grab my skates from the counter and find myself wondering what she's reading as she pulls out her Kindle without giving me another glance. I back away from the counter and slam into a mother carrying a tray full of sodas.

"Oh SHIT!" I shout. "I'm so sorry!" The woman looks at me with those parental, dead, lifeless eyes that say she hates her life and she hates that she's here on a Friday night. I pull a twenty out of my pocket and hand it to her. "For the drinks. I'm really sorry. I didn't see you there." I swear the woman only grunts before walking away. I refuse to look back and find out if Pepper saw all that. Refuse.

I set my skates down on the bench Allie picked and pull my button-up shirt off to let it dry out. My t-shirt will have to do. Allie starts squealing with delight next to me.

"What is it?" I ask, chuckling.

"You GLOW!" she gushes. I glance downward to find that my white t-shirt is indeed glowing in the black lights. Awesome. Just awesome. I haven't felt this ridiculous in years.

Allie holds my hand as she easily leads me around the roller rink. I'm not so great on skates and I feel like I've been clutching the rail or wall for most of the evening. I also feel like the biggest fool. If Pepper is watching me right now there is no chance for my manhood. None. I'm done for.

Allie tugs my hand, sending me full bore into the middle of the rink. I'm going to hit someone. I just know it. I'm going to take out a small child at this clip. Allie laughs as I flail and appears in front of me with her hands out to slow me down. I clutch her shoulders for dear life and let her lead me.

"I think I need a break!" I shout over the music to Allie who is pretty much dragging me along at this point.

"Okay. Will you get me a soda?" she asks, unaware of my embarrassment.

"Sure."

"Get it from Pepper," she teases, making googly eyes at me.

"Uh..." I let out, trying to focus on staying upright.

"She's pretty. I remember thinking she's nice, too. You should talk to her," Allie prompts. Sometimes I really wish the kid wasn't as smart as she was.

"What do you remember?" I ask, trying not fall on my ass.

"She got a big Magnolia tree. It was when you and Mom were taking different days at the shop, so, like, a while ago. Mom worked, I talked to her. She was nice but sad. She was really sad," she chatters.

"About what?"

"I dunno. I didn't ask."

I release her hand as we near a break in the wall for my exit and clutch the railing for dear life.

"Kay," I manage to say as I perilously make my exit and find a bench. I remove the roller skates with a sigh and rub my feet. Grown men were not made for this. We just weren't. A smile creeps over my face as I watch Allie whiz around the rink a couple times, bopping to the music and practicing something called "Shooting The Duck," whatever the hell that is.

Pepper looks lost in her book as I approach the counter. A few strands of her hair have fallen out from her bun and hang perfectly around her face as she reads. Her long legs are crossed at the knee and the kindle rests atop one. Even hunched over like she is, she's different. She licks her lips as she taps the screen, turning the page, and I stifle the groan that wants to come out of my mouth. She's got to have something very wrong with her. I never seem to be attracted to nice, boring chicks.

"Hey."

She looks up, startled from her reading.

"Good book?" I hedge.

"Uh, yes," she replies with a blush. A blush? Really?

"What is it?" I ask.

"What's what?"

"The book?" I ask.

"Oh, nothing..." she returns quickly, a small blush creeping up her neck. Hot. Why is everything she does so attractive? I must be really hard up. Maybe I'll call Kylie later.

"Ah, I see. Mommy porn," I retort.

"What?" she squawks, making me chuckle. She closes the case and sets the Kindle aside.

"I need two Sprites please, and a phone number," I order, feeling slightly cocky.

"Coming right up." She smiles before shuffling around to grab cups. When she returns with two full sodas complete with lids and straws, she blinds me with a radiant smile.

"Whose number would you like?" she asks while ringing me up.

"Yours," I say. Damn, wasn't that clear?

"I don't give mine out," she deadpans.

"Why not?"

"Because I don't date, so why would I give my number out?" Pepper is nothing but resistant. What am I doing wrong? She stares at me over the brim of my sodas, her eyes seeming to delve right into my mind with no effort at all.

"Why do you think I want your number for a date?" I say coyly.

"Because you've been thinking about me for the last month," she says nonchalantly. What the hell? How could she possibly know that? I do my best to hide my reaction. Women are strange. Their intuition is like pure magic.

"That's a rather bold assumption," I finally say.

"Maybe," she says, smirking. She has one perfect dimple on her left cheek when she smirks. I want to kiss it.

"What if I just want a repeat of our last encounter with no date?" I ask. She sighs and leans over the counter towards me. She eyes my lip ring lustfully as I lean in a little bit to make sure I can hear her. This is it. This is where she agrees to see me. I'm so pumped up I can hardly stand it.

"What if I don't?" she answers. Deflated. I am completely deflated. Had I read the signs all wrong? Wasn't she flirting? I know for sure she definitely had an orgasm that night. Yeah. Definitely.

"Pepper. Listen. I'm going to be honest here. I don't give a shit if you want a repeat or not. I don't give a shit if you want a date or not. I'm not able to take no for an answer." Maybe assertive alpha male is what she wants. Women totally go for that.

"Not able? Explain." There is a hint of a smile playing on her face. Good.

"I have thought about you. A lot. Just one date. No, wait, not a date. Will you please hang out with me for an afternoon? I'll take you on a bike ride and we can just talk." What am I doing? I sound like such a whiny douche. She's got my game all off. Hang out? I really want to slam my head on the counter but I resist the urge.

"Bike as in bicycle?" she questions. Her thumb traces her bottom lip as she waits for my answer. She is so distracting.

"No. Motorcycle."

"You ride." It's more a statement than a question but I answer anyways.

"Yes."

"What?" she asks.

"Harley Fat Boy." It never gets old saying that. I feel pride every time those words leave my mouth.

"I'm a Sportster gal myself," she counters. I think my heart just stopped. Like stopped and fell out my asshole. She can't possibly be real. Screw all my previous thoughts, I will take the chump's way and *hang out* any day of the week with her if that's what it takes.

"You ride?!" I say, completely shocked. She nods her head. I watch her nibble her bottom lip and mull something over.

"No date. I will, however, go on a ride with you if you promise to stop somewhere good for breakfast pastries," she says.

"Deal. When and where should I pick you up?" I am doing the biggest fist pump ever on the inside right now.

"I'll meet you. You're on your bike and I'm on mine. Got it?" she says, cocking her head at me.

"Uh, okay." I stumble over my words slightly. Not what I was hoping for but it's better than nothing.

"How 'bout tomorrow morning around ten? I could meet you here or at Bloodlines, since you know where that is?"

"Know where that is?" I scoff. "I co-own it with Clara. You know, the lady who did your tattoo?" Her eyes widen a smidge before she pulls her look back together. I wonder what she's thinking.

"Fine. Let's meet there then."

"Kay, well, see you tomorrow at Bloodlines," I say, grabbing my sodas and feeling like somehow I just won the hot-woman lottery.

"Hey!" she calls. I whirl back around and smile at her. She totally thinks I'm sexy. I knew it!

I smirk coyly.

"You forgot to pay," she states in a deadpan tone. Her head is tilted to the left and she's staring expectantly at me. I am the biggest idiot in the entire world. That is the only thought my brain allows at the moment.

Chapter 7

MIND BLOWN

I got almost no sleep last night. I think *maybe* from three to five I slept. Allie woke up to a full breakfast of pancakes, bacon, and eggs at eight a.m. By nine we were finished eating and I'd dropped her at her friend's house for a play date. I am an anxious wreck. Seriously. I want our non-date to be so awesome that she craves more time with me. That smile. She could light up a whole damned town when that smile reaches her eyes. I need a good plan for this date. I want it to be perfect. I want it to be so good she has no choice but to go on a second and third date with me. I don't know exactly how to do that, though, since she seems immune to my normal wooing. I've been pacing the shop for the last thirty minutes, driving Clara nuts.

"Jesus, Sawyer, sit the fuck down. If she sees you with your head pressed against the glass waiting for her she's going to think you're a total loser," Clara barks at me as I pace past her. "What's so special about this chick that's got your panties all wadded up anyways?" she snickers over the band *Adventure Club* filtering through the speaker system.

"Your talking isn't helping," I retort, irked. I hear the roar of the engine before I see the black Sportster pull up to the front of the shop. She's right on time. She swings a leg gracefully over the bike to stand. Her black leather pants leave little to the imagination and her cropped leather riding jacket hugs all her curves. I think I just came in my pants. Thank God I filled the saddlebags on my bike earlier with our brunch stuff. I'd never be able to remember everything I wanted with her here, distracting me.

She pushes through the door and waves to me as she comes towards the front desk.

"Hi," she breathes, blowing her bangs from her face. That gorgeous black hair hanging down her back shines under the lights.

"Hi," I say and grin stupidly.

"Magnolia, right?" Clara greets as she comes to a stop next to me. Pepper looks stricken with panic for a moment and she tenses noticeably. Clara doesn't usually make people flinch for at least the first year of knowing them.

"No. Sorry, name's Pepper," she finally offers, extending her hand. "You did a Magnolia tattoo on me, though." She smiles. "And I'm happy to report that I still love it."

"Huh." Clara looks perplexed. "I could have sworn your name was Magnolia, too."

"Nope," Pepper clips.

"Right. Okay then," Clara says with a smile. It's not a genuine smile, though. It's a catty smile. What the hell is going on right now? I watch the girls stare each other down for a moment before stepping in. I lean in and kiss Pepper's cheek softly. I know this isn't a date but fuck it. She recoils from me only enough that I would notice but still...it stings.

"You ready?" I ask.

"Yeah," she replies. I watch as she turns and starts for the door. Her ass is damn near perfect. Her black hair swishes as her hips swing back and forth in those leather pants. Damn.

"Sawyer!" Clara calls out to me. I pause and turn to her.

"Yeah?"

"We need to talk when you get back," she says seriously.

"Okkay..." I drawl. I hate it when Clara goes all cryptic on me. Just spit it out already. I turn around and meet Pepper at her bike. She keeps a safe distance from me, which irritates me, but I plan on wooing her with delicious breakfast treats once we arrive at the spot I picked. Plus, the blanket I packed will require us to sit snugly together.

"So I know a great mountain road that leads to a spot with a crazy beautiful view. Does that sound good to you? It's only about a forty-minute ride," I say. Her mouth rounds out then closes, and I swear she's mouthing something to herself.

"Yeah, that sounds nice. I haven't really explored the area much so it'll be nice to find another nice ride," she says before tugging her helmet on and straddling her bike. She starts it and flips her visor down, my cue to get on and get going. I pull on my helmet and pair my phone with it before starting her up. Softly, so I'm not too distracted to be safe, Klaypex's "*Lights*" starts playing. I turn the ignition and let the bike come to life under me. I flip my visor down, zip my jacket, and glance to my side. Pepper nods at me and I take off towards the outskirts of town.

She's a skilled rider. It's becoming difficult for me to keep my dick under control. Her outfit combined with seeing her on her own bike is doing ridiculous things to my gut. She's playful, pulling around me every once in a while until I catch up to her. The road bends and winds, but I don't speed on this particular road because it's a gorgeous view and it's not really safe. Pepper doesn't seem to care about either, though. She takes the corners fast, leaning expertly into the curves of the road and her bike. Although it's hot, it also makes me nervous. A straight shot is coming up so I throttle the engine and shoot past her. She turns her head my way briefly as I pass but otherwise pays me no attention.

Ten minutes later I slow and pull off to the side of the road onto a wide dirt patch. I kill the engine and wait for her to do the same. Her hair spills out around her as she removes her helmet and shakes it out. If I could pause time, rewind, and watch that moment all over again, I would. Repeatedly.

"So?" I ask.

"That was definitely a great road." She grins and hops off her bike. I do the same and grab the stuff from my saddlebags. She takes the blanket from me as I pile all the goody bags into my arms.

"Thanks."

"Sure." She shrugs.

"Do you mind a short hike?"

"No. Lead the way," she chirps.

I lead us up the half-mile path to a flat rock that overlooks the road we just travelled. You can almost see the whole of Blacksburg from it. When we reach the landing I set the bags down and reach out for the blanket. She hands it over without hesitating. I spread it out and sit.

"Are you going to sit?" I ask, admiring her perfect form. She nods and plops down next to me, careful not to let our limbs brush together.

"I don't bite, you know." I chuckle, trying to lighten the situation. Tension rolls off her.

"Sorry. I just..."

"It's okay," I say, cutting her off. I don't want this hangout to go bad before good so I grab the bag with the plates and napkins first and set them out before reaching for the other bag and putting out all the treats I picked up. I had no idea what she liked so I got a whole bunch of everything.

"Are those cheese Danish pastries? And scones?" she squeaks out in awe, her golden eyes large and round.

"Yes. Among some other things," I answer. Thank sweet baby Jesus that she likes some of these things. Her hand snatches one of the cinnamon rolls dripping with frosting and a cheese Danish. A small moan rises out of her when she bites into the cinnamon roll. Is it wrong to think watching a chick eat is erotic? I stare as she chews and delights in the food.

"Good fucking God this is the best frickin' cinnamon roll I think I've ever eaten!" she exclaims before taking another bite. I laugh and dig into my own selection. Masteron's Bakery has never let me down.

"So tell me about yourself," I prompt.

"Not much to tell."

"Okay, I know this isn't a date or whatever, but we can't talk? We can't maybe be friends?" I ask. Yup, that's right. I friend-zoned myself for the bigger picture. I have to have some angle to work myself into her life. She cocks her head to the left and blows her bangs up before laughing.

"Sawyer Crown, you do *not* want to be friends," she chastises. Always blunt. Always calling the situation out. I'm so fucking gone for that shit. It's so refreshing.

"Shut up and tell me something about yourself," I tease.

"Well, should I shut up or tell you something?" she volleys back at me. Damn. Add quick wit to the long list of things I'm already enamored with. I shoot her a look, a playful one. She smiles and pops another bite into her mouth.

"The view up here is really spectacular. How'd you ever find this place?" she asks curiously while taking in the view.

"It was an accident, really. A couple years ago the bike broke down right where we parked. I had time to kill while I waited for a ride. I saw the path when I was peeing." She snorts and covers her mouth with her palm. "Anyway," I continue, "I was bored, so I followed it and this was what I found."

"That's a nice story."

"Your turn," I say.

"Huh?"

"Tell me a story about you." I hand her a bottle of water and open one for me as I wait.

"Um, I moved to Christiansburg a year ago. You already know where I work. What else is there?" she says plainly.

"What else is there? My guess is a whole lot. Where are you from, how many siblings do you have, what's your last name? Favorite color, food...I could go on," I say with a chuckle.

"Jesus," she sighs. I sense maybe I went a little too far but I didn't really ask anything too personal. "I'm from around. No family, they've all passed. Black, I guess, and ice cream. Oh, and my last name is Philips," she finishes, shoulders dropping. I watch as she holds eye contact and takes a long, deep breath.

"Pepper Philips, huh? I'm sorry to hear about your family," I offer up, feeling really shitty for obviously bringing up a sad subject. Way to go, Don Juan.

"Listen, Sawyer, you're really hot. I actually like you. You seem...I don't know...like a good man, but I don't date. I have one friend, my bike, work, and the gym. That's my life. That's all I want." I start to speak but she holds up a hand to stop me. "I understand that doesn't really sound appealing to many people but for me, well, for me it works," she finishes rather passionately.

I want to kiss her. I want to change her mind. I want her to let me be in her short list of life inclusions. We stare at each other in silence a few beats. There is nothing up here to distract us. Just the sound of the wind and rustling leaves. I lean in and wrap myself around her. Without warning, I plant my lips firmly on hers and kiss the shit out of her. It takes only a moment before she gives in and kisses me back. I trace my tongue over her bottom lip and she opens for me. Her hands find their way around my neck and she pulls me down with her as she lies back. My erection is out of control and painfully cramped in my jeans as her hips come up and grind against me. Her legs wrap around my waist as I move from her mouth to her ear and dip further down, following the tendon that runs from her jaw down to her collarbone. I palm one breast over her jacket and curse the day leather-anything was made. She sighs loudly as I hungrily nibble and kiss her exposed areas. I work my way back up to her mouth and hover just out of reach from her lips.

"Seems like you want me," I whisper at her, grinning.

"I like a good fuck," she counters seriously. Not gonna lie, that hurt. I push up, unwrapping her legs from me, and sit back on my heels.

"What's so scary about the idea of letting me into your life enough to see if this goes somewhere?" I ask. I instantly want to take the question back. Pepper stares at me, looking horrified. I feel like I've crossed some personal line.

"Why does it mean I'm scared or have some sort of issue just because I don't want the same things you want?" she grinds out angrily.

"It doesn't!" I shout back, flabbergasted. I have no idea how I was just making out with the hottest thing on the planet and now we're fighting. She huffs and leans back on her elbows. Staring off into the distance, her lips move just barely.

"What are you doing?" I question. Her gaze snaps to mine and she brings her fingers to her lips. She looks slightly embarrassed.

"Counting," she says quietly. "It helps me stay calm when I'm anxious."

"Counting..." I repeat. She nods her head and then starts laughing, hard.

"What the hell is so funny?" I ask. Maybe she's crazy. Really crazy.

"I just...God dammit, Sawyer! I like you. I don't know how to do this, though. I keep everyone out on purpose. I'm not really a good person to be around," she explains rather cryptically.

"Explain that," I demand.

"I...fuck," she says and blows out a breath. "Just trust me, please. I don't have much to offer. If it weren't for Greta I wouldn't even be here with you right now. I was going to bail but she talked me out of it at the gym last night."

"I like Greta." I smirk. She smiles back. That's a good start I guess.

"She's like me. Detached. It's why we work together as friends. She doesn't ask questions and I don't either. I really know very little about her except that she likes ice cream as much as I do and she also does MMA training. That's rare in a woman," she explains. I decide to let our previous conversation go for now. She's talking about herself and I'm going to run with it.

"You train for MMA?" I ask, stunned. That would explain the rock-hard body but shit, if she decides she hates me she could probably kill me with little effort.

"Not *for* the MMA. I don't fight. I just train with the guys. I like being able to defend myself." She shrugs. Defend herself from what?

"Ummm...kinda don't know what the hell to say to you right now," I throw at her. She giggles and grabs my hand.

"I like that about you. You just tell it like it is," she says with a lingering smile.

"I thought that was what I liked about you," I counter.

"Oh?" she says and arches an eyebrow at me.

"True story," I state. She throws her head back and laughs. I think I might be willing to do close to anything to see her do that again and again. Her laugh is mesmerizing. I'm convinced it really does hold the secret of life. She stops and enjoys the view for a moment. A light breeze blows long strands of black hair across her face as she looks around. There is one strand blowing across her lips and I reach up to tuck it behind her ear. A tiny smile forms on her lips and one eyebrow rises.

"I will let you be my friend one condition," she says, smiling. "If I ever feel like it could be more, I'll make the first move. You don't get to lay a finger or lip on me until then." I groan as she finishes. This is going to be torture. "You can't kiss me. Friends don't kiss."

"Okay," I answer.

"You can't do things like tuck hair behind my ear; that was romance."

"Okay," I repeat.

"In fact, I don't think you should touch me much really at all because, um, well...it affects me," she says.

"Okay."

"Are you just going to agree with anything I say?" she teases.

"Probably. I like you. Being here with you makes me feel good." Her face goes soft. She looks up at me through her lashes and gives a timid smile.

"Okay then," she blows out.

"Can I get a blow job before we agree to this?" I joke. She moves like lightning and pushes me onto my back. The rock is hard and unforgiving underneath me. Holy shit. What is happening? Please don't kick my ass. Please. It was just a joke.

"I think that the arrangement can start tomorrow," she purrs as she unzips her jacket and tosses it aside. I can feel my eyes bugging out of my head now, like my head is going to explode. She's stripping down to nothing on top of a fucking rock out in the open.

Holy hell, I'm the luckiest man on the entire planet. That's the last thought I have as she undoes my pants and yanks them down my legs in one swift motion. She leaves my boots on and I don't think to take them off. I struggle to remove my boxers fast enough to keep up with her. She crawls, up my legs, stopping at my cock, which is standing painfully at attention. One long lick from base to tip makes me shudder but when I watch her pouty lips wrap around the head of my dick I think I black out from pleasure. This chick is crazy and slightly reckless. Maybe too wild for me. The thought leaves my brain as quickly as it entered when she cups my balls with her free hand. Her black hair drapes around my crotch, tickling my thighs as she bobs her head up and down. When she groans, the vibration is almost too much to handle. Her hand tightens and she sucks harder. Shit. I'm going to come.

Her hand reaches out to the bag of pastries as she licks my penis clean. Arching up she crawls slowly up my abdominals, Danish in tow.

"So, I kinda have a thing for desserts." She purrs. She pushes the Danish into my mouth slowly, allowing me to take a bite. Leaning in she licks the frosting off the corners of my mouth. I dip my finger into the middle of the frosting and rub it across her lips before kissing her deeply. Her hips rock against me. I want to please her but she stops when I move my hands from her arms. Pulling back, breaking our kiss, she smirks and rubs Danish frosting from the back of my ear down my neck. I'm about to protest when her mouth comes to my ear and slowly starts licking the frosting trail clean. Desserts are definitely cool with me. Definitely.

I barely make it back to Bloodlines in time for my appointment, let alone with enough time to hear Clara's "talk." Pepper seems wild. A wild driver and just...wild. A blow job on a mountain top? That's something I hadn't experienced before. I think I like that about her, but part of me wonders if maybe it's too much. No one can sustain a real relationship on just wild. I don't want to burn out. I'm torn between wanting to hold onto the reckless feeling she gives and knowing the responsible option is what's best. She's a thrill ride. I like that, yet I know I'm drawn to broken women. I want this to last awhile. I didn't get to kiss her goodbye. As soon as we finished our public fuck-fest it was back to friends-only territory. Going from hot to cold was insanely difficult. The only silver lining was that I finally got her number.

"Dude. I thought you bailed on me!" Carmine squawks at me as I enter the shop.

"Uh, sorry. Got held up," I say distractedly.

"With who? Clara told us you were on a date. Really, bro? A brunch date?" he chatters on. I run my hands through my hair and notice something sticky. Shit. I push into the bathroom without answering Carmine and look in the mirror. Frosting. I knew using Danish pastries as body frosting was a bad idea. Grabbing a wad of toilet paper and wetting it, I try to wash off any evidence of our kinky roll on the rock.

"So?" Carmine pushes, voice elevated so I can hear him.

"Yeah. She's...different. I like her," I hedge, exiting the bathroom.

"Clara says she rides."

"Sportster," I fill in.

"Damn. She gotta sister?" he says and chuckles.

"Nope. Sorry, man," I answer. I clean the area I'll be working on and settle into the task at hand. Hoot comes in forty minutes after I start on Carmine's leg piece and Clara and I settle into our little world of tattoos. Music blaring, needles buzzing, and money coming in.

"So tell me more about this chick," Carmine says as I'm nearing the end of his work for today.

"Name's Pepper. Says she has no family. She's pretty tight-lipped," I explain.

"Pepper huh?"

"What kinda name is Pepper?" Clara chimes in.

"Yeah." Hoot laughs.

"Shut up, Hoot, your name isn't any better," I call out.

"It's not my given name, though. Hers is."

"Maybe not," Clara says.

"What are you on about?" I ask her, trying to stay focused on the tattoo.

"I went back and looked up the paperwork she filled out. She put her name as Magnolia. I knew I was right," Clara declares, looking pleased with herself.

"Magnolia?" Carmine all but shouts. Jesus, what's with him? I pull the gun away from him so I don't screw up my work.

"Yeah," Clara laughs. "I guess that's not much better than Pepper, really."

"Cut the shit, guys. It's her name. It's cute. I like it," I defend in her absence.

"Describe her, bro." Carmine is boring a hole through my head with his eyes. What the hell is his issue? Maybe she had a one-night stand with him once, too? I push the thought aside. That is one thing I don't ever want to picture.

"Gorgeous black hair. Golden skin. Hard, tight little body. Big tatt that Clara did on her back." I know my voice sounds dreamy and I feel like a schmuck for it. Carmine's eyes glass over a little and his expression is hard.

"You said she rides a Sportster?" he asks a little harshly. His eyes are lit up and intense.

"Yeah. Shit man, what is it?" I push.

"Nothing," he says but then shakes his head and softens his features. "She just sounds hot, man. You're one lucky fuckin' dude."

"Does no one give a shit that she lied about her name?!" Clara cries out in irritation.

"No!" all three of us shout back. Lots of people lie when they get tattoos. Names, age. It really doesn't matter. It was a long time ago.

"You guys suck," she deadpans. The three of us fall into a fit of laughter that really pisses Clara off.

Chapter 8

WORK IT OUT

I waited two entire days before attempting to contact Pepper. I get the feeling it wouldn't take much to scare her off and I'm not going to take any chances. I'd really hoped she would contact me first. Anything. A text, a call, a stop into the shop, but no, there's been nothing but radio silence. I'd paced around the house for thirty minutes before Allie just told me to suck it up and text her already.

"Why are boys so dumb?" Allie asks with a huff, crossing her arms over her tiny chest. I bite back the smile and laugh that want to happen and ask what she means. "It just seems like adults make everything so hard," she starts. "If you want to talk to someone, just talk to them. Aren't you and Mom always telling me to just be honest and follow my gut?" she asks, exasperated. This kid has infinite amounts of wisdom that she doesn't even realize.

"We are, but what does that have to do with anything?"

"If your gut wants to call, then call. It's like you're just..."

I wait patiently as she struggles to find her words. "It's like you don't trust yourself to do the right thing," she finishes.

"Adults ARE complicated, and maybe I don't trust myself," I state, watching her sloppily put a giant bite of pancake into her mouth.

"That's stupid," she mumbles through a mouthful of food.

"It is, isn't it?" I say. She nods her head while swallowing and grabs the last strip of bacon from the plate. My jaw drops and my hand shoots out, grabbing the bacon from her small grasp.

"See!" she laughs. "You didn't hesitate on that."

"Life's easy when it's whether or not you want bacon," I say back to her.

"Stupid," she grumbles and sticks her hand out to me. I bite off half the bacon strip and hand her the other half.

"At least you're a good sharer," she says and smiles.

"Oh, Allie, please share your infinite wisdom with me; if I were going to text Pepper, what should I say?"

"Easy. You say, 'Hi, what are you doing today?'" she rattles off. It's not lost on me that I'm asking my eleven-year-old for girl advice. I think I've hit a new low.

"Easy, huh?" I grumble.

"Easy," she repeats.

I think that maybe Allie is right. Maybe this could all be easy. Maybe I am making this harder than it's supposed to be. I swipe the screen on my phone and open my text messages while Allie clears the table and rinses our dishes.

"Hi. What are you doing today?"

I hit send and instantly wish I could take it back. That has to be the lamest text in the history of men hitting on women. When did I lose my game? Do I have no swagger left in me? I just let an eleven-year-old girl dictate my next move. I groan to myself and toss the phone on the table.

Three hours later, as I'm meeting Clara at the shop to send Allie home for the day, my phone dings with a new text. I feel like a schoolgirl. My heart races and I'm deliriously hopeful that the message is from Pepper.

"Gym in an hour. You?"

Not exactly flirty or exciting as far as responses go, but what did I expect? I'd lamely asked her what she was doing today.

"Want company?"

I type back and hit send before I chicken out. I'm a little scared to join her at the gym. I work out three times a week but mixed martial arts training sounds a little more intense than what I normally embark on.

"So, Tuesday night. Sawyer, are you even listening to me?" Clara's voice admonishes. What? Crap. I missed everything she said. When did she even start talking? Allie raises her eyebrows at me mischievously and tries to stifle her growing smile.

"What's Tuesday?" I ask. Clara's nostrils flare.

"What's with you? Tuesday, Allie's chorus concert," she says pointedly.

"RIGHT!" I bellow. "Of course I'll be there," I answer.

"Great. So we'll see you then," she states dryly.

"Yup." I turn to Allie and hold my arms out. She rushes into them, squeezing me tightly.

"Love ya, kiddo. See you Tuesday."

"Love you too," she says, tilting her head up. I lean down, giving her a big sloppy kiss, which she squeals and wipes off with her shirt sleeve.

Straddling the bike, I start her up as I watch Clara and Allie pull away safely. My phone dings, then vibrates, in my pocket.

"Sure, if you can keep up. World's Gym, Christiansburg."

Shit. I have the distinct feeling I've bitten off more than I can chew. But maybe she'll feel bad for me, though, and rub my muscles down later on. Her perfect lips and strong but soft hands wreak havoc on my mind before I tuck my phone back into my pocket and head home to change.

I make it in record time. Pulling up to the gym I notice that it's a little defunct-looking. The concrete building has no windows besides the glass front door and it's not in the best part of town. This is where she chooses to work out? Strange. Clicking the button on my key fob, I lock the doors to the truck. It's not exactly fun riding home on a motorcycle sweaty and tired.

I don't see Pepper's bike here either so I'm not sure she's here yet, but instead of waiting around like a chump I decide I should just go inside.

Smelly. Gross, old-gym smell.

It's musty and smells like sweat. The rancid odors assault me the second the front door closes behind me. I make a sour face and look around. I see a roped ring, heavy bags, speed bags, and some weights. This isn't the kind of gym I'd expected. There are no cardio machines, no fancy front desk, no hot chicks milling about. This is like a bad, run-down boxer's gym from a B-list movie starring Marky Mark. Interesting.

I let my gaze wander until it lands on a spread of mats to the right of the ring. Two women are sparring. They move effortlessly around each other. The punches they're throwing are powerful and skilled. The kicks, shit, the kicks are insane. Both women seem to move like water across the mats. One blow in particular sends the other's head snapping backward with a sick, cracking sound. They both wear headgear and gloves but that had to hurt. I cringe and watch as the one who took the hit rights herself and attacks back.

"They're something," a deep voice says and distracts me. I glance left and find myself eye to eye with a thoroughly jacked up dude.

"Yeah," I answer.

"Pepper and Greta could take down half the guys here if they tried," he muses.

"What?" I find myself saying. I realize as I look back to the mats that Pepper is indeed one of the women. Her hair is tied up behind her and despite the mouth guard, if I'd looked hard enough, I would have noticed it was her. The tank she has on showcases her crazily ripped arms and shoulders and the loose mesh gym shorts show off her toned thighs. Everything clings to her slick, sweaty body.

"I've never had two women in here before they showed up. But shit, they are badass," the dude says. "I'm Jim. Owner," he introduces himself. I take his hand and shake it firmly.

"Sawyer. I came to meet Pepper," I say. He flashes me a devious smile.

"Good luck," he says before he chuckles and wanders off. I turn my attention back to the mats as I edge closer to them. Greta throws a sick combination of punches and kicks that sends Pepper reeling backwards, landing on her ass on the mat. She smirks at Greta before jumping up again. I catch her eye and wave at the same moment Greta throws a jab. Shit. Pepper's head snaps back and she lands on her knees with a thud. I hurry the last few steps to them.

"Shit! Are you all right?" I call out, worried. Greta spins around to face me. Her eyes are icy blue and deadly. I hold up my hands in surrender. It seems like the right thing to do.

"She's fine. Buzz off," she snaps. My jaw drops and I stand, stunned, unable to think of a retort. Honestly, women don't usually talk to me like that. I've even been known to make them stutter and flustered. This one, though, she's totally immune, it seems. Figures. She's every man's wet dream. Perky breasts, long, golden blonde hair, frosty blue eyes, and a figure to kill for.

"Greta, easy, that's Sawyer," Pepper says and chuckles as her friend offers her a hand up. Greta's eyes take me in, giving me a once-over from head to toe. It makes me fidget. She's not warm or friendly. I get the impression that she'd rather kick my ass then fuck it. I shudder at the thought.

"Sorry. I thought maybe you were another one of those gym rats trying to get in our pants," she drops flatly. "Although, I guess you *are*..." She winks and hits me with a blinding smile. It doesn't exactly seem genuine.

"Pepper and I are friends," I state. Greta snorts at me and turns back to Pepper who just shrugs.

"Hi," Pepper says, slightly out of breath.

"Hi." I grin back at her. A tiny bead of sweat drips from the hollow of her throat down her collarbone and disappears into her cleavage.

"You ready?" she asks. Am I ready? Shit, no.

"I'm gonna be honest, I've never boxed before," I admit, feeling like a pussy. I hear another snort from Greta. God, that bitch is annoying.

"We can show you the ropes. I promise to take it easy on you." Pepper smiles. Mush. I've been reduced to mush with just her smile.

"Okay," I answer.

Two hours later I am sore, bleeding from the nose, still, and hating life. What the hell was I thinking? Greta had suggested that Pepper coach me while I sparred with Greta. Needless to say, most of my time was spent dodging and holding my hands in front of my face. The woman was out for blood. Pepper had tried to call out instructions to me as we sparred but I'd been too in tune with my instincts to be reactive rather than proactive. Pepper had stopped Greta and swapped places with her an hour or so into it but I wouldn't exactly say she'd gone easy on me. I'd found myself so distracted by the way her tank clung to her, by the way she moved so gracefully around me, that I hadn't even heard Greta's calls of instruction. Pepper pinned me three times, legs straddling me, fists raining down on my face and chest until I'd tapped out each time. The feel of her body atop mine had made it all worth it, though. Loose strands of hair hanging haphazardly around her face, beads of sweat dripping down into her cleavage—it was hot. I would have let her pound me for hours if it meant I got to be that close to her.

My muscles ache in a way I didn't think was possible. My head feels like it's on fire and my nose throbs with pain. Greta towels herself off, sneaking glances my way and snickering. Pepper throws a towel to me and grabs one for herself.

"You did pretty good for your first time," she says.

"Right," I say shortly, feeling like my manhood has disappeared into some unknown crevice in my body.

"No, really," she pushes, looking adorable. Her bottom lip is sucked in between her teeth and she's trying not to smile.

"She's right," Greta says matter-of-factly. "I expected you to bail after the first fifteen minutes."

"Gee, thanks," I snort. Greta is a total boner killer. I think it's definitely possible that she has more testosterone than I do.

"I didn't mean that to be rude. We've both been in this a long time, years, and it's not easy for men to realize a woman or women can kick their ass. You did it rather gracefully," she explains.

"Sawyer, I'm sorry, I should have...I don't know, eased you into it. That was mean of me. I wasn't really thinking," Pepper says, looking a little sheepish. Seeing her with a shred of remorse kills me. Showing emotion doesn't seem to come naturally to her. Her guarded nature makes any sudden emotion seem like something meaningful.

"It's fine. Really," I state.

"So, drinks?" Greta asks, tossing her towel in a bin.

"We usually go for drinks after our workouts. To unwind," Pepper offers.

"You don't go home to wallow in sore muscles and ice packs?" I scoff, trying to make light of the beating I endured. Pepper chuckles and Greta snorts loudly, both women smiling.

"We do not," Pepper says.

"Lead the way, ladies. I'd love to drink with you." I chuckle as I toss my towel on top of Pepper's.

After we've all showered and dressed, we meet in front of the building. Greta throws an ice pack at me which I happily accept and gingerly press to the side of my nose. After a quick conversation about cars, Pepper decides to drive with me in the truck while we follow Greta to their normal bar. Pepper sits quietly next to me as we drive, hands folded in her lap, staring out the window.

"Penny for your thoughts," I say.

"My thoughts?" she asks.

"Yeah."

"They're boring. How 'bout yours?" she deflects. Why is it so hard to get her to just talk? Most women chatter on about anything, even if you aren't interested in hearing it.

"No way. I wasn't the one staring out the window pensively," I push.

"I was just...I don't know. I was just lost in thought I guess. Nothing in particular. Life," she answers.

"Life?" I question her vague response.

"Yeah, Sawyer. Life," she says flatly and resumes looking out the window. Greta slows and pulls into a spot along the road. I pull in behind her and shut the truck down.

"I wasn't trying to impose," I say, breaking our silence.

"I know," she answers before exiting the truck. So Goddamned cryptic. I think maybe she's got me hooked on her simply because I need to complete the puzzle.

The bar is a seedy little hole in the wall, a five-minute drive from the gym. The walls are dark beadboard and the lights buzz with fluorescent bulbs. It's not large and there are only three other people here. I find it strange that two women voluntarily come here. As they take their places at the bar I see the bartender nod in their direction and start pouring. He slides their drinks to them as I sit next to Pepper on one of the cracked vinyl stools.

"You're new," the bartender says, eyeing me.

"Allagash White, please," I answer. He nods and turns to get my beer. I notice that Pepper has what looks like bourbon, the same drink she had at the bar where we met. Greta is drinking some vodka concoction. Heavy hitters as far as drinks go. I'll stick to my beer. These two seem to do everything with a "go big or go home" attitude.

"So Greta, are you from around here?" I ask, trying to make conversation.

"No. I'm from Maine originally. Just moved here a few months ago," she answers easily.

"How'd you and Pepper meet?" I ask as the bartender returns and slides me my glass.

"The gym. She's the only one who can kick my ass, occasionally," she says and laughs.

"I'm lucky to have met her. She's made me a better grappler," Pepper interjects proudly. It's appears that Pepper seems to need Greta in her life more than Greta needs her. I watch them intensely. Their dynamic is so yin and yang. Pepper, although aloof, vibrates warmth while Greta puts out nothing but indifference, bordering on anger.

"So then what brought you to Virginia?" I ask Greta.

"What brings any woman anywhere? A man, of course," she answers.

"Oh. Nice. Maybe we could all go out sometime?" I offer.

"Not likely. We didn't work out," she shares. Pepper frowns and looks at me.

"Sorry," I answer.

"So, Sawyer, tell me about you," Greta says.

"I think maybe I'd bore you," I say honestly.

"Nonsense. I'm sure you're anything but boring. Come on now, wow me." She deadpans. Great. This doesn't seem to bode well for me.

"Well, I own Bloodlines tattoo parlor over in Blacksburg. I own it with my ex—well, not really my ex—shit, I don't know what we were. Anyways, we own it, and we share custody of her daughter, Allie. I'm not Allie's biological dad. But I've raised her since she was just a toddler—she's eleven now—so I'm still her dad even though Clara and I are done. I, ah, guess that's it really. I love motorcycles. I'm in Mayhem MC and I like this lovely lady sitting between us," I ramble. It's like diarrhea of the mouth. Make it stop. Greta is staring at me, face blank, and Pepper is smirking.

"Not boring at least. An MC huh?" Greta responds. Pepper continues to stare at me.

"Yeah."

"You gotta nickname yet?" she asks, eyes sparkling with curiosity.

"No." I smile.

"How's that?" Greta asks as she pushes her gleaming blonde hair over one shoulder.

"Haven't done anything yet to warrant one I guess," I answer. I bring my beer up for a sip and wince as the glass hits the bridge of my nose. Pepper's brown eyes flash and her hand comes to the side of my face, turning it slightly to face her better. Her touch makes my skin burn. It's so tender. It's so soft and caring, so not simply friendly.

"Does it hurt much?" she asks, looking a little worried.

"Yes," I answer. I might have lost most of my manhood today at the gym but, fuck, this does hurt and lying about it isn't going to save face at this stage. Her brows furrow together a bit and she frowns.

"I'm sorry," she pouts.

"Don't be. I should have tapped out long before but you sitting on me was distracting, in a good way." I wink. She grins quickly and drops her hand from my face. Turning back to her drink, she picks it up and chugs the contents. The bartender looks to her and she nods.

"Well kids, I'm out," Greta announces before standing. She tosses a twenty on the bar top and pats Pepper on the shoulder.

"See you tomorrow, yeah?"

"Of course," Pepper answers.

"See you around, Sawyer. Try not to fuck up this thing with Pepper or I'll have to kill you, and that'd be a shame since you're so easy on the eyes," she says as she passes me. I feel my eyes widen. I was sure that she hates me. I don't know what to make of her comment, though, since there's a part of me that actually believes she *would* kill me. Or, at the very least, beat me within an inch of my life if anything ever happened to Pepper. I don't know what to make of Greta. Something's definitely off about her but I can't pinpoint it and quite frankly I'd rather invest my time in Pepper.

"So, as friends, what are your plans for the rest of the evening?" Pepper pipes up.

"I have none." I shrug.

"Do you like movies?" she asks. Her eyes are playful.

"Do you like eating?" I say and laugh. "Of course I like movies, who doesn't?"

"Well, smartass, I was going to see if maybe you wanted to watch a movie?" She smacks my arm gently.

"What movie?" I ask, ignoring the smartass comment.

"What do you have to choose from?"

"Oh we're watching one at my place?" I quirk an eyebrow at her.

"I'm curious about where you live," she states. Well, all right then. Game on.

"Interesting. Does that mean you've been thinking about me?" I ask, trying to flirt.

"Don't friends do that?" she questions.

"I guess," I lament. Damn. She's too quick for me. My stomach's all knotted up with rejection that somehow wasn't really rejection.

"So, what do you have?" she pushes.

"Do you like The Hunger Games? I have the second one, but haven't watched it yet."

"Oh! Yes. Love!" she says excitedly. I need to figure out how to keep her in this mood. I like happy, lighthearted Pepper.

"Let's go then." I'm excited but still walking on eggshells. I need to weasel my way in deeper with her. I want to. Shit. *I want to.* When did that happen? I haven't thought about Clara for almost the entire day. My lips pull up into a smile as we head out.

Chapter 9

I'M NOT SMITTEN

The twenty-minute drive to my house was silent. I was on edge the entire time. Pepper seemed perfectly comfortable in silence, though. She didn't fidget or wiggle or sigh or anything. She just took in the scenery that flashed past the window and smiled. I wanted to ask her why she was smiling but I was terrified that I'd say something wrong and she'd tell me to can the entire evening and take her home.

She finally spoke when I pulled into the driveway, gushing about how lovely the house was and how on Earth does a man pick something like this out. I laughed loudly. If she only knew. I explained that I had picked the house out almost six years ago. I'd moved out when Clara and Dom started dating but when she moved in with him I'd moved back into the house. It seemed silly to sell it if one of us still wanted to live in it.

"So you kept it for Allie?" she says wistfully.

"Well no, I mean yes, Allie's grown up here but I love the house too," I state. The tension between us is confusing. She keeps her distance from me but just barely, like she's daring me to try and make a move. To touch her. Honestly, I just want to feel her. I want to twine her fingers through mine. I want to feel her torso pressed into mine. What would her slender arms feel like snaked around me? Does she nuzzle into the neck or arm area? What does she look like when she sleeps? All these questions buzz around in my head as we stand in the kitchen chatting about a house. A stupid house.

"But it didn't make you sad to live here, with all the memories?" she asks seriously, watching me.

"For a little while, it sucked. I was pretty messed up over the entire situation, but Allie and I made the house ours. We redecorated, moved bedrooms, the whole nine," I explain. She watches me carefully when I speak. It's nerve-racking sometimes. I want to know what she's thinking or if she's silently judging me.

"Is that the back patio?" she asks, looking behind me to the French doors.

"Yup."

"May I?" she asks, gesturing to go check it out.

"By all means. I'm just going to grab a new ice pack." I watch as she moves around me and pushes through the doors. The evening light creates a glow around her body that makes her look angelic. I think I could get used to her being around. I throw my used ice pack into the freezer and pull out a new one. I wrap a dish towel around it before heading outside to check on Pepper.

As I shut the door behind me the distinct smell of pot attacks my nostrils. Pepper sits on one of the lawn chairs smoking a joint. She blows out a large, white cloud of smoke and hands it towards me as she watches the billowing white cloud.

"Want some?" she offers, looking up at me.

"No," I answer more harshly than I meant.

"Okay then." She shrugs and takes another hit. Pot. Goddamned pot. I'm not against it. I don't really care if people are into that, but honestly I don't want the person I'm involved with to be a pothead.

"So is this a special occasion?" I ask as I sit in the chair next to her.

"Huh?" Pepper responds.

"The joint." I nod towards it.

"Oh, this?" she asks, looking at it. "No. I like to unwind sometimes. I get so anxious and tense. It helps." She smiles. Right. Sounds like an excuse to me.

"I'm going to get the movie ready." I push out of my seat and head back into the house. Tossing the ice pack and towel into the sink, I brace myself on the counter and wonder what the hell I'm doing. She's fucked me outdoors on a mountaintop, drinks hard stuff—obviously regularly—and smokes pot. I know I'm older than her but maybe this one is out of my league. She's young. We all did that when we were young, right? Dragging a hand down my face I try to push all those thoughts aside. She intrigues me. I like that. I like her. I like not thinking about Clara. I like that Pepper is different.

"What you got there?" she asks curiously from behind me as I pull down a bag of chocolate.

"Cadbury Mini Eggs. You want some?" I ask. Her hand snaps out and she steals the bag from me in record time. I watch, stunned, as she tears the bag open, swiftly walks to the couch, and sits hunched over while popping them into her mouth. Apparently she *really* likes them. I follow her to the living room.

"You look like Gollum from Lord of the Rings eating those," I tease as I reach over for one.

"Hey!" She slaps my hand away and pulls them to her opposite side. "It's okay, my precious..." she whispers to the bag. I can't help it. A bubble bursts and I let out a deep belly laugh. She looks at me and smiles a real smile. Wide and bright. She's funny. She's so beautiful.

"So as a friend, what am I allowed to know? Can I ask like, when your birthday is? Or if you go to church? I don't know what topics are safe," I ask honestly.

"I don't do birthdays," she states seriously.

"What?! Preposterous! Birthdays are meant for celebrating," I declare.

"A birthday is just another day. Christmas, too. Holidays come and go. I don't celebrate. I haven't had a reason to. It's fine. It's not like I've been missing out. Who would I buy for? Celebrate with?"

she asks. Her body language says she's comfortable with her statement, like it's well-rehearsed, but her eyes show a hint of sorrow.

"But all those holidays are pretty much an excuse for sweets, and I'm pretty sure you're addicted to sweets. First pastries, and now Cadbury Minis."

"Touché, Sawyer," she admits with a grin, "but I don't need an excuse to indulge in sweets. Any day of the year is a dessert holiday if you ask me."

"I'll give you that, for now," I answer with a grin.

"Good. Cause I'm really ready to watch this movie you promised me," she says and laughs lightly.

"Bossy little thing aren't you?" I say playfully.

"Little?" she challenges. We already know she can kick my ass without trying.

"As in...young," I explain.

"How old are you?" she asks.

"Thirty-five. You?" I can feel myself cringing, waiting for her response.

"Twenty-five, but my non-celebrated birthday is in three weeks," she answers, unaffected by our age difference. Twenty-five is definitely better than "I'm still in college." I'll take it. Ten years. That's not so bad. But I'm sure it can be a hurdle for a relationship, too.

"Are you trying to tell me you're twenty-five and three quarters?" I laugh. Her entire face lights up, eyes sparkling, shoulders shaking, and dimple showing.

"Yes. Yes I am," she says and chuckles. "Now, if you don't mind, I'd really like to watch the movie you promised." She raises her eyebrows at me and bites her lip to stifle a laugh.

"As you wish, milady." I bow to her and head to the DVD player to load the disc.

It happens about one hour into the movie as we're munching on popcorn; she stretches out and rests her feet over my lap. I'd like to report that I'm not smitten or totally over the moon about the small gesture of familiarity, but I am. I grab the blanket from the back of the couch and spread it carefully over her legs and my lap and slowly let my hand come to rest on her shin. I see her glance discreetly at me but she doesn't move or say anything so I feel all right about it. She snuggles down into the couch deeper and adjusts the pillow under her head.

"You comfortable?" I ask quietly.

"Yeah. I am." She smiles faintly. My thumb moves in slow, small movements over the blanket on her leg and I feel like I've gone to heaven. Maybe thirty-five and twenty-five aren't so different.

It's past eleven when the movie finally ends and I couldn't tell you a damn thing about it. I was so caught up in Pepper being in my house, on my couch, legs over my lap, that I couldn't pay attention to the movie at all. I could feel the heat from her body as my hand rested on her leg.

She yawns while throwing the blanket off her and stands stretching. "I need to use the bathroom before we leave," she announces.

"Yeah, sure, it's that way." I point behind her through the kitchen. I guess she's not staying over. I was hoping she'd fall asleep. I could just leave her on the couch tucked in. Like that's not creepy. Hey, fall asleep at my place so I can watch you sleep. Ugh. I need to get this fixation on her over and done with. Creepy me creeps me out.

"You ready?" she asks from the hall near the living room entrance.

"Of course." I stand, grab my keys, and rub my eyes to wake me up before we head outside.

Her house is adorable. It's a little cape that probably has two bedrooms and a bath. Perfect for being single. The yard is well maintained and there is a small front porch with a cute little "Welcome" sign over the door. Flowers line the house in colorful masses on either side of the porch. I shut the truck off and hop out before she has a chance to undo her seatbelt. Opening her door, I hold out my hand.

"Friends, eh?" she says and chuckles.

"I'm a considerate friend!" I say, feigning disdain.

"I wouldn't have it any other way!" she says, mocking my tone.

"Are you sure you don't want me to drop you at your car?"

"Nope. I'll walk to the gym tomorrow and drive it home then. No biggie," she says.

We walk side by side to her front door and pause. I want to kiss her. Friends don't kiss, though. She turns to me after her key is in the lock. Her lips curl upward in a half smile. Our eyes bore into each other's and I dip my head until our lips are a whisper apart. Her breathing picks up and she intently watches me. Her eyes trained on mine and mine on hers, both of us puffing breaths onto each other's mouths. It feels like every fiber of her body is crying out for me to just kiss her, but I don't. She opens her mouth to say something and that's when I claim her mouth. I'm soft and gentle with her as she worships me with her kiss, demanding and giving all at the same time. I can't help but melt into her just a little.

Then reality sets in. No, no, no! She pulls away, drawing in a calming breath and brushing the hair out of her eyes. Damn, she packs a killer kiss; it has my body tingling with awareness and begging for a lot more. I cross my arms over my chest and wait. I know she's going to scold me. I just know it. I'm ready and I don't care that I'm in trouble.

"Damnit, Sawyer! What the fuck was that?" she groans while staring at her feet.

"Just giving you a taste of what you're missing. You go on in and have a good night now," I reply smugly. I lift her chin so she's looking at me, smile, and brush a feather-light kiss on her cheek, and then turn and walk back to the truck. She stands on the porch with her hand at her lips and an arm wrapped around her waist as I pull away. My body is on fire. It's going to be a long, sleepless night.

My mind races the entire drive home. What does she want? Why is she so resistant, cryptic? How do I get more of her? My motorcycle needs an oil change, the yard needs to be mowed, the house needs a good cleaning, and the shop needs me to catch up on paperwork. I have a thousand things that need to be done but I can only focus on one right now: the way she looked at me after I kissed her. I'm thinking about everything I shouldn't be thinking about.

She's everything I shouldn't be thinking about.

When I get home I strip down to my boxers and fall hard on my bed with a delirious smile on my face.

Chapter 10

WORST. NICKNAME. EVER.

Beau Hawley, the Mayhem President, has been here for the last hour. I'm doing a pretty intense sleeve for him and I expect that I'll be here for another three hours or so. It's a good chance for me to suck up and hopefully find out when I can patch in.

"Down!" Beau bellows at his dog, Butch. Butch isn't so butch, really. Butch is a labradoodle or some poodle mix like that and is full of energy. Why Beau brought him in I'll never understand.

"It's okay." I chuckle as the dog tucks its tail between its legs and comes to sit next to Beau.

"No, it's not okay. Damned dog isn't trained for shit. The kids, the ol' lady, they spoil the damned thing like he's one of us!" Beau complains. I smirk and try to focus on my work. The buzzing helps keep thoughts from lingering in my mind, like thoughts of Pepper and our makeshift movie date the other night. She'd looked so stunned when I'd kissed her goodnight. I've made a point of not calling or texting her for the last twenty-four hours so I don't seem too eager. She's sent one text since then, the morning after. All it said was, "Friends huh?" I'd laughed out loud to myself and decided not to reply. It was a good sign, right? She was still thinking of me the next morning.

"So, Beau," I hedge, "any chance I'll be patching in soon?"

"All in good time my little one." He laughs deeply. I feel like a petulant child for asking. I huff and continue with his tattoo. "Yes, Sawyer, you will patch in soon. You're coming right up on a year and we've had no issues. You're loyal, the ladies like you, and our kids seem to hit it off." I jerk the gun up and away from his arm at the mention of "*our kids*." Hell no. Beau's deep voice booms with laughter at my response. "Take it easy. I was just messin' with you."

"Right," I say dryly.

"You're gonna have a tough go of it with her if you stay this protective." He chuckles at me.

"You're implying that I shouldn't be this protective?" I question.

"Not at all. You're a smart man and a good father," he answers. I grin and get back to the job at hand. I would do anything for Allie and I intend to.

The small bell at the door jingles and Butch goes nuts with excitement. Beau calls after him as he sprints to the front of the shop but the dog is a lost cause. I stop what I'm doing and glance up to see Clara making her way towards us, Butch in tow, leaping and licking her hand. She shakes her head, smiling, and pets his head for a moment. A neon green streak of hair hangs down from her shoulder and she's revealing just a hint of her tattoo at the exposed part of her collar.

"Hey, boys. Just picking up Allie's backpack," she greets happily.

"She's getting real good at leaving it behind to get out of homework," I admonish.

"Yeah. Tell me about it. I fought with her for thirty minutes the other night over doing homework that would have taken her fifteen to just sit down and do! Dom had to step in and take over." She shakes her head and throws her hands in the air, looking frustrated.

"What do you mean?" I question.

"Relax, Sawyer. I was flustered and getting angry. He stepped in to keep us from killing each other," she explains.

"Right."

"What's your problem? Beau, what is his problem today?" Clara asks sarcastically.

"Seems to me the man doesn't much like another man in his kid's life," Beau says. Shit. The last thing I need is someone meddling in our lives. Clara is already glaring.

"HIS kid?" she squeaks. Bad sign. Squeaking is a sure sign we're about to get an earful. I want to diffuse the situation but there isn't much I can do at this point. Clara wants me in Allie's life. I know this, she knows this, but Allie isn't legally mine in any way. I just...stuck around and after seven years, Allie thinks of me as her dad just as much as I think of her as my daughter. Blood be damned.

"Clara," I butt in.

"Allie is MY kid. I grew her. I birthed her and I'm responsible for her. Is that clear?" She's boring holes into Beau's head but he seems completely unaffected. Her small hands are fisted at her sides and she's turning pink in the face.

"CLARA!" I shout, breaking her concentration. Her face snaps to mine and if looks could kill I would surely be dead. "He's right and you're right. Allie is yours. Allie is also mine. I love her as my own. I'm protective. It's hard sharing her with someone new. That's all Beau meant. Chill, love," I finish and regret throwing "love" at the end but Clara's face softens and she breathes again.

"Right. Sorry, Beau. I'm a little protective of my marriage and Dom. Sawyer," she says, facing me again, "there's no need to explain to you that for all intents and purposes you are the only father Allie has known and you've always been a good one. Try to keep your friends' mouths shut 'cause I really don't want to hear their opinions on our arrangement." She snaps her mouth closed and grabs Allie's backpack from the corner before storming out.

"Damn. She must have been wild in the sack," Beau says and chuckles.

"She's not really so bad. She's soft and warm when she lets her guard down. But yeah—she definitely has serious attitude and sass. It's kinda what drew me to her," I ramble. "I liked the challenge. I liked the reward, too, getting to see her softer side. It's almost like two different people. Oh well, though." I bite my lip to keep myself from saying more and start back in on Beau's sleeve.

"You love her still?" Beau asks.

"Do you ever really stop loving someone you loved?"

"Deep, man. I guess not, but we all move forward and try again," he says wisely. Like he's trying to tell me to move the fuck on. I am, dammit! Pepper is the perfect distraction. She makes me feel. She makes me want to feel things that I haven't in a very long time.

"True enough. Everyone wants to find their slice of the pie," I say with a grin.

Butch, who followed Clara to the front door, comes prancing back to us. He stops, looks up at Beau, then at me, then moves closer to me. Before I have a chance to think about it any further Beau starts yelling, "NO! Stop!"

I pull the gun from his arm just as Butch lifts his leg and pisses all over my leg.

What. The. Hell.

"What the shit man!" I scream like a little bitch and push my stool back harshly while standing. Butch cocks his little cockapoodledoo-whatever head at me and wags his tail. Beau takes one look at my pant leg and bursts out laughing. My pant leg is drenched in dog piss and it's not even from my own dog. I groan and set the gun down, all the while Beau's laughter fills the shop. I can't help but start to chuckle too. The dog looks so Goddamned happy and Beau's laughter is contagious.

"Hydrant!" Beau laughs.

"What?" I squawk.

"Hydrant! You, son, just got your nickname!" he explains before falling into another fit of laughter. It's deep and loud. I groan through my smile. The moment is too funny not to share so I pull my phone from my pocket and send Pepper a quick text.

"So, while trapped mid-tattoo for Beau, his dog came over & pissed all over me.

All over my pants & shoe."

My phone dings with a response moments later.

"OMG-YOU GOT PISSED ON AT WORK?! I would have left! I mean @ the very least to change clothes for Christ's sake! WTF!"

I type a quick response to her.

"Working on it...Was just coined 'Hydrant'"

Almost instantly my phone dings at me again.

"No way. no. effin. way. DISGUSTING. And...worst. nickname. ever."

I chuckle at her response and tell Beau that I'll be back in a few; I need to grab a change of clothes before we can continue.

Carmine and Hoot are at the bar chatting it up with two rather skanky-looking chicks. Carmine's wide, white smile makes his dark, slicked-back hair look even darker. He looks like a greaser straight out of the fifties. The redhead next to him titters, placing a hand on his chest while she leans in to whisper something in his ear. His face lights up, part elation and part danger, looking at her secret words. Hoot and the brunette at his side look to be having a deep conversation in the form of shots. My brothers will not be driving home tonight, and I have a feeling whoever they take home won't be either. I push my glass across the dinged-up wooden bar top and nod to the bartender to fill me up again. Club soda and cherry juice. The Kaboose isn't known for its high-class clientele but it's a great spot for people watching. Leaning my elbows back onto the bar, I relax into my spot and glance around the place.

Twenty-somethings gyrate and grind all over each other on the dance floor. House-like music pumps from the speakers. Women line the bar, perched, really, waiting for someone to hit on them or offer up a drink. In the back corner, where we are, Hoot, Carmine, and their selected dates for the evening play a game of pool. Carmine's hand slides up the back of the redhead's thigh as she lines up a shot while bent over the pool table. Her lips turn up coyly as he slides his hand up higher to rest on her rear. He pulls his hand back and as she executes her shot he spanks her, hard. Her eyes bulge, her cue stick misses the ball, and she lurches forward. I watch as she tries to regain composure before spinning around and snarling at Carmine. Hoot shakes his head just barely and steps in front of his date. A protective move. I stay glued to my spot watching carefully.

Carmine smiles a slick smile at the redhead and yanks her by the hips to him roughly. Her body, stiff and rigid, releases as he drunkenly mumbles something into her ear. I can honestly say that I absolutely don't like the way he treats women. I will not, however, make that statement out loud to him.

By eleven I'm tired of people watching but I'm driving my two trashed friends and probably their women home and they show no signs of being ready to leave. Carmine prowls over to me, a cocky grin on his face, and slaps my shoulder as he leans a hip against the bar.

"Have a drink."

"I am." I hold up my glass.

"Something that actually has alcohol in it," he responds.

"I'm not really big on driving buzzed," I reply dryly.

"You gotta problem with me tonight?" he asks, head cocked.

"No," I clip. Hoot dawdles to a stop next to Carmine and smiles at us.

"We shoulda waited to pick ladies," he says, nodding his head in the direction of the entrance.

I follow his direction and smirk at my insanely good luck. Greta, in all her blonde-goddess beauty, followed by Pepper, a stark contrast with her luscious black hair and tanned skin, are pushing through the crowd to the bar with shit-eating grins on their faces. They stand out here, looking too classy for the joint but not caring in the slightest. Greta's pale yellow silk shirt and tight white pants show off her impeccable body and every guy here has taken a gander. Pepper though, damn, she's wearing black leather shorts with a white top that exposes her front and back precariously. How the shirt doesn't just slip off either one of the breasts it's covering is beyond me.

We're at the far end from them and they haven't noticed us yet which makes me smile. I like watching Pepper do her thing when she's comfortable and relaxed. Greta scans the bar and I turn my back to them for a moment not wanting to be seen just yet.

"Blonde," Hoot calls. Carmine's eyes are slits, his face twisted up like he's trying to recall details of something long forgotten as he watches Greta and Pepper.

"Not sure you want the blonde," I answer.

"Why's that?"

"She's a wee bit scary," I reply.

"You know her? Hook a brother up!" Hoot exclaims, forgetting about the woman he just spent the last two hours with.

"Who's her friend?" Carmine demands.

"That's Pepper." I smile. Carmine's eyes meet mine, a blank expression on his face. His eyes turn cold before turning away. I swear I hear him mumble "fuck" before stalking back to the redhead with his beer.

"What's his deal?" I ask Hoot.

"Dunno. PMS maybe. Sometimes I wonder about him," he says quietly.

"Me too."

Chapter 11

SHOULD HAVE STAYED HOME

Hoot flags the bartender down and orders another beer. I order a glass of bourbon and have it sent to Pepper and vodka for Greta. I watch from my spot as Pepper's eyes scan the bar meticulously searching for the drink sender. Greta spotted me moments ago but I'd put my finger to my lips and she'd played along. Pepper's shirt rides up slightly as she leans forward to see my corner of the bar better from her spot. When her eyes meet mine they show surprise before morphing into a pleased expression. She waves just slightly and smiles. I return the gestures and turn my back. She will have to come to me tonight. I need to retain a modicum of willpower in this game of "friends only."

Thirty minutes pass and my willpower is zilch. I'm watching Greta and Pepper dance together seductively, like a pervert. Hoot is practically foaming at the mouth next to me. He's already asked me three times why the hell I haven't gone to her or waved them to us. I attempted to explain that I was testing the waters and seeing if she'd give in first but he told me I was stupid and laughed. Greta drags a finger from Pepper's collarbone down between her breasts as they dance. Three men circle them, lustful sneers on their faces. Over my dead body.

I push off of the bar as one of them places his hands on Greta's waist and tugs her rear to his crotch. Pushing my way through the crowd, I stalk purposefully to them. I'm not sure what I'm doing but I'm not going to sit back and watch other men manhandle my girl. Shit. *My girl.* I chastise myself and reinforce "friends only" silently before placing a palm on the second man's shoulder and tearing him away from Pepper. He glares at me but I imagine the look I'm sporting tells him that I'm not backing down. Pepper spins to face me.

"Hi." She smiles coyly.

"Hi," I grind out.

"Dance with me?" she asks, looking up at me through thick black lashes. I reach out and spread the palms of my hands on her hips before pulling her closer a little more roughly than anticipated. Her small hands come up and rest on my biceps as I start to move us to the music. "*Tambourine*" blares from the speakers. I'm not the best dancer but I'm not the worst either. Pepper shakes her hips, sending shock waves through me straight to my dick. Greta watches me from the corner of her eye as she shimmies with a tall, strapping guy next to us. I glide my hands up to Pepper's waist, my thumbs almost able to stroke the sides of her breasts. From my height I can watch the sway of her breasts as she moves perfectly. A long, gold chain hangs between them, a ring hanging off it. The diamond glints in the blinking lights surrounding the dance floor.

A ring? She twists just as I'm about to make contact with the soft, full mounds, pushing her rear into my crotch just slightly. My dick jumps to attention and a groan falls out of me. My hands grip her waist tightly, trying to hold her in place as she dances. Her hands cover mine and squeeze gently. She turns again, facing me, hands on either side of my neck, and pulls my face closer to hers. Thank God. Her lips graze the shell of my ear as she says, "You're a good dancer." I laugh and shake my head at her. Her hands drop to my forearms and slide lower until she takes my hands in hers. I release one hand and use the other to twirl her. She cackles with laughter as I pull her back to me and rock us back and forth.

"Who's that?" she shouts over the music, eyeing Hoot who is now dancing with Greta. Unfortunately Greta looks bored.

"Hoot. MC brother," I answer.

"Boys' night out?"

"Girls' night out?" I ask.

"Fun night out," she states. "Blowing off steam." Her eyes gleam with mischief. I lean closer to her. Her eyes are mildly bloodshot. I wonder if she's high again.

"Ditto," I mouth in her ear. Goose bumps break out down her neck and arms. I push in a half an inch further to kiss the spot under her ear but she pulls away before I make contact. Damn.

"Control yourself, *friend*," she chastises playfully. A light sheen of sweat coats her face and cleavage. I want to taste it. She looks wild with her hair tousled, her dark, stormy eye makeup, her revealing outfit. Her legs appear to go on for days in those heels. And those pouty, full lips...

"Working on it," I mutter, discouraged. Her hand moves like lightning, cupping me. Her eyes widen with mine as she feels my obvious hardness and then she smirks, removing her hand and backing up a step. I feel like I'm going to explode. She doesn't seem to play fair. Carmine slams his hand on my shoulder, hard, jarring me.

"Pepper, this is Carmine," I say, trying to discreetly adjust my erection. Carmine nods and extends a hand to her. Pepper's eyes narrow at him but she quickly shakes his hand. I don't like the way he's looking at her, like he wants to consume her, but not in a sexual way, in a way that screams rage. Greta obviously picks up on this too because in an instant she's stepping in front of Pepper, introducing herself. Carmine tears his gaze from Pepper and smiles at Greta.

"You ladies want a drink?" he asks.

"No thanks. We're about ready to leave," Greta answers.

"Shame," Carmine replies.

"Not the way I see it," Greta responds coolly. Carmine's lips lift into a faint snarl. What the hell is going on? I really don't like drunk Carmine. At. All. This is embarrassing.

"You got something to say?" he questions menacingly. I need to get them apart. Greta, although trained to do damage, would never forgive me if anything happened to her or Pepper at the hands of a man. My instincts are screaming at me, shouting that Carmine would absolutely put his hands on a woman. It makes my stomach roll.

"Dude. Let's bail. It's last call anyways," I shout over the music. Greta looks ready to pounce and Pepper wobbles, slightly buzzed, behind her with Hoot at her side.

"I wanna hear what blondey here has to say," Carmine bites out, not backing down. I slap a hand on his shoulder and spin him to me.

"What the fuck, man. Grab the redhead and let's go," I state firmly. Carmine stares me down for what seems like an eternity until finally nodding his head and stalking off.

"Some friend," Greta spits viciously.

"I'm not sure we're friends after tonight. He's a Mayhem prospect too but..." I trail off. The music abruptly stops and a loud pop explodes from the speaker. I flinch at the unexpected noise. Greta whirls around, looking for the source of the sound, and Pepper crouches, eyes wide, terrified. Hoot reaches his hand to her and she cautiously stands, eyes trailing over every dark corner of the bar. Curious. Most everyone in the bar jumped, flinched, or was already too drunk or deaf to react. Greta grabs Pepper's hand and tugs her towards the door in a rush. You'd think by their reaction that a gunshot sounded off. Pepper halts and turns back to me.

"Night," she calls out. I raise a hand at her, signaling my goodbye as Greta tugs on her hand and she disappears out the bar door. I'm rooted in my spot wondering about too many different things. I've been cockblocked, turned on, shot down, and offended by someone who's supposed to be a friend. I should have just stayed home tonight.

Chapter 12

COUNTER RESISTANCE...KINDA

Saturday morning I had the brilliant idea to see if Pepper wanted to hike Cascades Waterfalls with me. After a witty exchange of texts she said that Greta and she would happily join me after their morning gym session. I called Hoot to see if he wanted to come along too so it's not just Greta and Pepper picking on me the entire time. Hoot agreed and we all piled into my truck around ten a.m.

A little over twenty miles northwest of Blacksburg are the Cascades, one of my favorite places to go and clear my head. It's a beautiful spot. Normally I enjoy the ride on my bike, but today I'm taking the truck so we can all ride together. There is a picnic area by the river where you park that has bathrooms. I shell out the three dollars to park and we pull into a vacant space near the restrooms.

"The trailhead is at the upper end of the parking lot." I nod towards the trailhead as I pull my hiking pack from the bed of the truck. Hoot grabs his bag and turns to Greta.

"You might need to hold my hand in a few tricky places," he says and waggles his eyebrows. I quietly chuckle and make a face at Pepper. We both know Greta won't need help with anything. Pepper and Greta hit the restrooms before we get going.

"Hoot, man, you gotta lay off Greta. I'm telling you, she could do serious damage."

"I think she likes my sense of humor. Until she lays me out, I'll stick to my tactics."

I snort at him, rolling my eyes. He's a great guy, just not so fast at learning how to talk to women.

After the ladies use the restrooms we start on the trail. The weather today is perfect, seventy and sunny. Pepper's khaki shorts and loose-fitting tank make her skin look even more tan than usual. I purposely walk behind her a step to take in the glorious view that is her ass. A few long, wispy strands of hair that have fallen loose from her messy bun curl in the light humidity. The trail follows Big Stoney Creek upstream, forking into an upper and lower trail. Pepper walks silently with swift, weightless steps, taking in the views before her.

"This place is stunning," Greta comments.

"So are you," Hoot retorts.

"Please, stop the drivel," Greta remarks, sending Pepper into a fit of laughter.

"Ouch, that was harsh," I say.

"Flattery is useless to me," Greta says as if that explains something deep about her.

"But nice to hear sometimes," Pepper chimes in optimistically. She pats Hoot on the back and winks. It's adorable to watch her try and motivate him even though Greta is clearly rejecting the kid.

"Greta, you're a tough nut to crack," Hoot says and then chuckles.

"I'm an acquired taste is all," she smirks. I grab Pepper's hand and tug it gently until she pulls back from Greta and Hoot, falling into step with me.

"Are you having fun?"

"This place really is amazing. I love the sound of the rushing water. It's really peaceful," she answers.

"Good." I grin.

"You're decent company too," she admits and smiles back at me.

"Just decent huh?" I ask. Her response comes in the form of a wink.

When we finally cross the second bridge, we've reached the halfway point to the waterfall. The trail follows the stream closely past beautiful cascades and pools. Pepper stays close, shoulder brushing my arm and occasionally taking my hand to help her across tricky portions of the trail. I want to grab her hand in mine or wrap an arm around her as we go but I know that I'm supposed to be friend-zoned so I don't. I let her lead. Shared smirks, brushing limbs, and the peacefulness that surrounds us make me hard and I have to keep mentally picturing baby seal clubbers to stifle my raging hard-on. The sexual tension between us is palpable. Every casual touch lingers just slightly too long, every shared glance meaning just a little too much. She'd be a fool if she thinks I haven't noticed her eyes wandering, following the movements of my muscles as we hike.

After the trails rejoin, they snake their way through the narrow gorge between high cliff walls, winding through moss-covered boulders and cutting through rhododendron thickets. The roar of Little Stony is a constant companion as we climb toward the main waterfall. The trail clings more desperately to the steep banks of the gorge here. Raised stone walkways, held together with steel pins, make it passable. But the rougher the terrain gets, the more impressive the sights. And the more Pepper looks to me for help navigating the terrain. Her quiet nature and natural beauty draw me in with every step we take. Furious white water rips between boulders to fall, churning into a pool below. Up ahead, a small stream tumbles down the side of a cliff into Little Stony.

After passing an old stone building, the falls come into view, a stunning climax to the trek we've just made. The base of the sixty-six-foot waterfall reveals lots of people relaxing and picnicking, just as we're about to do.

"Pick a spot ladies and let's have lunch!" I shout over the roaring water. The waterfall reigns in a bowl-shaped arena it has carved from the mountain. The rushing waters leap from the edge, cascading down the rock wall, landing in churning turmoil in the pool below. The sight is spectacular. I'm hoping that Pepper thinks so, too. I want her to enjoy herself. I want her to see that she can have a life that's full *and* inclusive of me. It doesn't just have to be friends or fuck buddies.

Pepper plops down on a flat rock near the water's edge and tucks her knees up under her chin while taking in our surroundings. Greta and Hoot are still bickering good-naturedly but the sound of the water pummeling into the pool drowns them out. I set my pack down and crouch next to Pepper.

"Penny for your thoughts."

"It's really amazing. Like a little slice of heaven tucked away in the woods. Do you think the water's warm?" she asks, staring at it longingly. A bead of sweat trickles down her neck. I reach out and wipe it away with a finger. Goose bumps break out along her skin. Her pupils dilate at her body's traitorous reaction.

"Care to find out?" I ask, still crouching next to her.

"What are you doing?" she asks carefully. Her mouth forms a perfect "*O*" as I hoist her up into my arms swiftly.

"Checking the water temperature." I laugh and swing her up in a bridal hold and leap off the rock, clothes on, into the water. She pops up, still squealing and wiping water from her eyes. Looking around furiously, she spots me and swims over.

"You shit! It's cold!" she says, trying not to let the smile creep over her face.

"That it is." I laugh, swimming away towards the shoreline. She follows, climbing out behind me, her clothes saturated and clinging to her body, the white of her tank, sheer and skin-colored—it makes my heart race. Her perky breasts stand at attention from the cold water and a pale pink bra does little to hide her.

"Eh hem..." she clears her throat, hand extended outward. I snap my eyes to hers, embarrassed that I've been caught staring at her chest.

"What?"

"Your shirt. There are kids here," she says, eyes bugging out, alluding to her see-through top. I strip off my sopping wet black tee and hand it over. Her eyes linger on the ridges and plains of my stomach a little too long to just be friends. Although her six-pack totally rivals mine, she seems fixated on my naked upper half. I stretch, flexing my muscles and enjoying inflicting a little sexual-tension torture on her.

"Damn, Sawyer, you're making me look bad!" Hoot calls out on a laugh. He's topless, propped up on his elbows, catching some sun. He does not have a six-pack, but he's not pudgy either. He simply is firm with no definition. I snort and sit down on the rock next to Pepper. She looks adorable swallowed up in my tee. Her shorts are lying flat on the rock next to her, drying in the sun. When did she remove her pants?

"No pants?" I question.

"I think your t-shirt covers all my bits," she says and chuckles. I stifle a groan as I lean back on my arms and tilt my face up to the sky.

"I am starving," Greta declares with a sly smile. "What'd you bring for lunch?" "Well you're in luck because I didn't let Hoot pack the food," I answer. "Otherwise we'd be enjoying a twelve-pack and some salt and vinegar chips." Greta cackles and scoots closer to Pepper, leaning in and whispering something in her ear that brings a brilliant smile to her face while I rummage through my pack, pulling out our lunches.

We're all packed up, full and mostly dry from our lunch at the waterfall. "Tradition states that the upper trail be taken back," I announce to the group.

"Says who?" Pepper questions.

"Tradition."

"But that view was really pretty, why not do it again?"

"Why not try something new?" I push.

"New is overrated sometimes," she says, looking away.

"The lower trail is definitely the more beautiful of the two but I think you'll like the upper trail too. And new is really good sometimes," I say, nudging her playfully. Her lips turn up just slightly before we all start our trip back.

From its lofty perch on the side of the gorge, this trail gives a new perspective of Little Stony. The hike ends where it began, at the parking lot. The girls scurry off to the bathroom to relieve themselves as Hoot and I toss our now empty backpacks into the bed of the truck.

"Think Greta will say yes if I ask her out?" Hoot asks.

"Maybe?" I shrug.

"She's so flippin' hot. Like, I want to maul her every time I see her." He smiles.

"So, all two times?" I laugh. He punches my arm and laughs with me.

"It's five already!" Greta declares in mock horror.

"It took three-and-a-half hours to do the hike both ways. But we also stopped to eat."

"Felt like six but then I don't do a lot of hikes," she grumbles good-naturedly.

We pile into the truck, Greta and Hoot in the back and Pepper and me up front. The drive is quiet and rather uneventful as everyone's tired from a day out in the fresh air. Pulling into the driveway at home, Hoot files out first, helping Greta down and slapping her ass as she walks to her car. She glowers at him while Pepper and I laugh at their ridiculous antics. Greta pulls out of the driveway followed by Hoot, leaving Pepper and me alone.

"Need any help bringing anything in?" she asks, hands tucked into her damp pockets. Her hair blows in the wind, sending it swirling around her face. She looks angelic. I fight the urge to tuck her hair behind her ears.

"Nah. I'm good," I answer, holding the empty backpack up.

"Okay," she says more to her toes than to me. I want to tell her to come inside. I want to take her in my arms and kiss her. I want to do a lot of things but I don't. I won't. She wants to make the first move. So I'll let her.

"Thanks for coming today. It's better with someone else," I say. Her eyes meet mine, holding them. I feel like I have the world at my feet but I'm tripping over it somehow. I try to look away from her, from the need and want I see her warring with, but I can't. Trapped in silent warfare, I wait, poised to strike if she gives me just the faintest of signs that she wants it. A faint scar runs the length of an inch near her temple, and another at the crook of her armpit. I want to touch them, kiss them. I want to know where they came from. She takes a hesitant step towards me and I war with my body to stay still.

"Thanks for a really nice day, Sawyer," she says, stepping into my space. She wraps her hands around my torso and squeezes. A hug. I let my disappointment out on an exhale and wrap my arms around her shoulders. Her arms linger around me just a little too long for friends. She releases me with a timid smile and heads to her car. "Bye," I call out. We talked. We laughed. We sat real close and held hands. By the time she pulls out of the driveway, I know I'm already a goner.

Chapter 13

SICKNESS BRINGS TENDERNESS

Fuck. My head feels like it's going to explode with pressure. My nose is thick and swollen with mucus, my throat's burning, and my chest is tight. Sick. As. Fuck. I hate being sick with a passion. I am a whiny baby. I want someone to dote on me and baby me. I roll to my side and grab a tissue from my nightstand, tossing it to the floor with a groan when it's used. I sit up gingerly, wondering how in the hell a full-blown cold can develop in the course of twelve hours. I felt just fine yesterday. The house phone rings. Its shrill noise makes me cringe. I shuffle to the nearest portable and grab it. Who the hell is calling at seven thirty a.m.?

"What?" I snap into the receiver.

"That's mean," Allie scoffs. I drag a hand down my face and toy with my lip ring.

"Sorry, baby girl, I'm sick," I answer.

"You sound funny."

"It's the cold."

"I want to come over today after school," she states.

"Tell your mom I'm sick and see what she says. I don't want you getting an infection or cold from me."

"I'm not weak anymore, Sawyer," she says in a snit.

"Babe, you know what I mean. Stop splitting hairs and just run it by her first," I say sternly.

"Fine," she huffs and hangs up the phone. I take it back to the bedroom with me and fall into bed. I can still remember the first time Allie got really sick. I'd panicked like a new parent.

Allie was almost five and had a fever of 104 that Clara and I couldn't manage to bring down. We didn't know what was wrong. We'd finally rushed her to the Emergency Room. After a night spent pumping her full of fluids the fever broke and she was all better. I snort a little at the memory of myself running around frantically, trying every known natural fever reducer Google had to offer. Clara had laughed at me and told me to start the truck because Doctors know best.

Two hours later I wake up sweating in damp sheets. I sit up and rub my face. This is bad. I'm freezing yet sweating. I check my cell and have two texts from Clara, saying that Allie will pop in after school to check on me but isn't to stay. After the kidney transplant we're both still cautious with her when it comes to colds. One close call in this lifetime is more than enough. It's hard to adjust to her being back to good health after watching her struggle for months to recuperate from her transplant.

A third text is from Pepper, bored at work, just saying hi. I type out a quick "hi" back and toss the phone on my nightstand. I should brush my teeth. That always makes me feel better but I just don't have the energy to get up and do it. Maybe I'll just sleep until Allie gets here. I set my alarm for three thirty p.m. and bury myself under the covers again.

When I finally wake up it is dark out. I leap out of bed and call for Allie on my way down the stairs. No one answers me. Crap. Wrapping my arms around myself as a shiver runs through me, I hit the landing and turn to the kitchen. Pepper moves silently between the sink and the stove, stirring something on the burner.

"You're up," she says over her shoulder. I think I'm hallucinating. I must be. Shaking my head slightly, I close my eyes and reopen them.

"Pepper?" I sound like I'm underwater. Distorted and far away. She moves towards me, reaching a hand out and placing the back of her hand on my forehead as I stare down at her concerned face. Her hand is cool and soft.

"Jesus, you're burning up," she says. "Allie texted me from your phone. She said you were sick and sleeping when she checked in on you. I told her I'd stop by, too," she explains.

"Allie was here?" I ask, confused.

"As far as I know. How else would she text me from your number?" she asks and cocks her head and pouts. "Why don't you go lie down on the couch? I'm making some soup for you," she states.

I try to shake the cobwebs from my brain but it proves impossible. I feel so out of it. I tug the throw off the back of the couch and lay down with it. My lips hurt, my skin hurts. I hurt. It feels like hours have gone by when Pepper emerges with a bowl of soup.

"I hope you don't mind that I came over," she says, setting it down on the coffee table.

"No, I just wish Allie had woken me up," I pout. I can't believe I missed her.

"From what I gathered she didn't stay long, Clara was coming to pick her up. Something about paranoid parents?" She waves her hand dramatically.

"For a reason. She had a kidney transplant. Two years ago now. We try to keep her healthy." My sentence sounds gritty and a coughing fit racks my body. Pepper rushes to the kitchen and brings back a glass of water.

"Thanks." I lift the glass and chug the contents.

"I'm glad I came, you are really sick. Eat your soup. It's butternut squash bisque. I made it from scratch," she says and smiles. I reach for the bowl as she disappears in the house and I try to enjoy the fact that someone made me soup. Shuffling back into the room, she sits at my feet with her own bowl of soup and flicks on the TV. It calms me having her here, knowing that I'm not in this house all alone. I watch her easy, bright smile and feel my chest tighten with contentment.

"What do you like to watch?" she asks casually.

* * * * *

Pepper stays through dinner, cleans up, and brings me tissues, Nyquil, and cool cloths for my fever. Basically she dotes on me like no one ever has, not even my mother when I was little. After finding nothing on TV we'd decided on putting on a movie, to which I promptly fell asleep.

When I rejoin the world of the waking, Pepper is curled into a tiny ball at the far end of the couch staring blankly at the credits rolling.

"I have a guest room. If you're tired," I croak, throat tight.

"Naw, I don't really sleep well," she admits.

"I also have sleeping pills or Nyquil." I laugh even though it brings on a coughing fit. She tutts and rushes off to bring me a fresh glass of water before sitting again.

"Sometimes I wake up crying at night or screaming. I just don't sleep well," she admits quietly.

"What do you dream about?" I ask.

"I...I don't know. Never really remember them." She shrugs. She's lying. I know and she can sense that I'm about to call bullshit. "I should get going. I work tomorrow but...I'll check in on you Tuesday evening, yeah?" Her attempt at distraction is lame but I'm too tired and out of it to bother digging deeper.

"It's okay. I am a grown man," I answer.

"I don't mind. Sometimes...well, sometimes it's nice to be needed. Have a purpose. But if you don't want me to stop by I won't." She looks down at the worn rug.

"I just meant I didn't want to be a burden. By all means, stop by. I'll gladly take homemade soup any day of the week." I push up and reach out, tilting her chin back up. "Thank you. It was actually really nice to wake up to someone being here, even more nice to have someone doting on me," I say with a smirk, dropping my hand. The moment feels like its gaining intensity and it would suck to be denied a first kiss based on possibly being contagious and having disgusting breath.

"Okay, well, it was nice to just be around someone else versus home alone. So, we're even." She grins. As she pushes off the couch to walk past me I grab her hand. She stops and eyes our connected hands wearily.

"Really. Thanks," I say gently. She nods, clicks off the TV, and heads out, nothing but the sound of the door clicking into place as she exits. This entire situation is so frustrating.

* * * * *

The morning comes too quickly. I feel like I've been run over by a semi. I gather all the strength I have and call my appointments for the day to reschedule. I haven't had to do that in almost three years. Sick is not something I do well. As promised, Pepper texts me mid-day to check in. Lacking the energy to respond any way other than curtly, I let her know that I'm still feeling terrible but that I'll live. Allie stops by after school to sit with me and it ends up being the highlight of my day. At seven, Clara arrives to pick up Allie.

She breezes through the door and plops down on the couch next to my head, wiggling her butt in for purchase.

"How you holding up?" she asks, looking mildly worried.

"I'll live," I grumble.

"Do you need anything?" Her hand reaches out to me, pushing hair from my forehead gently. It's an intimate gesture that somehow only makes me think of Pepper. Pink lips, full and lush. Dark chocolate hair tipped with purple hanging at her shoulders. The ceiling fan turns lazily overhead. I used to covet these moments.

"No, Allie's quite the nursemaid." I grin, nodding to the other end of the couch. Allie's white teeth gleam in the mellow light as she smiles.

"I got him water, made soup, and put the tissues right next to him. Just like you do for me," she tells Clara, a proud tinge to her little voice. I smile even though it makes my chapped lips hurt. She is so damned cute.

"Perfect, babe. Just what the doctor ordered," Clara responds lovingly.

"I think if you are ready to go, I might hit the sack," I interject.

"Of course. Allie, pack up your backpack and let's let Sawyer get some rest." Her fingers thread my hair just slightly before she gives me the "*mom*" once-over and retreats. Allie gives me a whopper of a hug and then they're gone.

Silence.

I shouldn't, but I lie in bed and wish Pepper was over again tonight, just sitting in the house with me. Just someone else to help take up the silence.

Chapter 14

FAMILY MOVIE NIGHT

Four. Days. It took four days but I finally feel like myself again. Slightly weak but no more cold sweats, hot chills, or general discomfort. Pepper, true to her word, checked in on me via text twice a day. I'd grown really used to seeing her name appear on my phone's screen. I like it. A lot. I learned more about her dessert addiction, her love of long bike rides, bourbon, and live music. Last night we had a long text conversation about dying hair. Not very manly but it was entertaining to say the least. She'd asked if Clara always dyed the same chunk of hair new colors and that she'd be too afraid to do that repeatedly to the same area because eventually your hair would fall out. She cited not wanting to be bald by Monday from over-dying.

Then we got on this whole topic of hashtags and how to make #baldbymonday trend on Twitter. I'm not very social media friendly and had to ask what the hell a hashtag was, but that got us going on a whole new conversation. Needless to say, she had me smiling and entertained for the night. I look forward to her messages. I smile preemptively when my phone dings just at the thought that whatever message is, it could be from her.

Allie and I are gearing up for our weekly movie night, one of her favorite playlists blaring through the house speakers. We're taking turns showing off our freakishly good dance moves to each other. Don't all line up at once, ladies, I know I am beyond a catch, if you like dork. Miley Cyrus's *"Hoedown Throwdown"* is blaring and I am lip syncing using a spatula as a microphone and trying to do the dance to it. Allie is in stitches laughing at me. Seeing her face light up the way it does when I goof off with her is well worth the effort.

"Sweet dance moves, but I come bearing dessert," a voice quips at me. I jump, grunting, and spin towards the sound. Allie rushes around me with a smile and squeals.

"SHIT FUCK CRAP SHITTY MCSHITTERTON!" I scream at Pepper in pure horror. Pure. Horror. Pepper stands in the entrance to the living room, the music still blasting from the surround sound. Allie is twirling around oblivious. I've just been caught dancing to Miley Cyrus with an eleven-year-old girl. Pepper's smile is wide and mocking but in a good way. Her smile reaches from one ear to the next. I am so embarrassed. Her body shakes softly as she tries to hold in her laughter.

"Hi! You brought dessert?" Allie asks, peering inside the bag Pepper is holding.

"Yes ma'am, I brought ice cream sundaes for your movie night," Pepper preens.

"Yes!" Allie fist pumps the air.

"Ahhhh, Pepper? Hello?" I call.

"Hi. Want ice cream?" Pepper says, holding up the bag in her hands.

"You really brought dessert?" I ask.

"All the fixin's, too!" She nods.

"You really shouldn't have."

"Well, I did. Let's make some sundaes," she suggests. Allie squeals again and runs to the kitchen to grab three bowls and three spoons.

I pull Pepper aside. "Pepper, in front Allie we're nothing but friends. I don't want her getting any ideas or attached. She already likes you," I whisper.

"Understood." She nods, heading to the kitchen. She drops the bag on the counter and pulls out chocolate and cookie dough ice cream, hot fudge, and peanut butter sauce and cherries and sprinkles. Jesus. This woman can do no wrong.

"Whoa, Sawyer! Check. It. Out. She brought everything!" Allie cries out in pure delight.

"I see that, Allie. Geez, Pepper, these are going to be the best sundaes ever. Mmmmmmmm. Peanut butter sauce, my favorite!" I moan, licking my lips. It takes all of my willpower not to sweep her up into a kiss. *Friends don't kiss*, I mentally remind myself.

"Allie, this is my friend, Pepper, remember?"

"Yeah. Of course I remember her. You like her." Allie snickers. I moan and shake my head at Allie. Pepper turns three shades of red and opens the drawer to her left, digging for something that she never finds. My chest shakes and I can't stop the laughter from rumbling out. Pepper's head snaps up and her eyes narrow at me as her nose wrinkles. Cute.

"Your dad's a sweet guy, Allie," Pepper says. Allie casts a curious glance at Pepper, me, and then Pepper again.

"I know." She shrugs like it's no big deal. We make three sundaes and invite Pepper to stay for the movie.

The couch is roughly big enough for me and Allie to sit on together comfortably. Including Pepper on it has my heart pumping. Should I sit next to her or should Allie sit in the middle of us? Or is that weird? Maybe I'll just stand. I have no idea what to do in this situation. I want to wedge myself in between them. I want to wrap my arms around them both but I know Pepper isn't there yet. I told her I could be her friend and I need to prove that or she'll never trust me. I *want* her trust.

"You two sit while I load the movie." I am biding my time and it feels weird. Why can't I just man up and make a move?

I pop the DVD in and push the play button. Then I stand up, grab my sundae, and eye the couch. I decide to sit on the floor in front of the couch and lean back against it between Pepper and Allie. That's safe, right?

"You can't see from there." Pepper's breath at my ear makes me shiver. Her hair brushes against my neck, she's leaned in so close to me. It smells delicious.

"Shhh. I can see just fine," I admonish. I can't focus on the movie anyways. The idea of a super gorgeous, super-hot, super funny woman sitting inches away has me completely distracted. Two slender arms slip under my armpits and I'm guided onto the couch in between Allie and Pepper. Her lips twitch and she leans into me. "Now you can see just fine," she whispers. I open my mouth to protest but then smack my lips together. She was right so I don't argue. Allie nudges my arm up and curls into me. This is nice. I catch Pepper watching Allie snuggling into me with a soft look in her eyes. I wonder if she wants kids.

At nine p.m. Allie is asleep, still curled into my side. I elbow Pepper who is actually watching the movie. "Yeah?" She sounds sleepy.

"Can you get up so I can carry Allie to bed?" I ask quietly. Pepper nods, standing to give me room to pick up Allie. There is an ease in this moment that feels so right, the three of us being here. Something warm slides through my insides and when her eyes catch mine they go warm like my insides feel. I stand up, making my way to Allie's room, where I gently set her in bed. I pull off her pants, pull the covers up over her, and give her a kiss before heading back to the living room.

Pepper isn't there. Turning to the kitchen, I find her washing the ice cream bowls and spoons. Wow. That's nice. Not just because I detest doing dishes, but because she wasn't even asked to do it. Thoughtful. She's hard and closed off yet opens up in the smallest of ways. I'm making progress. I feel like it's a victory.

"Woman of many talents I see," I tease as I lean a hip into the counter. She reaches out and wraps her hand around the back of my neck, pulling me closer. Surprise pummels me. Please God, please, let her kiss me. Let her finally make the move! She giggles and her fingers curl deeper into my neck before she says, "You're welcome," and crushes me to her chest in a long, deep hug. My hands work soothing strokes up and down the length of her back. I'm disappointed that this wasn't the defining moment, yet I haven't been handled with this much care by a woman in a long time. It feels amazing. I pull away and look down to her, admiring her. She's breaking down. I can feel it. I am going to win her over.

"You really made Allie's night bringing the ice cream," I admit.

"She seems like a good kid and you had a shit day," she says, referencing my back-to-back frat-house clients who all wanted ridiculous tatts today.

"She is and I did. But sometimes being a dad is like, 'Hey, Dad, let me know when you want to go to the bathroom and I'll come stare at you and ask for food,' versus the Norman Rockwell ice cream sundae picture you created tonight." My statement earns me a full-blown belly laugh from Pepper. Her eyes sparkle, crinkling just barely at the corners.

"I should head out," she says.

"Allie and I are going tubing tomorrow. Come with us," I state as she gathers her stuff. She pauses and hope flares in my chest.

"Tubing?" she asks, cocking her head sideways just so.

"You know, inner tubes, a river, sun," I say, walking with her towards the door. I'm trying to make this sound like a casual invite, not a date.

"Hmm, what time?" she asks, staring at me.

"We'll pick you up at ten and have you home by seven," I answer.

"What if I have to work?" She raises an eyebrow at me.

"Call out," I say as she palms the doorknob. She pauses, contemplating her options silently. I'm sure she's going to just leave without answering when she pauses in the doorway.

"See you tomorrow then." She laughs lightly before stepping through the door and shutting it softly behind her. I'd be lying if I said I didn't fist pump the air as soon as the door shut.

Chapter 15

BUBBLE OF BLISS

"Do you have some CDs to bring for the car ride?" Pepper asks, moving around the truck.

"Why, where are we going, 2001?" I joke. Her eyes shoot daggers at me but laughter bubbles out of her throat. God, her smile is addicting. I need to see it more.

"That was rude," she chortles at me.

"So was asking if I have a CD. I'm not *that* old," I quip, making a face at her.

"I never said you were old. Sounds like someone has a complex." She arches a brow at me playfully.

"Har har." I shoot her a pointed look. Piling into the truck, Allie sits in the middle spot of the back seat so she can hear all the conversation happening during the thirty-minute drive to the launch point.

"Let's play a game. I spy!" Allie chirps adorably. She's in a great mood today which makes me happy. Lately she's been sulking and full of attitude. Clara assures me it's normal for her gender and age but Jesus, there are moments when I'm ready to beat the kid.

"I spy..." I say and start looking at the scenery around us. Got it. A bug squashed into the windshield. "...something black," I say smugly. Looking over to Pepper, I notice she's not looking around for said object, nor is she smiling. I reach out, covering her forearm with my palm, face clearly asking "what's wrong" silently. Her eyes are blank and she just stares at me like she's a million miles away.

"The mileage sign!" Allie tries excitedly.

"Nope," I say, still focusing on Pepper. She shakes her head just barely, eyes swimming in sorrow, and turns to stare out the window. My gut says to leave it. If she wanted to explain she would have, and Allie is here, so maybe it's not the right time.

"The car ahead!" Allie tries again.

"Nope." I wink to her in the rearview mirror. She frowns back at me and looks around.

"Pepper, help me!" Allie pleads, reaching forward and playfully poking Pepper in the arm.

"I'm not big on car games," Pepper answers flatly.

Oh hell no. Do not make my kid feel like a fool for wanting to pass the time with a fun little game, no matter how annoying it is in reality.

"Yeah, Pepper. Help her," I push. It's an asshole move, I know, but I'd rather drive home the point that it's crap to shoot down a kid. Her eyes dart to mine and she scowls at me. I sense I've crossed some invisible line with her but unless she tells me what it is, how the hell would I know? I hold her glare, unwilling to back down. Communicate or pay the consequence.

"I have the new Miley Cyrus album on my Spotify, want to listen?" Pepper offers, removing her eyes from mine and looking to Allie. Allie squeals and hands the auxiliary cord from the back seat up to Pepper so she can plug her phone into the jack.

"Does no one want to know what the something black was?" I ask, perplexed at the one-eighty that's taken place.

"No," both reply in unison.

"Figures." I frown. I think I'm destined to never truly understand the conundrum that is the female species.

Clean, clear water, a shallow depth, and swift-moving current make this river perfectly relaxing. We couldn't have picked a better day to be out on the water. The sun is beating down on us, making the river feel absolutely perfect in temperature. Beers, beer floaties, inner-tubes, sun, Pepper and Allie, a perfect way to spend an afternoon. It's peaceful out here on the water: kids laughing, the water murmuring as the current moves, and not a cloud in the sky. Two gorgeous females accompany me and I feel strangely at ease with life in general. I could get lost in this moment and be content. Pepper's nose is wrinkled up as she smiles, dropping her head back toward the bright sun.

The rock in the middle of the rapids has kids gathered, all waiting in turn to jump off. Allie stands at the top patiently waiting while Pepper and I float leisurely next to each other.

"Tell me what happened in the car," I hedge. I want her to know it's okay to talk. To expel whatever her mind is wrapped up in.

"Huh?" Pepper says and shrugs, swiveling her float towards me.

"Pepper, the 'I Spy' game. You totally were all grumpy about it," I remind her.

"Oh. We're still on that?" she asks.

"I am," I answer.

"The last time I played...things didn't end well," she answers cryptically.

"What is that supposed to mean? It's a game for crap's sake," I ask. She sighs and takes a slug of her beer before meeting my eyes.

"That's all I'm going to say about that. I'd rather not remember it." She means business. Her entire face, her body language, makes it clear this conversation is over. One hand pushes into the clear water and paddles her float just slightly away from me to face Allie who is now next in line to jump. For a moment I watch Pepper's hair float along the top of the water behind her tube. I'm baffled. Her response makes no sense to me at all. Her golden sun-kissed skin almost glows in the bright sunshine. So many oddities and so many things I want to know more about. Why she plays everything so close to the vest escapes me. I paddle up to her and latch our tubes together just before Allie steps up to the edge of the rock. She smiles brightly and waves to us. Pepper enthusiastically waves back to her as do I. Pepper reaches out, grabbing my hand, and holds it while Allie jumps. Her small, lanky body flails in the air, her eyes wide with adrenaline before she plummets into the water. I laugh at the sight. Pepper turns to me with a smile, squeezing my hand.

"I'm sorry, Sawyer. I'm trying. I know you don't understand. But, I am trying," she says, her voice small but sincere. I don't want to push her. I want answers to my questions but I'm willing to wait it out for now.

"Okay." I nod, squeezing her hand back. She releases my hand just before Allie paddles up to us in her tube.

"That. Was. EPIC!" she squeals loudly. Pepper bursts out laughing. Watching the scene before me sends a wave of appreciation through me. How right this moment is—life is a quiet kind of spectacular. I feel a strange bubble of bliss, safely shrouded from the nuisances of everyday life.

By the time we crawl out of the river, we're all tinged slightly pink. The sky is painted gold, orange, and blue as the sun starts its descent. Allie haphazardly tosses her tube into the pile of rented ones, making the entire pile undulate like a Jell-O cake. Pepper's follows next and lastly I relinquish mine. Everyone is smiling and quiet as we make our way to the truck.

"That was so fun. Thanks for inviting me," Pepper says, buckling herself in.

"You're welcome," Allie chirps. I chuckle and shake my head.

"We had a good time, you're welcome to join us on any adventures," I tell her. Allie nods her head vigorously while grinning and Pepper blushes.

I watch as Pepper hugs Allie, thanking her for a lovely day. Allie beams and leans in close, whispering something to Pepper. I can only imagine what. Pepper's eye widen before a white, toothy smile takes over her face. She kisses Allie's forehead and laughs before turning and walking to her door. She waves to me and Allie, who's tucked beneath my arm, before walking in the door.

"What'd you say to her?" I push Allie for details.

"Girl stuff," she says, shooting me a look.

"Allie," I say sternly.

"Sawyer," she drawls with pure Clara attitude before slamming the truck door shut. It crosses my mind that maybe I'm doomed to never truly understand the female species. As we pull into the driveway at home I notice a text notification blinking. I swipe the screen to read, hoping it's from Pepper.

"Thursday. Patch in. Congrats Hydrant."

I stare at the text message for longer than necessary. I am finally patching in. The parties they throw to patch in are legendary: booze, music, girls, a loud, all-night-long ruckus. I cannot wait. My mind instantly wanders to Pepper. I want her there.

"Thursday night I patch in. Would like you to be there?"

I hit send and hope like hell that Pepper will agree to come to the party to celebrate with me. I can't think of anyone else I'd want to invite. I set my phone on the counter and start to put away the gear from today's adventure, trying to quiet my mind of the hope warming my body. I can't wait for Pepper's response.

Chapter 16

FOUR-LETTER WORDS

I've been driving myself insane for two days now. A tortuous mix of self-doubt is battling my willpower and anger. I feel like an insecure little bitch. It's taken me thirty minutes longer than normal to wrap up my paperwork for the day because my thoughts keep wandering to Pepper and whether or not she will call. I look up from the last of my paperwork towards the distinct rumble I hear. Pepper's bike comes to a stop outside the shop. It's a quarter past six. I haven't heard from her since we went tubing. Two full days of radio silence. She never even responded to my text that night. I watch as she tugs her helmet off, sets it on her bike, and strides purposefully into the shop. Anger overwhelms me. I'm hurt and mad but I'm also not sure that I have reason to be. I don't get mad at other friends when I don't hear from them for a few days.

"Hi," I clip as she approaches. She doesn't respond or stop until she is toe to toe with me. I stare down at her, thoroughly confused as she shoots daggers at me. She can't possibly be mad at me. I sent her a text before she even got home on Sunday. Heat radiates off her body. My arms want to reach out and wrap around her shoulders but I will them to stay where they are.

"Have time to take a ride?" she finally asks, breaking the tense silence between us. I sigh and roll my shoulders.

"I don't know, Pepper. What's up?" I ask. I have a thousand questions running through my mind. Why'd you drop off the grid? Why are we playing this game? Why can't I just be a part of your life? I stay silent, though, refusing to budge. She shuffles her feet and opens her mouth but nothing comes out. I wait. I've had lots of time to perfect my bullshit meter and she's setting off alarms left and right. I've ignored them. I've let my hormones lead but now, now I need more. A soft sigh falls from her lips. Her hands are clutched tightly into themselves at her sides. Her chest rises and falls. I watch as a single tear spills from the outside corner of one eye and drips off her chin. It tears me up. She doesn't move to wipe it away. She's trying to tell me something but I don't know her well enough to know what. Instinct takes over. The protector comes out and I lean down, regarding her just a moment longer before kissing her softly on her forehead. A wheezy breath escapes her.

"You are pure. You're good, Sawyer. Sometimes, I get lost in our moments together. Sometimes I think you're my last chance at being human again." The words fall faintly from her lips, laced with remorse and sorrow.

"I don't know what you mean, Pepper," I push.

"I know you don't." She tips her face up to look at me. "I know I must seem all...cryptic. I don't want you to have to understand that. I want..."

"Are you high?" I ask, taken aback. Her pupils are dilated and her jaw's clenched.

"What?" she asks.

"Are. You. High," I say in staccato for emphasis.

"Does it matter?" she scoffs. "I'm trying to..."

"Yes! Of course it matters! FUCK, Pepper. You show up here out of the blue, start what seems like a serious conversation, and I'm supposed to be okay with it coming from you while you're high? What are you on?" I grind out, irritated and cutting her off.

"Ecstasy." Her lips tip upward just slightly on the word, pissing me off.

"Did you think you'd waltz in here, say some meaningful words, and then be able to screw me,

Pepper? Although I'd love nothing more, I have a few standards. I want you because I like you. I see what you're doing. Driving your bike around like you stole it. Like you have a death wish, drugs, drinking, fucking because you think that gives you power. Power is just an illusion, Pepper. Grow up." I step backwards from her, not caring at the tears streaming down her face now. I thought the pot was recreational, the hard alcohol occasional, and the driving, well hell, that kind of race driving is just stupid. Bikes are meant to be enjoyed, leisurely. But ecstasy? That's just one thing too many to overlook.

"You don't get to tell me how to live my life, Sawyer. You don't know jack about what I've been through, what pain I live with!" she clips.

"So tell me!" I yell at her. She flinches, counts softly, and looks up to me.

"I...I can't," she sobs brokenly.

"Why the hell not!?"

"I can't. I want to, I do. It's not possible." Her finger rubs the scar at the bridge of her nose lightly. Her lips move silently, counting again.

"Stop counting damnit!" I bellow. "You know what I want? I want to date you. I want my friends, the MC, to meet you. I want to know what your favorite fucking color is, how you take your coffee, where your ticklish spots are. I want to know what you wear to bed, or how you look when you wake up first thing in the morning. I want to make you shiver when I touch you." I take a step towards her and drag a finger down her arm. Her entire body jolts. I lean down until our mouths are almost touching. "I want to make your heart race." Straightening, I turn my back to her and slam my hands on the front counter in frustration. "I'm waiting for the day when your bark will lose its bite, Pepper, but I'm losing hope."

"Hope is a four-letter word, Sawyer," she breathes. Her words shock me. Such a sad way to think. Why on Earth would someone ever say that? I turn to her. Tears slowly drip to the floor. Her head hangs.

"Love. Live. Life. Hope. Baby. Hunk. Soul. Balm. Calm. Loss. Myth. All four-letter words. All full of meaning. You don't get to decide if they stand up to their definitions. You don't get to redefine them. There will always be pages that hurt to look back on in your life. There will always be regrets. Hope is hope, Pepper. It exists." Anger flashes in her eyes at my words.

"Hope kills souls," she grits out. Turning on the ball of her foot, she jogs to the door, letting it slam shut behind her. I start to follow but find myself unable to execute. *Hope kills souls.* What the hell could she possibly mean by that? The sound of her bike firing up brings me out of my thoughtful fog. Remembering she's high sends a panic through me. I rush out the door, locking it as quickly as possible. I can hear her bike still. She can't be too far yet. I hop on my bike and head out in the direction I think she went.

It takes ten minutes to catch up to her. She's speeding around the twisting corners of the mountain road without much regard for safety. The expression "*ride it like you stole it*" is how she rides. I ride for pleasure; she rides like she's being chased. She doesn't acknowledge me at first, but I choose to keep up with her. I'd never forgive myself if something happened because she was an idiot who rode off mad and high. A small clearing at a sharp bend overlooks a babbling, small river. She slows slightly, fishtailing into the clearing. My breath hitches as I watch her try to control her bike. I slow and pull up next to her. She's panting. She swings her leg over the bike, letting it fall to the dirt. Hands on her knees, helmet vent open. I put my kickstand down, kill the engine, and walk to her.

"Don't," she grits. "Just, don't." She holds up a hand to stop me from getting closer. I stop and watch instead. "I lost someone I love. It was tragic and fucked up. It...it wrecked me. I haven't made a single friend here outside of Greta until you. I have no personal connections because people who're near me get hurt." She pauses taking a breath and looking weary. "I live with that guilt every day. It eats at me. Drinking, E, pot, it makes me feel alive in a way I can't on a daily basis. It's short-lived and never true, I know that, but the thrill, the rush, it's all I have. You don't get to judge that, Sawyer. People don't get close to me. You, though, you've weaseled your way in, making me want more. I don't honestly think I'm capable of giving more, though. I war with myself about it daily." Her words are short and choppy now like her breathing. Hurt bleeds from her, sorrow and regret, leaking out from her pores. It's almost as if she's drowning in her emotions. I pull her helmet off gently so she can pull herself together. She straightens up and gazes at me with such intensity that I have the overwhelming urge to hold her, to take some of the burden off her shoulders. Whatever events and experiences she's lived through are painful in a way I probably don't or won't understand. It's evident in her eyes.

"I want to hurt whoever did this to you, whoever scarred you so deeply," I whisper as she sniffles. "Are you all right?" Her eyes stay trained on mine. Fierce and fiery.

"Every action has a consequence, Sawyer. That's what I'm trying to tell you. It doesn't matter if you run or hide or just try to live in the moment. Eventually it catches up to you. Being with me would end up having a consequence. Not a happily ever after."

"Pepper, the world isn't man-meets-woman; they fall in love, and are torn apart for one of them to rescue the other for a happy ending. You fall in love, sometimes fall out, but you always fall in love again someday. You're robbing yourself of that chance." Her hand clutches mine tightly. I look down between us, unsure of when we connected. She's holding my hand like it's saving her life. Her small hand is warm and I wilt at her touch. How do I get through to her?

"I'm protecting others from me, not robbing myself of chances," she says desperately.

"Protecting others from what, though? What kind of evil do you think you harbor in that head of yours?" My brows furrow and my face is twisted up tightly, making my jaw ache.

"It's not evil." She shakes her head. There is something forbidden in her eyes. "I felt so normal on the river that day. I felt so at ease. Peaceful, like we were in some perfect bubble of bliss. I didn't want it to end. But the guilt after I went home, the guilt of knowing I could ruin you, I could ruin Allie, if I gave into you...it ate me alive. The last two days have been awful. So many moments I wanted to text you or call or just show up. I'm sorry about today. I lost my willpower. I never should have stopped at the shop. I shouldn't be telling you any of this. It's impossible to ask anyone to just understand blindly and that's all I have to offer." She releases my hand; a chill runs up my arm at the loss of contact.

Her words frustrate me. I don't understand why she can't talk about things. She makes it sound like if she tells her story lightning will instantly strike her dead. It's irritating as shit and on some level it feels like a game. Except I'm the pawn. I drag a hand through my hair and bite my lip ring.

I guess this is over.

She has no answers.

I have no answers and neither of us is willing to bend.

"Let me at least follow you home so that I know you're safe," I mutter after a tense silence. She nods her head at me, accepting that the road ends here for us. There is nowhere left to go.

Chapter 17

FRIENDS NO MORE

Parties at the MC for patching in are wild, although I'm not exactly in the mood for a wild night out after the week I've had thus far. I refuse to let Pepper Philips ruin my night, though. I refuse to let the thought of her monopolize my brain. I've gone over Tuesday's conversation a million times in the last forty-eight hours. I cursed and paced and picked up the phone only to hang up a thousand times. It all ends the same way: me being confused and Pepper out of my life, even as a friend. Tonight I drink. Tonight I replace my prospect patch with a member patch. It's a big deal. I'm proud to be a member. I want to remember this night as an achievement. I push Pepper from my brain and focus on my surroundings.

The women are scantily clad, wandering around in mini-skirts and tube tops, most of them already buzzing nicely. Music blares from the speakers, revving everyone.

"Where's your girl?" Carmine asks, glancing around the room with a scowl.

"She's not my girl," I answer on a sigh. Carmine's eyes dart to my face, searching for an answer.

"She skip town? Know where she went? She seemed flaky anyways," he rattles off at me.

"No she didn't skip town! What the fuck kind of question is that? We just aren't hanging out anymore," I reply, annoyed at his oddities.

"That was a compliment, bro, figured if she left you, it musta been cause she wasn't around anymore. Who could stay away from you, pretty boy?" he teases, but it doesn't feel good natured. It feels like he's looking for information. On what, I have no idea. I stare at him blankly, trying to figure him out.

"Why are you so interested in her?" I ask after a few moments.

"I'm not," he says and stiffens.

"You *are*, though. Always questions about her, and then you're all in her face when we do see her. Like at the bar. What's your deal?" I ask harshly as my anger grows.

"Bro, settle. You have it all wrong," he says heatedly.

"I don't think I do. Stay away from her," I bark. Carmine leans back, shocked, before sneering at me.

"It's not me you should worry about," he mumbles before stalking off. I want to reach out and throttle him but it would serve no purpose outside of making me feel temporarily better. He is so strange. I don't know why Beau keeps him around. After Hoot and I told him about the bar scene I thought for sure he'd let Carmine go, yet here he is at my patch-in party. I order another tequila shot and slam it before my brain decides to think or feel anymore.

"Hydrant, my boy, you've been a poster boy as far as prospects go. We're happy to have you as one of our own, officially," Beau bellows to the room, shot glass raised. A round of cheers rings out as the brothers gather around me. Beau rips off the prospect patch, tossing it to the floor. Kitten hands him a member patch. "Boys, it's time." Beau holds out my cut, allowing me to slip into it. As soon as I shrug it on and beam at the crowd they all laugh and toss their shots on my new cut.

"What the?!" I sputter. Beau slaps me on the back, hard. I stumble forward a step and glance around at everyone. They all seem to think it's normal to throw liquor on someone.

"Just breakin' it in for you," he says and chuckles. "Tradition is tradition," he muses.

I'm sticky and smell like tequila but the night is sailing right along. Five beers in and multiple shots have my mind foggy but I'm not driving myself anywhere tonight so I enjoy the feeling, hazy and relaxed. A hot little blonde sits on my knee, purring about something in my ear. I'm far too concerned with the conversation Hoot, Beau, and I are having, though, to pay attention to her. She lightly taps my shoulder and pouts. I missed something apparently. I blink twice and try to hold her gaze.

"Awww. Don't be like that," I flirt. She titters and says she'll be whatever I want if I want her. I smile but my gut tells me the only thing I want isn't here and won't be here. I shake the stupid thought from my head and hug the blonde into me. She smells kind of good.

"*Trip Like I Do*" starts to play from the speakers. My mind wanders to Pepper. I shake her from my brain and focus on the girls around me. All of them flirting, willing. A shot is handed to me. I take it and slam it back. The door to the club bar swings open, letting in a refreshing blast of night air. It's after ten and most everyone who's coming has been here for hours. The blonde on my knee nibbles the shell of my ear. It makes my skin tingle. I turn to the bar to order another shot.

"Get off," a soft voice commands.

A leather-and-lace corset hugging every single perfect curve, leather pants that look like they've been painted on, and black heels appear before me. Pepper's black hair is teased out to epic biker proportions. Her eyes are lined heavily with black liner, making the caramel color of her eyes pop. Her lips are cherry red and glisten like she's just licked them. She's every biker's wet dream. I'm too drunk to bother wondering why she's here. I want to lick her. I want to devour her. I just want her. I am so done being friends.

"'Scuse me?" the blonde says tartly.

"Get off him," she repeats with calm fury. I disengage the blonde's arms from me and push her gently until she's standing, mouth agape at me. Don't care, though. Pepper is here. Here and demanding full attention. I shouldn't give it to her. I know I shouldn't but I'm going to. The boys are catcalling Pepper and offering to buy her shots or drinks. She doesn't take her eyes from me, though. It's like we're the only two people in the universe right now. The music makes me feel like I'm in a trance. In a trance and staring at the most beautiful creature to grace the planet. She steps between my legs and opens her mouth. My vision is hazy, though. She sets something on the tip of her tongue and grins wickedly.

"Trip like I do, Sawyer," she breathes into my mouth as her lips meet mine. Her breath is minty. Her tongue pushes something into my mouth and I know I should care. I should ask what it was. I should spit it out, but I can't. Velvet lips massage mine until my hand is knotted in the hair at the nape of her neck, holding her firmly to me. Her pelvis pushes against my groin, sending shivers through me, synapses firing, neurons receiving too many conflicting feelings. The beat of the music is fast, and the loud chatter at the bar is providing a white noise of sorts. Pepper's smell infiltrates my nostrils, her lips are on mine, and the taste of her overwhelms me. My heart feels like it's going to pound right out of my chest. I can hear my pulse in my ears, whooshing. I can feel Pepper's pulse in her neck. Fast and hard. Exhilaration courses through me and I squeeze her tighter, the leather and lace providing a tactile experience. She's kissing me with a deep, greedy want. It feels good to be wanted. To be chased, instead of chasing.

"Who's hottest?" she asks, ripping her mouth from mine.

"Huh?"

"Look around, Sawyer, pick a girl," she pushes. I don't know what game we're playing but I drag my eyes away from Pepper and scan the room.

"That one." I smile sloppily. Everything feels different. She looks over to the blonde that was sitting on my knee previously and sighs. Untangling herself from me she struts over to the blonde and starts talking to her. I try like hell not to punch every guy here in the face as they blatantly stare at Pepper's ass. Tugging the blonde behind her, she comes back to me, making me feel lighter somehow. The room spins and tilts a little but Pepper remains steady.

"Where's the bed?" she asks. I can feel my face scrunch up at her question. I don't understand. Her hand cups my jaw and it feels like heaven. Gentle, warm, soft. "There is a bedroom here, right?" I nod and take her hand, leading her. Brothers whistle and scream as I lead Pepper to the guest room. Both girls enter the room and Pepper shuts the door. The music is now muted but still audible in the distance. Pepper instructs the girl to sit on the bed. The blonde follows her orders without batting a fake eyelash.

"Sawyer," she says, holding my gaze. I nod to let her know she has my attention. My tongue doesn't seem to be able to help my mouth form words. "I'm giving you a congratulatory gift. There is only one rule. You with me?" she asks. I nod. "You are to watch. No touching. Do not join in and do not touch yourself. Do you understand?" she asks. I nod. I have no idea what's going on. My mind is hazy. I feel too much right now or maybe not enough. I can't be sure what's happening. I think I'm on drugs. No wait, I am. I know I am. She pulls a chair next to the bed and motions for me to sit. A steady thumping reverberates through the walls, creating a beat that she seems to move to.

She stands the blonde up and starts to strip her clothes off slowly. So slowly. It takes my brain minutes to catch up to my eyes. Everything has a strobe light effect. Pepper's small hands caress the blonde's milky white breasts. My dick leaps to attention. I groan and shift in my seat. What were the rules? There were rules. Why is Pepper massaging another woman's breasts? Wait, do I care? *No.* No, this is awesome. Pepper is awesome. I want Pepper. Why is the blonde even here?

The blonde watches me with fascination but I don't return the eye contact. Pepper's pouty, full lips wrap around a nipple and suck as she guides the blonde onto her back on the bed. Her hands trail down the blonde's body slowly. Those small, soft hands. I need to touch her. As if sensing my thoughts she glances at me and shakes her head no. I stay rooted in my spot. Pepper trails kisses and licks down her body until she's poised between the blonde's legs. I gasp and wonder if she's really going to do what I think. Am I the king of the world? I think, yes, yes I am. Two fingers slide in and out slowly. The blonde's eyes roll back in her head. My pants are too tight. My brain is going to explode. I've never experienced something like this. My eyes are heavy but I force them open wider. I rub my palms on my thighs to keep them from grabbing my cock. Pepper's tongue comes out and licks the blonde's center. Slowly she licks up and down the length of her. The blonde's hips buck and she moans, hands finding her own breasts and massaging. Pepper works two fingers in and out in a steady rhythm while she licks the blonde with determination. Sucking, licking, in repeating patterns. My pants are wet with pre-cum. I think the slightest touch from anyone would make me explode right now. The blonde screams out as her legs try to snap closed. Pepper skillfully keeps them apart and keeps going through the tremors until the blonde is babbling utter nonsense.

Pulling back from between her legs, Pepper slaps the blonde's crotch and tells her to get dressed and then get lost. The blonde shoots me a look but I ignore it. There is only one person I want. She quickly tugs her clothes back on and curses us both as she hauls ass out of the room, shooting dirty looks over her shoulder at us. Pepper wipes her mouth on the back of her hand and stalks to where I sit.

"Take me home," she says into my ear. I sprint from the room, frantically looking for Hoot. Finally finding him, I tell Hoot to fire up the truck and drive us home now. I pull Pepper onto my lap in the truck, enjoying the feel of our bodies touching. She is soft. Light and warm. Hoot hollers at us to take it in the house, making Pepper giggle. The ride was consumed with making out like teenagers. If Hoot hadn't been driving I would have taken her in the car. It takes no time to get us into the house. I hear a horn honk, probably Hoot signaling his departure, but I don't pay mind to it.

Gripping her hips, I lift her, setting her on the countertop. Resting between her thighs, I lean in for the kiss. Those lips. I need them. Now. Her legs wrap around my waist, pulling me to her, nails raking down my arms fervently. She tastes sweet, like pink lemonade, but she's wicked, wickedly devious with her body. I pull back slightly; those big, brown eyes framed by perfect black lashes looking up at me all half-mast would do any man in. I'm quite certain that in this moment the bliss I feel will never end.

"Can't blame a man for being a little over excited can you?" I rasp as she breaks our contact to come up for air. She tips her head sideways and smirks.

"I guess not. I did go from friend zone to threesome in under a minute," she says, biting her lower lip. Her eyes darken, changing from caramel to milk chocolate.

"So damned hot," I growl, leaning towards her sweet, pouty mouth.

"Addicted already?" she whispers before licking my lip ring.

"I prefer the term habit, but yeah. Pepper, you're an addiction I don't *want* to kick," I whisper back.

"Let's see how this plays out," she murmurs. The green light. I'm getting the green fucking light. Finally.

"I missed you," I groan as she massages the back of my neck.

"Not as much as I missed you," she says between kisses. I pull back and take a step away from her. Taking her hands in mine, I flip over her hands until they're wrist up and kiss the inside of each one before dropping them and moving away from her.

"Lose the pants, keep the corset and heels, and follow me," I command with a crook of my finger. Her eyes darken again, stormy with desire and lust. She shimmies out of the leather pants and prowls after me. She better have stamina because I am not giving up a moment of the next twenty-four hours for sleep. I intend on taking Pepper to places she's never been before.

We crash into my room together locked passionately in a soul searing kiss. Tearing myself away from her I look her over. She makes a move to kiss me but I back up. I'm hard as a rock but I want to take my time.

"Touch yourself." I command. "Eyes on me." Her eyes darken as she bites her lip and slides a finger down herself until reaching her sex. I grab my cock and stroke as her finger slides between her folds. Tonight's going to be epic.

Chapter 18

WHO THE HELL ARE YOU?

I feel like crap. I'm hungover from shots and something else. Aww yes, drugs, perhaps. I roll to my side and stare at Pepper's naked sleeping form. Her olive skin is slightly flushed and her full, pouty lips move just barely with her breaths. Gorgeous. I mash the heels of my hands into my eyes to relieve some of the pressure in my head and think back on last night. Damn.

"Touch yourself," I'd commanded. She'd complied. "Eyes on me."

She'd bit her full bottom lip and rubbed herself for me. I'd watched her slide a finger inside herself while I stroked myself. It dipped inside, came out wet, and slid back up to her clit.

"Sawyer..." she'd mumbled in pleasure.

"Do. Not. Speak," I'd told her, crossing the short distance between us and laying her back on the bed. I'd propped her legs up over my shoulders, spread her wide, and tasted her. Repeatedly. Her entire body trembled and shook until she let out a guttural, incoherent scream. I'd slowly unlaced her corset on my way back up her body. One breast at a time I'd lavished with attention. Perfect, full breasts that were like silk under my tongue. She'd reached between us, grabbing my dick, and stroked me until I nearly came. I'd pulled her hand away and plunged into her tightness before finishing. I didn't want to come in her hand, I wanted to be inside her. She'd pouted for a moment before arching her back and thrusting her hips up to meet mine. I'd watched her come with such force that a tear leaked out from her eye, sliding down her temple. It'd tasted salty and sweet.

Reaching for the bottle of water on the nightstand, I sit up slightly and chug half the contents before setting it back in its resting place. A hand comes to my thigh, a thumb making lazy passes on the skin. I turn to her and Pepper's grin is huge and lazy and *hot*.

"What'd you give me last night?" I ask. I'm trying not to stay mad over this one small detail of an amazing night but it needs to be talked about.

"Ecstasy," she says and winks. Winks! I groan and pinch the bridge of my nose.

"Never again, Pepper." Her smile falters and she pulls the covers up over her naked body.

"Excuse me. I was just trying to give you a good time. A congratulations for patching in," she defends.

"Don't need drugs to do that. Also, don't need you eating out another woman. I'm not going to lie, that was *hot* as shit, but I only need you." I roll on top of her. She pushes. Hard. But I don't budge. "You want to give me a gift, go for it, but the only thing I *want* is you, naked, under me." Her eyes widen and she looks taken aback.

"It was supposed to be...fun."

"It was, but I don't need drugs for fun. I don't need my girl offering herself to another girl for fun. You want fun, I'm happy to give it to you anytime, anywhere, any *way*, as long as it's just you and me." I pull the covers down, exposing her breasts, and nibble her nipple. She gasps and tries to make me look at her. I continue my plight on her breasts. When she's squirming under me I stop, taking her face in my hands.

"You are enough for me. Just you." Dipping my head, I trace her bottom lip with my tongue while sliding one hand down her body until I find her clit. She bucks under me, her hands coming around my

146

neck and pulling me closer. "Do you understand?" I ask into her mouth. God, she feels good.

"Yes," she answers breathlessly. I move my fingers lower, sliding inside of her.

"You sure we're clear?" I ask.

"Crystal."

Curling my fingers just so, hitting that coveted spot, and she groans loudly while thrusting her hips upward.

"Good. Now roll over." She obliges instantly, ass up, head down, and I smile. She gets it now.

* * * * *

In the last week Pepper has spent all but two nights with me. We never stay at her place. I don't push to know why, but on some level it irks me. We'd spent my patching-in night and most of the next day rolling in bed together, ordering take out for fuel or discussing the over-the-top method she used to get my attention. I'd laughed when she said she felt like she owed me "the male fantasy" to make up for friend-zoning me for so long. Of course it was a fantasy of sorts, what straight male doesn't want to see some girl-on-girl action? Truth be told, though, I'm more turned on by the fact that she's in *my* bed with me and told her as much.

A lot of good things have started. She talks, not a lot, but enough for now. The love of dessert has been prevalent from the start but let me tell you, when a chick adds cheesecake to the bedroom, it's mind blowing. I have half a mind to keep a slice next to the bed whenever she's here in hopes that she'll wake me up with a "'dessert BJ" every time.

Allie's been over the last two nights so Pepper's stayed at home. It's been torturous and good at the same time. It allows us time apart to cool off. I don't want to risk burning out too fast. I want her to keep opening up. To keep talking. She'd mentioned that

Greta would be away for business for a week or so and that she wanted to hang out with her and get her workouts in before she left, so our schedules actually meshed pretty well. I have club business tonight and she has to work so our two-day dry spell is extending a third day. I'm really looking forward to this weekend, though. I want to take her to the Parlor for ice cream and maybe take a day trip with her on the bikes up into the mountains. I'm a total sap, thinking about ice cream dates and long bike rides. I want her on the back of my bike but I know she'll want to ride next to me on her own. I'm not really sure which is hotter.

I intended on driving home but I found myself steering the opposite way as I left the MC. It's well after midnight and I'm a total creeper for what I'm about to do. I slow as Pepper's house comes into view. I'm not even sure how I ended up here. It wasn't a conscious choice. Slowing more, I let the bike idle. I feel like a total stalker watching her house. Why did I even come? Someone's jacked-up truck is parked in her driveway. Who would be over at this hour? A knot forms in the pit of my stomach.

Two lights are on that I can see from where I'm parked. I squint, trying to focus on the inside of the biggest window. Pepper's long, black hair comes into view as she strides purposefully into what looks like the kitchen, her arms flailing, her face screwed up tightly. What the hell? A man appears behind her. Tall and broad and stiff in posture. Arms gesturing wildly. She spins to face him, leaving me with a view of her back. She points towards the door. The broad man slams his hands down on the counter, shaking his head no. Grabbing something next to her, she hurls it towards the man. I can hear the shatter of the item as it hits the wall. Not on my watch. Kicking the kickstand down, I hop off the bike and race up the steps to her front door. Blood rushes in my ears as my brain thinks up the worst scenarios possible.

"Pepper!" I roar. Silence. Oh shit. "Pepper!" I pound frantically on the door. What has that asshole done to her? Taking a step back, I notice a window cracked and decide to go for it when I'm hauled backward and flung onto my ass roughly. Before I have a chance to look up, catch my breath, or figure out what the hell just happened, my arm is yanked up and back. I squeal in pain as I'm hoisted to my feet.

"Shut up and get inside," a burly, sandpapery voice orders. Not that I have much choice in this position. I'm pushed through the side entrance, into the kitchen. Pepper is on her hands and knees in a tiny nightie cleaning up glass and spilled liquid. Her face lifts, splotchy from crying, takes me in, and blows out an annoyed breath. I feel like an outsider instead of the hero.

"Let him go, Bentley," she commands. To my utter surprise, he does. I rub my arm gingerly and step away from him with a glare.

"Pepper? Are you all right?" I ask, confused as hell.

"What are you doing here, Sawyer?" she asks, pushing up from the floor with a dustpan full of glass shards. I look between the two of them. Nope. Still confused.

"I...shit. I don't have a good excuse," I admit. Moments pass and I begin to feel more and more like an intruder.

"You shouldn't be here," Bentley grits out.

"Who the hell are you?" I whip back.

"BOYS!" Pepper shouts, drawing our attention to her. "Sawyer, follow me." She turns and stomps out of the kitchen. I follow Pepper down a dimly lit hall to a bedroom. She walks me inside what is clearly her room, motions for me to sit on the bed with her, and turns to me.

"I need you to wait here. I'll come get you in a minute," she says sternly, not giving up anything.

"I think maybe I should just go," I mutter while dragging a hand through my hair roughly.

"Too late for that," she laments, standing. "Just...just wait, okay?" she asks. She leaves, closing the door behind her.

Everything feels wrong. I get up and pace. Her walls are a gray color and her bedding a soothing blue. Everything spa-like and calm, but I don't feel calm at all right now. There are no family photos, no friends depicted anywhere on her walls or her dresser. Clothes lay strewn on the floor and the bed looks as though it's been slept in. Is that her boyfriend? Oh fuck. What the hell have I gotten myself into? Gripping her dresser for support, I see a note resting on the top, catching my eye.

"Eyes open. Escaped. Coming for you."

The choppy lettering looks like my handwriting, a man's handwriting; maybe it's that guy's out in the kitchen. How did things get this gnarly this fast? I haven't had time to think, to work any of this out. I stumble backwards until the backs of my knees hit her bed and I lie down. Stretching my arms behind my head to relieve the tension growing in my shoulders, my hand connects with cool steel. I flip over, gripping it, and pull it from under the pillow. A pistol. Heavy and dangerous. A gun, under her Goddamned pillow. *Who is Pepper?* Emotions whirl around deep in my gut. Allie pops into my mind and I can't shake the feeling that Pepper has indeed been warning me about herself for good reason. Clinging to the gun, I've decided I've had enough. Who keeps a pistol under their pillow? Storming from her room, I stomp down the short hall, their murmuring voices growing louder as I approach. I quiet my steps and my breath to listen better.

"I won't do it. I won't sit back again and watch you try and kill yourself," he grunts.

"That's awfully dramatic," Pepper drops sarcastically.

"Is it? Jesus, I watched you almost drown in bourbon once before and now you're adding drugs to the mix?" he grits.

"Pot, Bentley. I hardly think that's a death sentence," she quips. So the drugs thing is new. Somehow that sets my mind at ease just a bit. I agree with him, though, it seems like she's ruining her life purposefully.

"Oh so the X was just a onetime deal?" he asks. I can hear the caustic tinge in his tone.

"How do you even know about that!" she squawks.

"Honey, I'm ATF, and you're you. How did you think I wouldn't know about it?"

I can hear her feet drag along the flooring and she huffs but otherwise remains silent. It feels as if time has paused.

Tick tock.

I'm about ready to step out from the shadows when he speaks.

"And this Sawyer guy?" The sharp intake of his breath is trenchant. "I knew this would happen but why didn't you tell me?"

"Bentley, please. I'm just...we're just friends." At the word *friends* my gut sinks. A bilious noose tightens around my chest. I truly am a fool.

"Mags, you're allowed to move on. Start a life. WITSEC isn't a death sentence." He sounds defeated and tired. Like this conversation is nothing new between them.

"I...I don't know what to say," she whispers as my head spins. What have I stepped in to?

"There isn't anything to say." His tone is harsh, accusing, even. "We need to clean this up. Get your story straight," he clips, all business.

WITSEC? WITSEC!

Pieces are falling together and not in a good way. Little did I know things would get so crazy so quickly. Who is she? I step out from the shadows, still clutching the gun. Instantly Bentley draws his weapon and aims at me. The gun clatters to the floor as my hands rise upward, stunned.

"Pepper?" I croak.

"Bentley, for fuck's sake," she snarls. He withdraws his gun, setting it on the small kitchen island. He doesn't withdraw his glare. What the hell did I do to him?

"Who are you?" I ask, voice faltering. Her face morphs into so much defeat it tears at my insides.

"I'm Pepper," she says and sighs.

"WITSEC. Gun. Cryptic note. Mags?" I grind out, anger bubbling.

"Fuck," Bentley grits, running a hand through his hair. "Time to sit."

He brushes past me into the dark living room, switching on a lamp. Pepper follows suit and I'm lost in the chaos. My thoughts swirl like a tornado. Can I do this? Should I do this? Is it time to cut and run? I can't form a solid thought. It's odd. There's how you feel, and then there's how you think you *should* feel. I need, no, want answers. I want to know what the hell I've unwittingly gotten into.

"Sit, Sawyer," Pepper orders. So I do.

"Magnolia was my name. The gun is registered to me and I can't sleep without it. The note is from Bentley." She jerks her thumb at him. Understanding dawns and I suck in a sharp breath.

"Clara was right. You lied to her, to me." My mind races back to dancing together at the bar. The gunshot sound.

Her face.

Terror.

When she took care of me while sick. Calm. Her playfulness at the Cascades. Memories, all conflicting, run rampant.

"Mags, or rather Pepper, is in the Witness Protection Program. She didn't lie. Her name is legally Pepper Philips now. And simply divulging this information could cost her her safety," Bentley cuts in, looking pissed. So now I'm putting her in danger by demanding the truth? Please. This asshole is riding my last nerve.

"Why are you in WITSEC? Who's coming for you?" I ask. I'm concerned for her now. The anger and betrayal I felt is now changing, shifting into care and concern.

"Can't share that information," Bentley snaps.

"Maybe you should let her answer," I snap back.

"Boys, come on. It's late. I'm tired. So tired," Pepper says, her voice full of regret. Her hair hangs in long falls over her shoulders and catches the lamp light just so. It almost looks like a halo around her head but she's no angel.

"I don't do secrets," I state. I won't. I can't.

Can I? After Clara, I have to wonder if there is any relationship that can be successful where secrets reside.

"They aren't secrets. Don't you understand? I *can't* tell you. I would, Sawyer. I would. I want to, I want to let you in." Her face falls and she sniffles. "Bentley, you should go. Please. Think about your job. You're not supposed to have contact with me." Interesting. He stares at her, nostrils flaring. "Bent, you aren't a marshal. You aren't my contact. You need to go. I won't let you ruin your career because of me."

"Screw you," he grinds out as his body jerks and anger rolls off him as he stands. Without a word he's to the front door, swinging it open and striding out, slamming it behind him. The picture on the wall rattles with the force of the slam. Headlights flood the living room as he starts his truck up. Pepper shoves out of her chair and stares at me. Silence engulfs us. She pinches the bridge of her nose. Her white nightie clings to her curves in a way I can't seem to ignore even though, right now, I should. I should have more questions. I should walk out. I don't want to, though. I want to stay and find out what might be between us. I want more answers. It's obvious I'm not going to get them right now.

I lick my lips and stare at Pepper just to intimidate her. I know Bentley is watching from the driveway. The shudder she emits is just what I wanted for a reaction. I know it makes Bentley want to smash through the living room window and grab me by my throat. I need to stake my claim, though. Jealousy is an ugly thing. I'd know.

I'm to her in three long strides, mind made up. I want nothing more than to kiss her, to hold her. I need to feel her. She stumbles back a step at my approach. Her face registers surprise when she notices her feet aren't on the ground anymore. When my lips crash down on hers my skin sizzles in every place where our bodies touch. I gently slip my tongue between her lips and I can feel her tremble in my arms. Tilting my head, I deepen the kiss. Her lips are soft like cashmere. She winds her arms around my neck and threads her fingers through the hair at the nape of my neck, pulling me closer. I tear my lips away from hers and look into her eyes. The headlights fade as Bentley finally pulls out and peels rubber on the road, signaling his departure.

"What's wrong with having a little faith in what you're feeling in your heart? Why be so afraid?" I ask. I set her down softly, but keep a strong arm wrapped around her waist, crushing her to me from chest to hips. Her smile. I feel it in my belly. Her caramel eyes are the most beautiful eyes I've ever seen but when they're warm and her lips turn up into a smile, making her whole face warm, it's almost too much to take. Her face falls as she lets my words sink in.

"I don't have faith in life," she answers brokenly, "and I can't answer your questions. They aren't secrets being kept from you, they're questions that *have* to stay unanswered. Please, Sawyer, I'm doing this to protect you."

"You think I need protection? From you? Pepper, I promise I would never let you do anything to harm me or yourself. I will protect you from all your demons, real or imaginary."

She sighs, resting her head on my chest.

"I still can't tell you anything."

"I don't know if I can live with that. But for now I'm willing to try, on one condition."

Her face lights up with delight as she clutches my arm.

"Shoot."

"Stop the drugs. Bentley's right, it's like you're trying to kill yourself."

Her face blanches and her eyes snap shut while she inhales.

"All the dangerous things make me feel alive. Just for a little while. It's like a flash flood of *feeling* something. Without that, life just seems corrosive. We're all headed for the grave anyways." Her words scorch my heart. I can't imagine having such a bleak outlook on life. Although, if I did, I suppose I'd want to get baked daily, too. Or worse.

"Pepper." I search for something to say but she shakes her head, suggesting this portion of the conversation is over. She scrutinizes me in silence as we both eye each other.

"I will stop everything but my bourbon if it makes you more comfortable," she announces sincerely. Relief sweeps through me. It's a start.

"Fair enough," I chortle at her conviction. "I mean, we all have one vice in life. I'm not asking you to do anything but show some moderation." Leaning down, I cup her face and kiss her lightly. She kisses me back tenderly, but with a deep, underlying passion. I need her to be lying down in bed with her legs wrapped around my waist. Before I do something stupid, I turn towards the front door. It's definitely my time to leave.

"Stay," she says.

"What?"

"Stay the night. Please." Her eyes are innocent and pleading with my own. How could anyone say no to her?

"I'm not sleeping with a gun under the pillow." I arch a brow at her. She titters passively but stands, motioning for me to follow her.

"Fair enough," she chirps, allowing a small smile to grace her lips.

Chapter 19

TRUTHS

I lie down on the bed next to her. She sets the pistol on her nightstand, kills the light, and rolls to face me. My eyes adjust to the semi dark room. The nearness of her body makes my body sizzle, and the warmth from her body makes me woozy. This day has been too long and too dramatic for me but there is so much that needs to be said.

"Pepper," I start. My voice sounds dry and crackly. She sighs.

"I know. This is why I push you away," she answers.

"You don't have to, though. Things make a little more sense now that I know you're in witness protection."

"Do they, though? Because I wouldn't have been able to tell you that if tonight hadn't happened. My life is all lies, Sawyer. I'm in danger, maybe. I've been struggling. I don't know how to live a normal life. I don't know how to move on. I want those things, but as you can see it's almost impossible to forge true friendships or relationships when you're living a lie. I don't want to memorize a cover story. To pretend to be someone else. The guilt eats at me, Sawyer. It eats me up knowing that you have this whole, complete life and that to have me in it means concealing who I actually am. It hurts. It reminds me that I can't have what I want. That I can't have what you have." Her voice is furious with regret.

"Don't say that. You can lie *about* your life all you want but it doesn't change the truth about who you are as a person. It doesn't change your soul," I whisper into her ear. She inhales sharply, body wooden, but stays silent. "Tell me a truth," I say quietly as I bring her hand up to my mouth and gently kiss the inside of her wrist. She mewls slightly but doesn't reject the idea.

"I'm lonely," she admits.

"We all feel that at some point but loneliness is not a permanent state. I'm here, Pepper," I promise.

"I've been so lonely. So out of control. I'm still so angry about things," she whispers like it's a shameful secret to feel those emotions. She rolls, burying her face in my chest, wrapping her arms around me. "Sawyer, your lips are so warm, so intoxicating. You taste like a fine wine and all the best life has to offer." No tears fall but her breathing is ragged. I hold her firmly to me and keep my mouth shut. It seems she needs someone to listen more than she needs someone to talk. I stay quiet.

"I like Allie," she blurts into my chest. I chuckle at her randomness and peel away from her slightly so I can see her face.

"I like Allie, too." I laugh. She shakes her head slightly and laughs lightly.

"Sorry. That was random," she apologizes.

"A little."

"I was thinking of more truths. That was one of them."

The corners of my mouth pull up into an enormous grin. This girl is not at all who I thought she was, yet she's everything I wanted her to be.

* * * * *

Light spills in softly through the curtains. Arms are wrapped around my midsection and black hair is strewn everywhere. Pepper's breaths blow out of her mouth in short, soft bursts. She looks like a completely different person when she sleeps. Soft, innocent, sweet. I like it. It's almost as if I'm seeing the real her. I want to touch her scars. Kiss them. I want to know where they came from. They highlight the beauty she already possesses. She stirs and I realize it's only a moment before she wakes and the mask comes back on.

"Morning, love," I mumble groggily as she stretches her limbs next to me. She glances at the clock. Surprise etches in her features.

"I haven't slept well, let alone late, in more than a year," she says into the early morning light as she stares at the clock. I stay quiet and hold her gently to me. "I don't know what you're doing to me, Sawyer but...it's working," she mumbles, it seems, to herself.

I lean over her and brush my lips to hers. I deepen the kiss. She presses her body closer to mine. I want more. I want more of her, of us, of the feeling in this particular moment, but I know I can't push too fast. I pull away gently, swiping the pads of my thumbs across her jaw.

"Breakfast?" I ask.

"Absolutely." She grins.

Chapter 20

BITCHES BE TRIPPIN'

It is a stunning day today. Mayhem is hosting a casual cookout that happens to be family friendly. There's something about the way the sunlight shines on Pepper. It brings out the abandon in her eyes. She's carefree in this moment and I can't tear my gaze from her. Everything from the grass to Pepper and Allie seems to be in Technicolor. I am too busy watching her to focus on the conversation around me.

"Beer?" Greta asks, thrusting a bottle in my face.

"Uh, sure. Thanks."

"She seems better somehow." Greta motions to Pepper who is giggling with Allie over something a few feet away from us.

"I guess," I answer, shaking my head slightly.

"You've done that," she states firmly.

"Have I?" I turn to face Greta. Her hawk-like eyes are taking in the scene before us with scrutiny. She's always so Goddamned alert. I know Pepper worries about her. Wonders about her quietly in her own way. It's hard not too when she barely gives up any personal information. Pepper's mentioned opening up more lately to her but Greta still keeps her life pretty tight lipped.

"Yes," she says and nods. "You have. Keep it up. She's a tough nut, but you'll crack her," she says seriously. I laugh at her odd choice of phrasing and she looks to me and smiles. "I am too I guess. Pepper's probably the only real friend I have and shit, we barely discuss personal things."

"Why is that?" I ask, genuinely curious. I still don't understand Greta. She's always watching, paying attention to her surroundings. She shrugs noncommittally.

"I guess some of us are just like that," she answers.

"No, some of you have just experienced things to *make* you like that," I retort.

"You could be right but I'll never tell." She laughs and moves in Hoot's direction. I guess that's the end of that conversation.

Allie nods at Pepper and runs off in the direction of a group of kids her age. She rolls back onto her elbows, face to the sun, and smiles. Gorgeous. I think I could watch her forever. Carmine plops down next to me and bumps his shoulder into mine. He's been handling family *matters* in Maryland and just arrived back. Outside of telling people he's handling matters, he never talks about family at all. They have no names. No stories about them are shared. No one comes to visit him. He has no pictures. It's strange.

"I thought you two weren't a thing," he says, nodding to Pepper. His eyes narrow as he watches her.

"We are," I state, already suspicious.

"She's trouble," he warns.

"What would you know about it?" I ask, getting angrier by the second. What is his problem?

"She's like cold product. Hot once, but used up."

"Who the fuck *are* you? It's rude to judge. You don't know shit!" I bark at him.

"I'm someone you should listen to," he hisses. "You got shit here that's good, shit to care about, a *kid*. She," he says and points at Pepper, "is going to bring nothing but trouble into your life."

"You got something you want to fill me in on, spit it out or leave it the fuck alone. Pepper is not your business," I snap. Pepper looks to us, brows furrowed at my raised voice.

"I can't spell it out any more than I have, man," he grinds out. His phone rings, he glances at the screen, looks to Pepper who's making her way towards us, then me, and says, "Gotta take this," before wandering off. The more shit he spews at me about Pepper the more my gut tells me to pay attention to him. Something's off about him and it makes me uncomfortable.

Her small hand touches my shoulder, drawing my attention to what's in front of me versus what's walking away.

"Everything all right?" Pepper asks, concern written in her soft features. I smile up at her warm face.

"Is now, love."

She smiles and sits next to me. I lean over to kiss her cheek but she shies away. *Okay.*

"Are you all right?" I ask.

"Yeah, great," she answers sincerely. Allie charges up to us, looking like she's on a mission. I shouldn't be, but I'm irked at the timing. I want to question Pepper more about this hot-and-cold business.

"Pepper," Allie states.

"Yes?" Pepper answers curiously.

"I have a concert this week. Will you come?" Allie asks, grinning. Pepper looks to me, unsure of how to respond. I nod, letting her know it's okay.

"I'd like that," she says softly. Allie does a little dance and high-fives me before darting off again to play.

"What kind of concert?" Pepper asks once she's out of earshot.

"Allie sings. Clara teaches chorus. Her kids are pretty amazing. During the summer Clara runs a summer chorus program for them. You'll love it."

"Will Clara?" she asks carefully. Clara will have to get over herself.

"Clara will love anything that makes Allie happy," I tell her confidently. I'm not so sure that Clara will love someone being in my life or Allie's but that's a different conversation altogether.

* * * * *

It's Friday evening. The shrill sound of the school bell rings. Pepper tenses at the unexpected sound. I wrap an arm around her and grin. She still has a long way to go but she's made so many leaps forward that I feel nothing but pride for her.

"Why are bells ringing if school hasn't even started yet?" she complains.

"I actually don't know." I shrug. I lead her to our seats in the front row. She looks around nervously before settling her eyes back on me.

"What's wrong?" I ask.

"I just don't want to step on toes. Are you sure Clara is okay with me being here? I mean, I don't want Allie to get too attached either. I'm not exactly good at sticking around," she mumbles nervously.

"Jesus, this again?" I bite out as Clara's husband, Dominic, arrives, taking his seat on the other side of Pepper. I shove all my irritation down and nod at Dom. This isn't the place or time for this particular conversation. I slap a smile on my face and hope it doesn't look fake.

"Dominic, this is Pepper. Pepper, Clara's husband, Dominic," I introduce.

"We've met," Pepper says, smiling shyly while extending her hand to him.

"Indeed. Lovely to see you again. I didn't realize you two were...seeing each other," he says. Pepper looks back to me before looking at Dominic again.

"We're friends. Allie asked if I'd come tonight," she responds. Friends. *Friends?* This is not going how I'd like it to. Not at all. I don't want to read Us Weekly together and drink wine. I want to have dirty sex together and tell everyone she belongs to me.

Clara strides in wearing a billowy silk blouse that's so sheer you can plainly see her butterfly tattoo through it. A light purple streak of hair cuts through her natural mocha color. Tight but flattering capri pants and tall heels make her look stunning tonight. She passes right by me and Pepper without a smile or nod, stopping only to give Dominic a kiss before settling in at the piano. What stick crawled up her ass and splintered? Women are seriously irritating sometimes.

I reach over, finding Pepper's hand, and pull it onto my thigh, keeping it covered with my own hand. I might as well just make my intentions plain as day. She looks down between us at our hands and squeezes my thigh gently before looking at Clara, then removing her hand. What is happening here? Am I being cockblocked by Clara? Is Pepper really pulling away now, after everything? My mood is deteriorating by the minute with this hot-and-cold business.

The kids filter in, finding their spots on the risers while the crowd murmurs and papers crinkle. Allie comes in last, stopping in front of the piano to kiss her mom on the cheek. She waves to Pepper and me and takes her spot on the bottom riser right in the center. The lights dim, Clara starts a simple melody on the piano, and Allie steps forward as a hush falls over the crowd.

The first lines of Pharrell Williams's "*Happy*" fall from Allie's lips and Pepper's face splits into a wide smile. I purposely didn't tell her anything about how Clara runs her chorus. The kids all join in on the chorus lines and different children take the individual verses solo. After "Happy" the kids do their rendition of "*Sweet Child O' Mine*" before diving into "*Love Somebody*", which Allie rocked with her solo portion. Three other fantastic renditions of popular songs are sung before the grand finale, "*Iris.*"

Pepper's hand finds mine midway through the song. I steal a glance at her, noting her eyes shimmering with tears. All these tiny voices melding together perfectly tend to do that to people. The words of the song linger in the air around us. I wrap an arm around her shoulder, pulling her into my side. She nuzzles in willingly, giving no resistance, and sighs. Much better.

Allie beams right at us as she sings her perfect little heart out. Pride swells in my chest. Allie, so confident, so beautiful inside and out. I know what's coming next, as Allie's been practicing nonstop for a week now. "*Iris*" morphs into "*Home*," and Allie steps forward off the riser. She walks past the piano, Clara, and stops in front of Pepper, who pulls up and out of my arms to rest her elbows on her knees and watch Allie closely. The chorus stops and Allie sings the middle chorus and verse alone. Each word seems to hit Pepper like a bullet to the chest:

Settle down, it'll all be clear,

Don't pay no mind to the demons,

They fill you with fear,

The trouble it might drag you down,

You get lost, you can always be found,

Just know you're not alone,

Cause I'm gonna make this place your home.

The kids all join back in after the line about demons and fear. Allie smiles at Pepper, gives a jerky little wave from her hip, and joins the kids on the risers as they finish the song perfectly. Nothing less ever happens at Clara's concerts. Pepper wipes a tear away quickly. She tried to be stealthy about it but I saw.

The parents in the crowd go nuts, clapping, hooting, and whistling. I stand, put my fingers between my lips, and whistle the loudest for my girl. Allie's face scrunches up in delight when she hears it. Clara stands and hushes everyone.

"Thank you all for making the time this summer to have your kids participate. It's a joy for me but, more importantly, it's fun for them! Okay, you can all get out of here!" she announces, flushed like always from the adrenaline of orchestrating one of these concerts. Allie runs up to Dom and he swings her up into his arms and squeezes, letting her know how proud he is of her. She kisses his cheek and he sets her down. She turns and latches her arms around Pepper's waist. Pepper rests a single hand on Allie's head and looks about ready to openly weep. Before anything can happen, Allie detaches herself from Pepper and throws herself at me.

As always, I kiss her face until she begs me to stop, all while swinging her around. The auditorium crowd dissipates until it's just the five of us, all pitching in to get things tidied up before we leave.

"Ice cream?!" Allie loudly whispers to Clara. It's a tradition, although, it's been less of a tradition for us all to go together lately. Clara nods her head as Allie squeals and does cartwheels up the center aisle.

"You'll both come, yeah?" Dominic asks Pepper and me. Clara shoots him a mildly irritated look that one wouldn't pick up on if you didn't know her like we did. He ignores her and waits.

"Pepper's generally *always* up for dessert, so yes," I answer. Pepper smiles hesitantly but doesn't protest.

Chapter 21

DOMINATION

Allie rides to the Parlor with Clara and Dom. Pepper is unusually quiet. She only stares out the window lost in thought like she used to do before.

"Tell me a truth," I say breaking the silence.

"I'm nervous," she answers.

"About what?"

"Having this celebration with Clara and Dominic. I feel out of place and I don't think Clara likes me," she says hesitantly.

"Clara doesn't like anyone that I date. It's not you. It's her."

"She loves you still," she says quietly.

"Not like that. She's just shitty at letting someone else have what was hers."

"It feels like more," she says.

"Trust me when I tell you this, Clara is in love with Dominic. The way she looks at him was *never* the way she looked at me. She's just a control freak who doesn't like to share," I explain. Pepper nods as I pull into a parking spot.

"You know, there's this guy who works here who is just about the funniest thing I've ever encountered," she changes the subject expertly.

"Johnny. Yeah. He is a staple here. Allie adores him." I laugh.

"I do too," she sighs.

"Should I be jealous?" I ask with humor.

"No, no. I've just...I like this place. It's perfect for an ice cream," she says. I want to ask for another truth. I want to know why she's staring into the picture window of the Parlor with such a dazed look on her face but we don't have time. Not now.

As always, we take the bench booth at the picture window, with Allie, Clara, and Dom on one side and Pepper and me on the other. Johnny comes round, all smiles and wit, to take our orders. He doesn't disappoint with his hot pink capri pants, black-and-white skull tee, and checkered Converse outfit. Allie points out each thing that's hilarious about his clothing and he plays right along saying he's lucky to have her to keep him in line. When he gets to Pepper for her order, he stares at Pepper with curiosity, like he's trying to place her, but makes no comment. Pepper keeps her eyes down while she orders.

"Allie, you did great tonight!" Clara beams. Allie smiles and shoves a bite of ice cream into her mouth.

"You're really talented. That was amazing tonight. Sawyer didn't warn me about how cool it would be," Pepper chimes in. "And Clara, I'm really impressed. You play piano beautifully. It must take a lot of work to put all of that together."

"I guess. I've been doing it for a while now," Clara replies dryly. Dom nudges her shoulder and she pushes her spoon into her mouth while she shoots daggers at him. Strike one, Clara.

"How long have you two known each other?" Dom asks, breaking the silence.

"A few months," Pepper answers, smiling. My chest literally gets warm when her face lights up. I should call the doctor.

"Interesting," Clara grumbles with a fake smile.

"Pepper is at a lot of the club stuff. She rides a bike, Mom!" Allie squeaks.

"Fascinating." Clara's words are dripping with sarcasm.

"She works at the skate rink! How cool is that?" Allie continues.

"Well it must be nice to not have a rigorous career. Some days I'd love to just have a fluff job." Strrrrrike two. One more and she's out.

"Clara..." Dom scolds before I can.

"No, it's okay," Pepper cuts in. "I didn't get to finish college, I'd like to go back but I need to save up the money first so that I don't have loans."

"That's a smart way to do it," Dominic says and smiles. "What were you studying?"

"Psychology originally, but now, I think maybe I'd like to change my major to Criminal Justice."

"That's a tough career to make decent money. Have you thought about what you'd want to do for work with either degree?" Dom asks.

For the first time ever, I'm grateful for Dominic Napoli. He is being gracious and easygoing in a situation where clearly Clara is not willing to do the same.

"I haven't had a chance yet to explore the options, really," Pepper answers.

"Have you thought about a business degree? I have some positions that will need to be filled in the next twenty-four months at the club I opened here in Blacksburg. You could call it an internship," he offers sincerely.

"Really?" she asks, bewildered.

"Absolutely," he answers. Clara snorts and I kick her shin under the table to shut her up.

"I hardly think slinging drinks while scantily clad can be called an internship, honey," she whips at Dom. He all but growls at her but keeps his mouth shut. Strike motherfucking three, Clara.

"I have waitressing experience, actually. I wouldn't mind," Pepper announces. Something new. Something I didn't know.

"I wasn't implying that you'd be slinging drinks, as my darling wife so nicely put it. I was thinking more of having you help out in the office. Accounting, orders, hiring, payroll, et cetera," he explains.

"Wow. Really?"

"If you're game and planning on sticking around, yes," he answers. Allie sticks her spoon into Clara's ice cream and takes a bite.

"Hey!" Clara exclaims.

"I wanted to try it." Allie shrugs.

"You've been spending too much time eating with Sawyer." Clara chuckles.

"Naw, he's only like that with bacon." The table, including myself, erupts with laughter. The kid is spot-on.

Allie looks like she needs someone to roll her out of the Parlor by the time we're all finished. Of course Pepper, the champ, took down her entire sundae with no issue. I have no idea where it all goes but man, that gal can eat ice cream. Dom and Pepper stand near his car, talking about next steps for a possible job while Allie climbs in and Clara and I hang back a step or two.

"Sawyer, is this serious?" she asks me quietly.

"I hope so," I admit.

"I don't think you should just bring dates around Allie. She gets attached," she starts.

"I'm not an idiot, Clara," I grit out.

"I do wonder sometimes," she quips.

"Listen, cut the shit. You were downright rude to Pepper in there and it pissed me off. She's not so different from you. She's reserved, doesn't trust easily, and has some baggage."

"Are you saying I've got baggage?" she squeaks.

"An entire ship hold's worth. You going to deny that?" I snap.

"No." She looks at the pavement, fidgeting. "I just don't like that she's hiding something. I can feel it. She's not good enough for you."

"You don't get to be the judge. I'll decide that. As for hiding shit, you are the queen of that. But trust me when I say you don't know what you're talking about. If she wants to share with you someday, she will, but I'm not talking to you about her personal stuff," I say, hoping to drive the point home.

"Fine."

"Fine," I parrot.

"Thanks for coming tonight," she says.

"I wouldn't have missed it for anything," I answer.

Clara steps away, approaching Dom, slinging an arm around his waist. He pulls her in tightly to his side. I step into Pepper's space and place a hand on her shoulder. She looks up to me and smiles shyly before thanking Dominic and Clara for the concert and ice cream. I grab her hand as we walk back to the truck, swinging it up to plant a light kiss on the inside of her wrist.

"She definitely does not like me," Pepper declares. I can't help it. I burst out laughing and sweep her up into my arms. She clutches my neck and squeals.

"Who gives a shit?" I answer. She smiles and kisses me sweetly.

"Good answer. Let's go have some hot sex. I could use a Sawyer Crown orgasm right about now," she whispers into my mouth. I set her down in front of her door, open it for her, and watch as she buckles in.

"One Crown orgasm, coming right up!" I say and laugh, shutting the door and trotting around to my side.

Chapter 22

TOO MUCH SEX?

Green, blue, and black whirl together, speeding past me. The sun is shining brightly and the air is warm and fresh. To top it all off, Pepper's on the back of my bike. I can smell the honeysuckle scent that I've come to associate with her whirling around us. The last week has felt off. She's hot and cold. Willing to snuggle or hold hands one second but then pulling out of my hold the next. Sex, though, damn. It's good. It's frequent and it's wild. But the thing is I want this to be more than sex. I want to feel connected to her through more than just the physical intimacy part. I want the conversations, the knowing each other through just a shared look. The easy way two people move about a house together through sheer practice and time. She's halfway there but retreating, little by little, outside of sex, day by day. It concerns me. I try to bring it up and she refuses to talk about it.

"Tell me a truth," I'd said the other morning. She'd stayed silent. I'd tried a different approach. I'd dropped my lips to the scar on her side and kissed it. "How'd you get this?"

"Car accident."

I'd kissed the next one, near her shoulder. "And this?"

She'd sighed. "Explosion."

"And this one?" I'd trailed kisses along the scar that barely shows on her face.

"Broken nose. Are we done?" she'd snapped at me finally.

"Pepper?" I'd asked, hoping she'd open up, talk to me.

"I should get home."

"You haven't even had coffee yet," I'd noted. She'd pushed out of my bed, dressed, and left without uttering another word. Car accident. Explosion. Broken nose. It was something. It was sharing, but it'd put her in a funk enough to leave abruptly. I'd rubbed my hand over my face and growled at the ceiling, frustrated. I should have gone after her. I didn't.

Frustration coils in my stomach as we speed along towards her house. I suggested this ride. I'd wanted to get out, the two of us alone, away from the bedroom, to connect. The ride has been silent, which is fine, seeing as it gives me time to think and Pepper time to just be wrapped around me. I'm running out of ideas on how to break through her walls. I know she's given me more than she thought she was capable of lately. I know that in her head that makes sense but I also know that she's got a lot more to give. The way she is with Allie says so. The way she is with me in those tender moments when she's not hiding herself away, I see it. I see more. I see what a good friend she is to Greta. How they take care of each other in a silent, strong way. The passion that goes into her workouts. She's all in. It's there, it's in her, more, but how do I convince her that it exists when she refuses to acknowledge it?

At the club gatherings, people love her. The only exception is Carmine, who's been missing in action for the last two days. Hoot thinks she's just about the sweetest thing, outside of Greta, who walks the planet. Beau keeps saying to "tie that shit down," because she's a good woman who's equally good with all the kids. How does she not recognize those parts of herself?

We pull onto her street and her hands slide to the insides of my thighs, slowly sliding their way up to my crotch. I know what she's doing. I pull into her driveway and kill the engine as she starts to massage me. Pulling her arms from me, I hop off the bike and reach out to help her off. I want her to know this isn't just a sex thing for me. I secure our helmets to the bike and take her hand as we walk up and into her house.

"Baby, help me out of these pants. We definitely have time before I have to be at work," Pepper says and winks. I sigh. I am all for sex. Lots of sex. But it seems like that's all I am to her. That that's all *we* are.

"I don't want to just screw you, Pepper. Why does it seem like all you want from me is sex?" I grate out. She stops, body stiff, and looks at me. I let her. I'm still holding her hand; I want to show her that I want the whole deal, not just the bedroom. She jerks her hand from mine and takes two steps away from me, glowering. Hurt.

"Sex is easy. Unattached and safe. If you fall in love it's no longer safe sex," she admits, moving to the kitchen. She pulls down the bourbon and a glass. I want to take that bottle and smash it against the wall.

"You'll regret it. Living behind your wall. You'll never fall in love if you don't risk it all. You have a choice," I push. She snorts at me and shakes her head venomously. She puts the glass to her lips and slugs back the brown liquid in one fluid motion.

"Don't you understand? I chose this life over the other one. I knew what I was getting into, no family, no connections, no PTA meetings or holiday dinners, no relationships. It was a tough call...but I made it. I had no one left. Not really. It was easy for me." Tears start to leak from the sides of her eyes. "But you— you have people. You have a whole network of people that love you...Allie and Clara and good friends who would miss you. Don't you see? I made a choice knowing I would miss out on all those things. I chose knowing my future would be permanently altered. That my dreams from before would just have to adapt to my new life. I can't drag you down that road with me. I'd never ask that of anyone. Adapt or die, Sawyer, that's how I live." She wipes her tears away with the back of her hand. I feel like I'm drowning in her words. "You will never have to make that choice. I will never allow you to put yourself in a position where you have to make that choice," she continues. "Your attraction to me is much like your love was for Clara. I'm another damaged, broken woman with secrets to save."

"Stop it!" I roar angrily, tension seizing my muscles. She's wrong and crossing a line. I could have compared her. I didn't. I didn't because there was something about her that made me look past those feelings, made me leave them behind. I will not let her do that.

"No! I won't. I'm not Clara. I'm not fixable. You don't get to know my past, my secrets. They. Are. Mine. I'm not hiding them in shame. I'm legally not able to divulge. You need move past that. I can only give you what I've been giving you. I have nothing else. I can't use you like she did. I'm not that selfish!" she yells at me, arms flying up dramatically and hair whirling around her shoulders. Anger rips through me.

"She's not as selfish as people think. You don't even know her! I won't stand for anyone bad-mouthing her or any of the people I care about for that matter," I push. She stops moving and stares wide-eyed at me.

"Oh shit!" she hisses in shock, "you still love her."

"No," I declare firmly.

"Yes." She shakes her head and says, "What am I, Sawyer? A distraction? A plaything to take your mind off of your reality?"

"No, Pepper. It's not like that. I've lived secrets. I've had the alternative relationship. It sucked. I don't want that. I want honesty and accountability. I want you and I want the truth," I grind out, irritated.

We're standing in the kitchen close together but the spaces between our words and each other seem so stretched out. Dread builds with the weight of every passing second that she's silent.

"I'm not her. I'm not her and I think you're still hung up on her. I think you're comparing me to her," she finally admits.

"I'm not comparing you. I'm not hung up on Clara! FUCK!" I blow out in frustration. "I'm pissed off because you're hiding something huge, Pepper. I don't know what it is but I know that it's big. You aren't in witness protection for nothing! I promised myself I wouldn't do secrets again!" I yell out. Shock registers on her face like a physical slap.

"Then don't," she replies simply, closed off. Her face grows stoic.

"How can you say that? I'm telling you I'm giving up on you...say something!" I shout in frustration.

"I've given what I am capable of. I'm sorry that's not enough for you." Her shoulders droop and her expression is broken but she won't budge. Resistance. Nothing but resistance. It's infuriating. Her eyes glisten with tears that she holds in. She's fighting the urge to cry. She's willing me to make this choice for us. For me to leave. She's proving a point, even if the cost is her own heart. Facing each other in a staring match, I need to know more, but she can't give it to me.

"It's not enough," I bark and stalk out of the house, slamming the door behind me. At the bottom step of the porch, I hear a glass shatter. The sound mimics the way my heart feels.

Chapter 23

CONFRONTING DEMONS

It's a terrible feeling, knowing that you're screwing up something important, yet somehow continuing to screw it up anyway. I regret storming out of Pepper's. I should have stayed. I should have forced her to admit her feelings. It was all there behind her eyes, plain as day. She thinks she's doing me a favor, but why, I don't know. I get the whole living-a-normal-life-in-WITSEC concern, but isn't the point of that so that one *can* live a normal life again?

I show up at the "cabin" that belongs to Clara and Dom. It's more like a log mansion if you ask me. I don't really recall how I arrived here but I feel like I'm slowly losing my mind. I raise my hand to knock on the impressive wooden door but it swings open before I have a chance. Clara stands in yoga pants and a tank, colorful hair swept up atop her head and hand on a hip.

"Sawyer?" her voice is cautious, reserved.

"I..." I don't get to finish my thought, not that I even know what I was trying to say, before Clara pulls me by the bicep into the house and pushes me onto the couch.

"What's wrong? Who died?" she asks, worried, concern etching her features. "Actually, I'm really glad you're here. I have something to tell you," she says, bulldozing the conversation. "Dominic wants to adopt Allie."

"What?!" I boom, tension coiling deep in my gut. Holy shit. What the hell is she talking about?

"Before you freak the fuck out, can I please explain?"

"Explain what exactly, Clara? That you want to make your happy new family legal? That you want to cut me out? What about Allie's best interest?! Jesus...I come here for...I don't know what and you spring this on me?!"

She stands, pacing, hands balled into tiny fists.

"NO! No one is taking Allie away from anyone. He's adopting her so that she feels a part of the family, so we all have the same last name. Nothing on your end will change. Same visitation, same role. Dominic is still her stepfather. I haven't talked to Allie yet because I wanted to talk to you first! If she abhors the idea then it gets tossed out the window, but Jesus, Sawyer, let's let her make the decision for what will make *her* feel connected with all of us."

Fuck. Now I feel like a total ass. I were in Dom's situation I'd probably want the same thing. A unified family.

"My role doesn't change? I don't lose *any* time with her?" I ask, feeling defeated.

"No and no. Sawyer, you're her father, I could never take her away from you like that," she says more softly.

"It would kill me, you know."

"I would kill me too," she admits.

"So a last-name change, essentially, and you'll have legal work drawn up to state that I have parental rights still?"

"Do you need that?" she questions.

"I want that," I declare. I do need that. I need it so I know that no one will ever take my little girl away from me whether or not I'm her dad.

"Then okay. I'd like to ask Allie next week. She'll no doubt feel conflicted so be sure to be ready for her to run to you. I want all three of us to be there for her while she thinks it through," she says.

"Of course," I answer.

"Now, uhh, why are you here?"

I suck in a sharp breath, feeling childish almost for having popped over for woman troubles now. Allie is about to have a monumental moment and I'm here because my woman loves to screw me but doesn't want commitment. What the hell is wrong with me?

"Pepper thinks I'm hung up on you," I blurt.

"Are you?" She inhales sharply. I shake my head, searching for the right words to explain this to Clara.

"I chose to feel it, my love for you, but you couldn't choose. Clara, you were what I wanted but I'm not sorry it's over. Not now. I gave what I gave and it wasn't reciprocated, not the way I wanted. I'm not sorry there's nothing left to say. There's no way back to how we were. This time it has to go right. My life. My love...it has to go right this time." I pause, trying to figure out what I need to say. "We have to stop hiding from the shadows we left behind. You kept secrets that I thought I knew. Every single silent moment felt like a debt we had to pay. I'm free of it all now. It feels good. Let me go. Let me have my life. You've taken up home inside of me and you'll never leave, but..."

Her broad mouth, always ready with a smile or wisecrack, smiles sadly at me. She understands.

"But you need me to say it," she finishes for me.

"I don't, Clara," I say bitterly. "That's why I'm here, I don't need to hear anything from you. I need you to be my friend, my best friend. I need you to be happy for me, but I don't need to hear that you approve or grant permission. You don't have a hold on me in any way to warrant granting permission."

Her eyes fill with tears and I know I've struck a chord.

"Sawyer..." she says voice faltering. "I'm so afraid to let go, really let go, because it means there is a possibility of losing you one hundred percent." Her voice waivers but she steadies it.

"Maybe, but you know me and you know I wouldn't do that. I think it's a control issue."

She cackles loudly, head dipping back. "You sound like my therapist."

"Your therapist sounds smart," I retort dryly. She takes my hand in hers and squeezes.

"I don't think once you've loved someone you ever really get to unlove them."

"I agree, but you love Dom the way a wife should love a husband, and I want to find that too. I think Pepper could be the one, Clara. You have to let her in. You have to share. There's enough of me for everyone," I say gently.

"How on Earth did I ever get so lucky to find you?" Her voice is thick with sentiment.

"Same reason I was lucky enough to find you. We served each other well, really well, until we didn't anymore, and that's okay," I push.

"True enough. Beer?" she asks. She's deflecting. I get that. It's hard to say what I said. It's got to be equally hard to hear it.

"Sure," I answer.

"Good, 'cause I guess it's time you tell me all about Pepper and let me see if I can help you out," she calls over her shoulder on her way to the fridge.

"If by some miracle I get another chance before all this is said and done I won't be such a coward next time," I quip.

"I'm sure you've done everything right," she says supportively.

"She has secrets, Clara...dark secrets."

She hands me a beer and plops down next to me. A wave of nostalgia passes through me. I miss our time together. I miss it differently than before, though. I miss my best friend. The closeness of having that person.

"Go on," she urges. I breathe in deeply and get started.

Chapter 24

BFFS FO-EVAH

By the time I'm finished with my hot-and-cold Pepper explanation, Clara is staring at me wide-eyed.

"Damn," she breathes.

"Is that good or bad?"

"Sawyer. Do you remember when we first met?" she asks.

"Of course," I answer.

"I barely spoke to anyone unless I had to. I used you for sex, which, for the record, was *ah-maz-ing*, and then realized I was so comfortable with you that I couldn't be without you. You accepted me as is. I was damaged. Broken. Untrusting. You've learned from your mistakes, and they *were* mistakes. You've pushed her, but gently, and she's still gun shy."

"Is there a point hidden in there?" I ask, resting my head on the back of the couch, frustrated.

"Har har asshole, yes. Keep pushing. Harder. Stop being gentle with her. I obviously don't know what shit she's gone through, but based on the "how I got my scars' conversation, she's got a lot of hurt in that head of hers. Be the knight in shining armor. You're actually really good at that. But also, be firm."

"Firm," I repeat.

"Firm!" she shouts, causing me to jump. "Dom puts me in my place. A lot. If you haven't noticed, he's a take-no-prisoners kinda guy. That does not exclude me. When I fuck up, act like a jerk, or do something rude, he lets me have it. Sure, he's polite and waits until we're alone, but he does not forget. He does not let it go. He addresses it and forces me to put it out there and deal with it. After the concert, I got a freakin' ear load when we went to bed. He laid into me. Hard. But, he was right, you were right, I was a bitch to Pepper."

"So I'm still not really seeing the point. I mean, I just told her we're over," I remind her.

"What was the point of her responses to you in that conversation today?"

"I don't know! To push so hard that I bailed?" I cry out, frustrated with all this woman logic.

"DING DING DING! We have a winner! What did you do?"

"I bailed," I whisper.

"You bailed. You played right into her mindset. You proved that she is worth walking away from," she whispers back.

"But I don't feel that way."

"DUH. I know that. It's plain as day. You're like a pathetic lost puppy right now. You still did it, though," she answers.

"Well what the fuck, Clara! What am I supposed to do now?" I bellow, completely aggravated by the situation that I clearly messed up.

"Go. Get. Her." She spells it out for me like I'm five.

"She's probably all mad and shit."

"I'll repeat since you seem to be deaf tonight. Go. Get. Her. NOW," she says again. "Make it count, Sawyer. Tell her the truth."

"And what exactly is the truth?" I ask.

"That you love her. That she can act like a jerk all she wants but you're not going to give up on her. That you are going to force her to see the beautiful side she keeps hidden from herself. That you're going to be like a leech until she does see it!" she rattles off quickly.

"A leech?"

"Okay, leave that part out, but..."

"I get it," I cut her off. "Go force her to be with me," I answer. Clara groans and smacks me.

"Do NOT say it like that to her. But, yes, go force her to be with you." She laughs.

"Clara," I state quietly.

"Sawyer."

"I've really fucking missed you," I tell her and lean in to kiss her forehead.

"Me too. I'm sorry I'm an asshole," she replies, hugging me.

"Me too." I chuckle. She swats me again and promptly yells at me to get the fuck out of her house and win back my woman.

I jog to the door, feeling like I need to rush to Pepper. I can't get there fast enough. I'm not sure if this is a brilliant plan or not seeing as she will be at work. Can this happen publicly? Maybe Clara's wrong on that small detail, maybe I should wait until she's home and we can talk in private. I stare at the bike, helmet on, and wonder what I'm forgetting. Clara yells from the stoop.

"Keys, asshole!" She tosses them to me and, surprisingly, given I feel like a nervous wreck, I catch them without issue and fire up the bike. With a quick wave of my hand I tear out of the driveway and speed towards Christiansburg.

Please don't let me be too late. That's the last rational thought that enters my head as I pull into the parking lot at Pepper's work. People are rushing out the door in droves and huddling together near parked cars. I hear the roar of a Harley and turn my head to see a SuperLow speeding away. It's a newer bike. I've only seen a couple around. Carmine. I pull up to the front of the building, kill the bike, toss my helmet, and jog to the front door. People are yelling at me not to go in. Sirens blare in the distance. What the hell has happened? My gut clenches. Pepper.

Darting through the doors, I head directly for the counter where Pepper usually sits. My feet skid to a halt when I see her facing a derelict-looking man in a standoff.

Chapter 25

OBJECTIVES

Fingers rest easily on the trigger of both guns. Quiet confidence rolls off Pepper. A standoff. There's blood in her eyes. Blood and fire. I watch her delicate shoulders rise and fall with determination. My stomach is a solid mess of knots. What the fuck is going on? Who is she? Who is he? Why the hell do they have guns trained on each other? The intensity on her face speaks volumes. She's eerily calm and blank. Intense, but calm and blank. Her body looks comfortable pointing a pistol. She looks comfortable. Why isn't she freaking out?

Her pupils look tiny and she stares at the man snarling in front of her but it's as if she's staring right through him. She's somewhere else. Her eyes aren't hers. No warmth lives in them. She's hard and calculating. Her stance is firm, unwavering. She's not scared. She looks ready, eager even. I'm sucking air. My heartbeat seems so loud I think it might give me away. She doesn't acknowledge my presence or maybe she's so focused she doesn't notice me. "*Titanium*" blares from the speakers. It's odd. It sounds too loud for the eerily quiet space.

"Pepper?" I call out, wishing my voice didn't sound so fearful and small. I can hardly breathe.

The man's head whips around to face me. His body jerks towards me, too, gun swinging in my direction. He looks soulless, evil. His eyes are black as coal. He is weathered and beaten down but his eyes are crazed. A cracking sound fills the air, deafening me, the sharp sound of a bullet leaving the chamber. The man's head explodes in a mass of red rain. It splatters everywhere in a wide path behind him as his head jerks unnaturally backward. He crumbles to the ground in a limp pile, eyes open. Well, the one eye that's left in his head. I want to look the other way, but my head won't turn, my eyes won't close. A man was just shot ten feet from me. He is there. Dead. I can't breathe.

I fucked the woman who just murdered in cold blood. No signs of remorse grace her features. In fact, no emotion shows at all as I turn my head toward hers in horror. She stares blankly, head tilted to the right just barely, and looking lost in thought as her shoulders rise and sink rhythmically.

Sadness fills the air around her. When her eyes meet mine, something like reality hitting, maybe, flickers in them. Everything feels like it is in slow motion. Frame by frame I watch as she drops to her knees, gun banging off the floor. Her lips move in a succession that resembles counting. I don't want to take a breath, don't want to exhale. I'm nailed to the floor, my fingers tightly balled into fists, my stomach gone to shit. I'm not equipped for this.

"It's done. It's done. It's done," she chants on a breath as if she's forcing herself to accept something. There's a rawness in her tone, like she's close to cracking open.

Her body trembles so harshly I think her bones will snap under the vibrations. With boldness I didn't anticipate having, I approach her. Her eyes look up to mine, wide and scared. The color has drained from her face. She looks like porcelain, fragile porcelain. Pain, deep anguish contorts her features. I sink to my knees, reaching out for her. Her arms come around my body and keep me firmly connected to her. What am I doing? What just happened? My arms form a protective cage around her, her face in the nook of my neck, our torsos fully pressed into one another, and still she trembles.

"Pepper," I start.

"It's done, Sawyer," she says, her voice so raw, the edges of her words blunt and warbling.

"What's done, love?" I ask softly. Sirens blare in the background. She's going to go to prison for this. The man looked scary but he made no move to harm her. His crime was being distracted by me. She shot in cold blood. Cold blood. One second he was alive, the next he wasn't. I feel ill every time I blink. The image of his head exploding won't leave. My gut says to listen to her words. She may be young and sometimes reckless with her own life, but I know deep down she's not a cold blooded killer.

"My objective," she releases, sighing deeply. Her hands clutch me hard, sweating. Looking up at me, she whimpers before the first tear dribbles down her cheek. I smooth it away with my thumb as she starts weeping.

Broken.

Something inside her just cracked. Split wide and shattered. I don't know what, but it's clearly something agonizingly painful. Splaying my legs out in front of me, I pull her head against my shoulder and hold her. The doors burst open as men in black vests and SWAT gear swarm into the lobby area, men with ATF hats and shirts, boots, and walkie-talkies buzzing. It's surreal as I hold this broken woman in my arms.

"I'm here, Mags."

I lift my face from her honeysuckle-scented hair to find Bentley. Motherfucking Bentley. Pepper lifts her head slowly. She looks drained and lifeless. Hollow.

"It's done." She sobs even more desolately than before, vicious tremors coursing through her body again. Bentley leans down, grabbing her by the armpits, and lifts her up and out of my hold. She melts into his firm frame without hesitance. Jealousy pumps through me.

Mad.

Hurt.

She's not mine. Dammit. I made sure of that. I didn't want lies. I didn't want broken again. I pushed. She pushed. We never found a middle ground. She turns her head to look at me while he holds her, stroking her hair and talking softly in her ear.

"Don't leave me," her voice softly calls out, stunning me. Her eyes lock on mine. She wants me here. No more resistance. Here with her. My head nods its affirmation before my mouth can compute something to say and I smile at her, the kind of smile that only happens in times of anxiety. I want this, right? I came to tell her I wanted her. But murder? Shit. Shit!

I follow Pepper and Bentley to the hospital, somehow managing to text Clara the limited information I know because I don't think tomorrow will be a good day to take Allie. She responds instantly, telling me to call if I need anything. Once we get to the ER entrance, I hand my keys to the valet and try to remember how I got here. I don't recall the drive. I don't recall anything but that man's head exploding in front of me. Bentley slaps me on the shoulder, hard, jarring me from my trance.

"If you can't accept her and be strong for her right now, you don't fucking deserve her," he grates, glowering. I stare coldly back at him and nod. I follow him into the bustling lounge area and wait as he talks with a fellow ATF agent before moving through a pair of double doors towards the private rooms.

Pepper lies on a gurney in stark room, looking pale and fragile. So different from how she normally looks. Emotions pummel me. I'm angry and confused, yet I want to be there for her. I don't know what to say to her, though. I don't know how to comfort her.

Chapter 26

SPILLING SECRETS

"Hi," she says, extending a hand to me. My feet feel leaden as I take the three steps necessary to reach her, trying to ignore the chaos of the hospital around us.

"Hi." The silence that follows is heavy. I can feel the weight of every passing second as she clutches my hand firmly.

"You're angry," she states with quiet confidence.

"I'm...I'm a lot of things right now," I answer bleakly. What the hell does she expect?

"Mags, we need to talk," Bentley cuts in from behind me, his voice sharp and loud in the silence between us.

"Bentley, I'm spent. I want to go home now," she says.

"Who the hell are you?" I snap at her. Emotions are welling up and spilling over inside me, my gut is twisted. Bentley sighs and pulls up a chair next to Pepper. I watch as they eye each other, silently having a conversation that only two people who've intimately known each other can. It's right there. That's exactly what I want with her.

"Tell him," she urges. "I want him to know who I am. I'm sick of keeping everything to myself. I'm sick of hiding," she mumbles.

"Mags..." He shakes his head. "Once you fire this bullet, it doesn't go back in the barrel. Are you prepared for that?" he asks.

Her eyes dart between Bentley and me.

"I was raped," she starts quietly. Her body shudders. My insides coil so tightly that I think I might snap. Rape. Jesus. "My boyfriend, no, that's not right, my...my soul mate, his family sold guns, illegally. His *uncle* raped me." Her voice is thick with emotion as my stomach heaves with disgust. "I shot him, after it happened. Except, except..." Her eyes fall to the floor and tears fall gently down her cheeks. She shakes gently with her tears. I know I should do something, but I can't. Not yet.

"She shot Cane, her boyfriend, instead. He was my contact inside the family. Cane was working with us, the ATF, to bring down the operation in exchange for being free of it all. Long story short," Bentley continues gently. "Mags here ran after she shot him. I followed her. She thought she killed Cane. Ezra, his uncle, went after her. Only he sent Cane, who hadn't died, to do the job. Turns out Ezra was higher up than we thought. Had information on an ATF sting that went haywire. That information was in a backpack that Mags here took with her when she ran. We made a play to give Ezra the intel back in exchange for his nephew but..." Bentley looks to Pepper. His expression is tortured. I'm not sure how to process all this information. Everything is flying at me so quickly.

"But I didn't save him. I didn't get to him in time. He died," Pepper wails, heartbroken. "He died because his own uncle tortured and beat him and left him to rot," she finishes, gasping for breath.

I'm trying my best to digest the words coming at me but my mind is reeling and all I can manage is a blank stare. My brain is numb, a fog clouding all rational thought.

"Because of the intel that Mags uncovered, we needed to keep her safe throughout the trial. Ezra was working directly for Torren Delanti, a big-time gun and drug runner here in the States. He's got connections. He's out the money Mags took. His top middleman was sent to prison and Mags here is the last loose end. Mags chose WITSEC, Ezra went to prison for life. He escaped during his transfer from a medium to a maximum prison. I warned Mags to stay alert." Bentley looks crushed as he scans Pepper from head to toe longingly.

Exactly what kind of relationship did they share before and for how long?

"How'd he find me?" Pepper squeaks, eyes coming alive. "How'd he fucking find me, Bent?" she demands, voice rising.

"We don't know. Delanti was somehow involved with the escape and there was chatter that he put out the word to locate you," Bentley answers. "You know I'm not privy to that information anymore. I'm not even supposed to be here with you now. I was taken off that case."

"So, you thought you killed your boyfriend, after his uncle raped you...then realized he was still alive and you tried to bring down the uncle once and for all?" I cut in, floundering in all the information I've been given.

"Yes, but I took the backpack when I left, it had a lot of money in it and the USB with all the information on Ezra," she answers.

"And that man you shot..." An image of a head exploding assaults me and I grimace. I think I might be sick.

"That was Ezra," she answers, eyes going cold and distant at the mention of his name.

"How many people have you shot?" I question. What do I really know about her? It seems like a moot point at this juncture but I feel the need to know.

"Three." She looks at Bentley sheepishly.

"Three?!" I bellow disbelievingly.

"She shot me in the leg at our meeting with Ezra. On purpose." Bentley laughs lightly and Pepper grins, just slightly.

"What the hell is so funny about that?" I grind out, irritated.

"Nothing. Everything. Sawyer, please. Please," Pepper says. "Magnolia will always be a part of me, but I stopped living for her a long time ago. What we're telling you is...what happened today means I can finally start to let go, put it in the past, babe. All the reasons I am the way I am, the reason I'm scared of...of life..." she says, choking on her words. "I was carefree, from a good family, I was a good girl, in college. It all changed in a millisecond. My world shifted and I became something else. But now, now it can be done. Right, Bentley...it can be done now..." she pleads, although to who I'm not sure. My brain can't seem to catch up with the news.

I blink twice. It's like being buried in an avalanche of detail. I still have so many questions.

"Haven't talked to the marshal's office yet, but my guess is WITSEC still stands and Pepper Philips still exists. Not gonna lie tho, hun, if we don't know who located you, you may have to start over again."

The pained look in Pepper's eyes as they bore into mine cut deep but all I can muster is a grim smile.

Bentley stands and exits the room, leaving Pepper and I alone. "Please don't leave. Please don't hate me," she pleads.

"I don't know how to feel, Pepper. I watched a man die. His head exploded!" I answer. She glances at the floor between us.

"I'm so sorry."

"I don't need an apology, Pepper. I need answers."

"Ask," she urges.

"Were you and Bentley together?"

"Yes, but not for long. He was one of the only friends I had at that point in my life. It took him the better part of a year to get me to even talk to him. Just when I thought I was falling for him, Cane found me." Her voice fades as she finishes talking. She shakes her head at herself.

"What are you thinking?" I push.

"Just that everything is such a mess. I'm a mess. I'm making you a mess. I've messed up Bentley's life and possibly his career, too. I'm not fit to be around." The look on her face makes my heart speed up. It's as if a bolt of lightning has struck me directly in the chest. If she's trying to let me go, I don't want her too. I came tonight to fight for her. I have all the details I didn't before and although they make me uneasy, I can't help but wonder what they've made her feel all this time. I won't give up. Not tonight, anyways.

* * * * *

Five hours later we're at Pepper's house. She's been cleared, for now. A U.S. Marshal stands in the kitchen near the side door and another is stationed at her front door but Pepper is in a daze, curled up on her bed. I am a train wreck of emotions. I waffle between going home and shutting the door on this relationship forever and staying here, never to leave her side. This entire situation is insane. Crazy. Not what my life usually entails. I refuse to pick an emotion just yet and run with it. Logic says, run. My heart says, stay.

"All this time I believed killing Ezra would stop the pain. The rage. I thought knowing he was dead, knowing I avenged Cane's death would free me. It's like a bubble burst but the ache I feel will forever be with me." Her voice cracks and tears spill sideways down her temples onto the stark white pillow of her bed. She's bleeding emotion right now. It's torturous to watch. There isn't a damned thing I can do about it.

"We never bury the good, not really. We keep them with us. That's the price of living. Whatever sins you've committed, you can't go back and undo them. You can let it go, even if nothing is wrong. You deserve love," I say. "Everyone deserves love."

"Silence suits me, Sawyer. Sometimes I worry that if I say too much, I'll start screaming and never stop." Her voice holds such pain and worry that it chokes me up inside. "I've been outta whack since Cane died. He passed away in my arms, you know. I couldn't stop it. I came unglued. I haven't really slept well since then, staring at the alarm clock on my nightstand night after night. Life's sucker punches keep coming, so you'd better get used to the pace of things. Adapt or die, you know?" Her mouth frowns slightly. "I actually look forward to death. At least then my mind can find peace. Life's not worth living without passion and I just don't have any left. The drugs, the drinking, it was..."

"Your way of coping," I cut in. She nods and curls into a ball, back tightly wedged against me. Against all my better judgment, I sling a heavy arm over her and let my head hit the pillow. I'm so spent and having her in my arms feels so right.

"It should have all worked out, but it didn't. He should be here now, but he isn't. It's hard to live with. All that time I ran...just when I let Bentley in...he came back. Alive. I had six days with him. Six days and he died, again. Both times because of me," she mumbles into the blankets.

"You build me up, then I fall apart—not because I want to, but because I can only take so much. You're trying to save me, but please, stop. You'll never save me from myself or the conflict that courses through me. The guilt. The very thing I loved is what's killing me. I've tried, but I can't conquer it. The best I can do is sleepwalk through life." Her eyes hold mine with intensity and fire. She *has* passion left, she just doesn't believe it, she doesn't feel it.

"The human spirit can bend an awful lot before it breaks," I answer, unwilling to just give up.

"I can fake a smile or a laugh. I can hold everything in—the guilt, the pain. I can carry the weight of it all. I have, I am, but I'm still human,

Sawyer, and I still bleed when you cut my skin. You have the world to offer someone. That someone should be able to share it with you. I cannot." She pauses, sucking in a deep, shuddering breath. "I tried. After Cane I tried, with Bentley. Then..." She trails off, lost in her own past.

"Pepper, I can't save you from yourself. I want to, but I know I can't," I state. "I don't know what to do here..." I squeeze her hand, bringing her back to me. Her words are knives in my heart. A tear drops off her chin. I kiss it away.

"After Cane died, I realized I have a mass of black tissue sitting in my chest where my heart is supposed to be. Watching him die, it killed me too. I died right there with him." Her eyes harden and the unshed tears in her eyes retreat into her.

"Pepper, you're the only one who doesn't see it. Bentley sees you. Sees what you *still* have to give. I see it. Allie sees it. Greta sees it. If you don't feel it, okay, but at least have a little faith in the people you *do* have. Trust us. Don't give up yet," I encourage. "Tell me a truth." She sighs, resigning herself from our heavy conversation and stares up at me. Flecks of gold and chocolate take me in with tenderness. Her body shakes as she gathers what's left in her. I can see something building in her eyes. She inhales deeply and takes my face in her hands softly.

"I don't need a lot of words, Sawyer. I don't need a conversation every moment of our time together. I don't need a promise from you and I don't need your life in exchange for me or my love or to show you how I'm feeling. I never knew how much I could care again, Sawyer. You did that. You showed me that. It scares me more than anything in the world. I've tried so hard to fight it, but I'm so tired of fighting against it." Her hands squeeze me tightly. My heart stops beating. Stops. Beating. Lungs. Don't. Work.

"Are you saying..." Warmth spreads throughout my body.

"I'm falling for you," she confirms.

"*Now* you tell me?!" I bark with mock irritation. I watch as Pepper's face moves into a beautiful warm smile wrought with relief. Her hands slip from my face so her arms can hold me even more tightly around my neck.

"I never said I had good timing," she muses. That is the understatement of the century.

"Pepper," I whisper, leaning down to her lips. "I've been a goner since we went hiking. I've been falling since the skating rink, and I've been wanting to hear those words from you since you swooped in to nurse me while I was sick." I brush my lips to hers. I forget everything the night has brought our way. I push all the crazy information and the gruesome scene at the rink to the bowels of my brain and I taste her. I drag my mouth from her lips to her ear. "Pep, since we're finally on the same page, let's do something 'bout it, what do you say?"

She nods, barely, and squeezes her arms around my neck. Her fingers thread through the hair at my nape, tugging slightly. Cupping her buttocks and bringing her snug against me, a moan of desire slips through her lips—the sort of noise that leads to naked bodies and hot sex.

I slip her t-shirt up and over her head quickly. I crawl over her, leaving a trail of soft kisses on her neck and across her collarbone. She arches upward until I take her breast into my mouth. She rakes her fingers through my hair, pulling my mouth closer to hers. I grin wickedly. I can't help it. Everything has fallen into place it seems. Swept up in a haze of desire, she arches her hips, urging me to slide into her. The heat from her body makes it nearly impossible to take my time. To savor this moment, to savor her. She'd barfed up all her emotional baggage to me, like somehow that'd restore her to a better, newer, purer version of herself. I know better. I know it's a long road for her. I *know* I need to guide her to a truly sound state of mind but right now I don't care about any of that. I care about her silky skin urging me on. The fire in her eyes, the fact that she basically said she loves me. I spread her legs more and push into her. The soft moan that puffs from her lips almost sends me over the edge. Slowly, I pull out slightly and thrust back in, filling her. Nails dig into my shoulder blades, but I don't care. I dip my head and lightly bite her neck. Goose bumps break out on her skin and she whimpers. Faster, harder, deeper.

Chapter 27

MIXED BAG

I wake up violently to Pepper's punch to my gut. Her voice is strained yet clear. "No. No. Not like this," she yells like a broken record. I wrestle her, pinning her arms at her sides, calling her name until she wakes.

"Shhh. You're safe," I whisper into her ear. Her breathing is ragged and she goes limp in my arms. "I'm right here. You're safe." I loosen my hold and she rolls into my front, burying her face in my chest. I run my fingers through her hair, over and over until she's settled. Breathing steady. Soundly asleep.

* * * * *

When morning comes I pad into the kitchen to start coffee for us, completely forgetting there are two ATF agents in her house. I scream like a little bitch when I see them, cover my exposed junk, and hightail it back to the bedroom. Pepper's awake and laughing. Loudly.

"You forgot." She laughs. I leap onto the bed, tackling her in all my naked glory.

"Yeah," I answer.

"You screamed like a little girl." She giggles more, squirming to break free of my hold.

"Did that too," I admit.

"I want to try, Sawyer" she says, not giggling.

"Try what?"

"I want try us. Really try us. What do I do?" she asks timidly.

"Pepper. All you need to do is talk to me. Don't pull away. Explain that shit. No more hot and cold. If you're overwhelmed have the balls to just say that. All I need is a heads-up. I can give space when you're feeling quiet. I can smother you when you need affection, but you have to at least tell me."

"Okay. I'll talk more," she says. "I need smothering." Her eyes well up with tears but before a single one can fall I lean down and kiss her senseless while holding her tightly to me.

* * * * *

"Clara is sitting down with Allie today," I chatter nervously. Pepper already knows this. I'd relayed the entire conversation with Clara yesterday. We've closed the shop for today and tomorrow to be available to Allie. It's the last weekend of summer before school starts back up. The timing seems off to me but I think that has more to do with everything I've been dealing with surrounding Pepper.

"Sawyer, I know it sounds like a huge deal, but Allie will be okay. She's a really smart, open kid," Pepper soothes.

"She is...yeah," I mumble. Pepper rubs my back in slow, gentle circles. It only drives my anxiety home even more. I shoot up and start to pace the kitchen.

"Should I go?" she asks hesitantly.

"No. Maybe. I don't know. I don't want to annoy you—but I'm a pacer when I'm anxious," I ramble.

"Noted." She laughs.

The phone rings. I dive across the kitchen for it. Fumble with it. Drop it. Almost punch Pepper in the head when she tries to retrieve it for me and finally get it answered.

"Hello!" I shout. Ugh. Someone shoot me now. I'm already messing this all up.

"Sawyer?" Allie hiccups into the phone. My heart breaks. Right there. Like never before.

"I'm here, baby. What do you need?" I coo into the receiver, wanting to take away every bad feeling she could possibly have.

"Pepper," she cries.

"What?" I ask, confused. I pull the phone from my head and stare at it like it bit me. Allie sobs into the phone some more before I hear Clara come on the line.

"She wants Pepper. She wants to talk to Pepper alone," Clara states, sounding as baffled as I feel.

"Okay." I turn robotically, stare at the woman beside me, and hope like hell this is the right move. I hand the phone to her.

"She wants you," I say drawing, my brows together.

I don't understand this. I'm not prepared for Allie needing anything outside of me or Clara or Dom. Pepper smiles nervously and takes the phone from me.

"Hello? Allie?" she speaks softly. "Uh huh." She pauses, listening. "No, actually I think it's wonderful." Her face lights up at something Allie says. "Oh honey, because, it just goes to show how many people truly love and adore you," she says, smiling at me. "Absolutely. We'll be right there."

I watch in shock as Pepper ends the call, hands the phone back to me, and slips on her shoes.

"Allie would like us to come over for a sundae-making contest. She said, 'I think it will make us all bond.' Have I ever told you that that little girl has somehow managed to steal a piece of my dead heart?" Pepper rambles. Everything slows down. Blurs together. She loves my little girl. She handled that flawlessly. She's going with me to "bond" with the rest of the family. I'm going to have a Goddamned heart attack right here. It's happening. I don't think I'm breathing.

"Sawyer!" Pepper shouts. "Did you hear me? We have to go." Her head is cocked to the side and a hand rests on one hip.

"Uh, yeah. Just, yup, we have to go." I smile. Content. I feel full with contentment. Pepper grabs my hand and tugs me towards the door.

"Let's take the truck in case she wants to come back with you and spend the night."

My heart explodes in my chest.

Chapter 28

BREAKDOWN

We make it to the cabin in record time. Pepper chattered on the entire way about how amazing she thought Allie was. I couldn't disagree, but I'd been quiet, Overthinking Allie's reaction. I'm nervous for the questions and the aftermath that we might be stepping into.

The truck is barely in park when the front door flies open and Allie comes tumbling out, running full speed at me. Her arms are splayed wide, ready to be held. Her small cheeks are red and tear stained. It takes everything I have not to cry. I scoop her up into my arms and crush her to my chest.

"You're always my girl, you know that right?" I whisper in her ear. She nods into my neck and sniffles. Pepper smiles and follows my lead into the house.

"Pepper, welcome," Dom says, looking worn out. Clara is splayed out on the couch with a glass of wine. She lifts a hand but utters no words. That's a first. Clara, speechless. I set Allie down and sit in the chair to the left of Clara and Dom. Pepper stands awkwardly.

"Pepper, can you help me get all the stuff lined up on the counter?" Allie asks shyly. Pepper nods happily and lets Allie lead her to the kitchen.

"So," I start.

"Well, it was awful at first," Dom starts.

"But then Allie...just...got it," Clara finishes.

"We explained that in no way does this option change anything between the three of us and how we all function now. That it's still her choice to accept it or not. She was so worried for you, Sawyer. It was heartbreaking. But," Clara stops talking and breathes deeply. "She said as long as you're still her dad then she'd like to take Dom's last name. That being adopted would be okay. Then she wanted to talk to you. We should have had you here I think," she whispers.

"She didn't even speak when I picked up," I state.

"She said that Pepper seemed like someone she could ask advice from, not a parent. Can you believe that? The kid is more emotionally stable than any of us." Dom chuckles.

"I think you're right." I watch as Clara sits up and watches Pepper and Allie move about the kitchen.

"She was really great, Sawyer. Supportive and honest. I think Allie needed that right then. I think she needed to hear it from someone that *wasn't* a parent to her," Clara says, smiling. Dom pulls her close to his side and kisses her temple. I ache to be able to do the same thing right now. To have that partner for support in moments like these.

"Sundae contest is ready! And I'll warn you, Pepper is the bomb at dessert," Allie chirps. We all push up from our seats to join them in the kitchen.

* * * * *

By ten p.m. Allie is tucked in and sleeping soundly upstairs. Clara, Dom, Pepper, and I are out on the deck having a drink and enjoying the view of the lake as the moonlight dances on the water. There's a slight chill in the air as summer is winding down and fall is creeping in. I watch the moonlight reflect off Pepper's long, black locks. Her skin is lit up and she looks stunning in the low light with her copper eyes sparkling.

"Can I comment on something?" Pepper asks.

"Shoot," Clara answers.

"I think Allie is amazing, and I think it's because of you all. She's open-minded, caring, and kind. I don't think if you and Sawyer had had a traditional relationship that any of this—you marrying Dominic, Sawyer dating, adoption talk—would have turned out the same. I think you've shown her love comes in many forms and I just think it's amazing how cool she is."

Dom beams at Pepper and nods his head. For the first time I'm actually enjoying my time at Dom's house with Dom present. The outdoor speakers are softly playing one of Clara's mellow lists and the company is proving to be really pleasant. It feels nice. Right.

"I've thought the same thing. Sawyer and I," he starts, pausing to look at me, "have had our...differences, but when it comes to Allie he's never ever let anyone down and Clara has made sure that Allie gets what she needs no matter what her personal feelings might be. They've done great and it shows in Allie's behavior and personality." Clara kisses Dom's cheek before pouring herself a refill. I pull Pepper onto my lap and squeeze her.

"Thank you," I whisper into her ear. She smirks at me before I kiss the spot just behind her ear. Her body tenses just slightly. It makes me wonder what I just did. She stands, declaring that she needs another bourbon, and moves to the outdoor bar Dominic has set up. I lean my head back in the Adirondack chair and soak up the easy moment of camaraderie surrounding me.

That awful country song comes on. The one Clara knows I hate. I make a face at her when I realize it's playing. She laughs.

"Suck it up. It's *one* song," she says and chuckles. A glass breaks on the deck. All eyes dart to Pepper's direction. She's frozen in place. Pale as a ghost. Her knees buckle, but before I have a chance to get to my feet, Clara is next to Pepper, catching her as she collapses. Tears are falling freely down her face. Her lips are moving. Counting. One. Two. Three. My gut hurts. The expression on her face shows shock and hurt as she clings to Clara through her violent shaking.

"Shh," Clara whispers to her. "It's okay." She holds up a hand to me and Dom, silently asking us to keep back. I don't want to keep back. I want to scoop Pepper into my arms and take away whatever pain is haunting her.

"The song," Pepper gurgles. Dom moves instantly to the iPod and changes it.

"Come with me," Clara urges, helping Pepper to stand. They move past me silently and swiftly. Dom appears by my side and slaps a hand on my shoulder.

"She'll be okay. Come on, let's clean this up." I hear him but the words don't compute. I don't understand. I walk to the iPod and look at the playlist. "*Hey Pretty Girl.*" That's the song. What happened?

Thirty minutes later Clara emerges from the bathroom. I rush to her, desperate to understand why it looked like Pepper had a mental breakdown.

"Well?" I ask, feeling detached.

"Jesus, Sawyer. It's bad. She's calm now. I gave her a Klonopin to calm her down." She pauses and stares out the window for a moment. "She talked. I get it. I get her. *You* need to get her. Get her help, Sawyer. A trauma counselor. I gave her my therapist's card. Make sure she calls."

What? A trauma counselor?

"Please explain what's happening," I say quietly. Clara pulls me aside, further from the bathroom.

"The song triggered a memory. Caused a panic attack. Do you remember my nightmares?" she asks.

"Of course."

"Okay, same idea. Just awake instead of dreaming. You said she had secrets. I didn't realize they were similar to things I've been through, but worse." She shakes her head at me. "She's young,

Sawyer, convince her to call the therapist. I'll help you however I can with that."

"Okay," I mumble.

"Take her home. She's tired and embarrassed. She needs to just be with you. She trusts you," Clara says with a sad, knowing smile. I always protected Clara from her demons too.

Chapter 29

WOLF IN SHEEP'S CLOTHING

"I'm so sorry," she whispers while staring out the truck window as we drive to her house.

"Pepper, for the last time, it's okay."

"No it's not," she answers quietly. Instead of arguing, I reach across the cabin of the truck and take her hand in mine. She clings to it tightly, as if she's afraid of letting go.

"Did Clara mention her counselor to you?" I ask as we pull onto her street. Small houses move past us in blurry detail. I don't know exactly how to help her. It's frustrating. Pulling into her driveway, keys still in the ignition, her mobile rings. She lifts it from her purse to check who's calling.

"Greta. I'll be quick," she says. She climbs out of the truck and heads towards the kitchen door. I follow a few feet behind to give her some privacy. Once inside, she goes straight to her bedroom, shutting the door softly behind her, and I plop onto the couch wishing I could do something, anything. I drag my hands through my hair, roughly massaging my scalp to try and ease the tension. I want to know why that song set her off. I want to know what she told Clara. I want to know what the hell it's going to take to help her. To stop the nightmares. To make her feel safe. To give her a place she feels comfortable calling home. She's permanently adrift. She doesn't identify with a place to call home. A place that brings comfort just by being there.

"Sawyer?" her voices carries down the hall from her room.

"Yeah?"

"I know it's not that late, but I want to go to bed."
She sounds small and distant. Worn down. I squeeze
my eyes shut before answering her.

"Coming."

I push off the couch and make my way down the
hall to join her in bed. She smells like fresh minty
toothpaste. I'm too tired to even consider brushing
my teeth so I strip down to my boxers and climb in.
She nestles into me and sighs.

"About the counseling thing..." I start.

"I'll call tomorrow," she cuts in.

"Really? Just like that?"

"Just like that," she answers. Silence engulfs us.
The faint light of the streetlamp across the street
barely lights anything up. Her black hair is
everywhere and her warm body is pressed close to
mine. With her breathing steady and even, I let
myself drift to sleep.

She wakes gasping for air. A strange strangled
garble leaves her mouth. I pull her to me, wrapping
my arms around her tightly. "Shhh. You're safe." I
breathe into her ear. Her body shudders one last
time before relaxing into my hold. "I'm right here
with you." She relaxes even more, nuzzles her face
into my neck, and breathes deeply until she falls
back asleep. I send a silent prayer to God, asking
him to help her through all this.

* * * * *

The morning light hits the windows and I'm
awake. Awake, staring at the most beautiful
creature. Her window's cracked and the chill from
the early fall overnight air has crept in, leaving
Pepper and I cocooned under the blankets together.

I crawl out of bed as quietly as possible. I don't
want to wake her. She needs the sleep and I have to
swing by the club today before opening Bloodlines. I
scribble a quick note letting her know where I'll be,

start the coffee pot for her, and head to the club for a shower.

* * * * *

Beau greets me at the bathroom door as I'm coming out. He eyes me warily.

"Kicked out?" he asks and raises an eyebrow.

"No, just didn't wanna wake her." I chuckle. He eyes me for a moment, debating whether or not I'm telling the truth, before he nods and palms my shoulder, leading me to the round table for our meeting.

Members sit, coffees in front of them, looking half asleep. It's unusual to have a morning meeting.

"We have a couple issues we gotta deal with now," Beau starts. "First off, have any of you seen Carmine? He's been off grid for days and it's not the first time. This, as I'm sure I don't need to tell you, looks bad on the club. It shows a lack of respect and my gut tells me to cut him loose as a prospect." Heads nod in agreement. "We've had two girls complain that he roughed them up a bit as well. I don't take these particular girls' stories too seriously as they have reputations, but I'm not gonna let that fly no matter what. We deal with our own, and that shit has got to stop flying around. Doesn't set a good feeling in the community when people get wind of that talk."

"I saw him a couple nights ago, I think. He was leaving Adventure World, round the same time they had the shooting," I chime in. I didn't really think about it then, but now that I remember, it seems odd he was there. He has no kids and doesn't generally get invited to anything kid-related.

"Hoot saw him earlier that day too, but no one has since then," Hurley says from the opposite end of the table.

"Eyes open. You see him, you bring him in. I got questions," Beau grumbles from the head of the table. We vote on whether or not to let Carmine continue to prospect. The vote is unanimous, he's out. Beau goes over a few minor club points and we're all released to go about our days.

Pepper's bike is in my driveway when I get home. A grin takes over my face at the sight of it parked. I like that she feels comfortable enough to show up here without permission from me. I want her to feel like what's mine is hers. I practically prance up the driveway and into the house.

"Pep? You here?" I call out.

"Out back!" she answers. I move through the kitchen towards the patio doors when Pepper comes flying at me full tilt. She lands in my arms heavily and I stumble backwards a bit, taking her with me.

"Hi," I whisper into her hair.

"Hi," she returns.

"How was your day?" I ask, moving her hair over her shoulder and kissing her neck. She groans and backs out of my arms.

"It was...productive. And before you start wooing me with your lips, let me tell you about it."

I feign hurt feelings and let her lead me to the patio chairs. A beer waits for me on the side table and a bourbon for her.

"So, I called that therapist today," she starts. "And she had me come right in. I spent an hour there. I really like her, Sawyer. She had a lot of insightful stuff to say."

"That's great." I can't even pretend to hide the elation I'm feeling. This feels like exactly what Pepper needs.

"Yeah." She breathes. "The best part is that she wants me to come in for a more formal session with her later this week. I guess this appointment was really only the intake stuff." Pepper's excited and nervous rambles are adorable. "I'm kinda nervous

209

though, you know? Like what if I'm really freaking broken?"

"Pepper, counseling is the best thing for really freaking broken. Don't overthink this. It's definitely the right step forward," I encourage.

"Yeah. Yeah you're right," she agrees before taking a big sip of her bourbon. I reach out, grab her free hand, and squeeze it gently. She squeezes back as we take in the sunset together in silence.

Chapter 30

THE PATH OF LIFE

The last three days have been torture. I think Pepper has been scared shitless of her appointment today with the therapist. She's been cleaning and rambling and occasionally whisper counting. I tried to quell her fears but she bottled everything up inside and didn't want to talk about how nervous she was. Her appointment ended about an hour ago and I'm anxious to hear from her. I don't want to text or call in case it was an intense session and she needs alone time to process. It is killing me waiting for her to call, though.

She finally comes to the shop an hour or so before I usually close up, looking red-eyed and splotchy. I rush to her and kiss her cheeks before pulling her into a bear hug.

"What's wrong?" I ask.

"I'm going to a retreat for trauma therapy," she starts. *Thank God.* I am so happy she's going through with this whole therapy deal. "It's supposed to be an intense treatment option or something," she says, sounding far away. "That appointment with the therapist was really hard. It led to this month-long retreat idea. She said it would be especially beneficial to me. I feel like an overstimulated clitoris right now," she sniffles. I can't help but chuckle at her. "I have no idea what I'm doing, but this sounds like a rational decision to make for myself."

"Admitting that you have no idea what you're doing is the best thing you can do for yourself. Maybe even the hardest thing to do," I tell her sincerely. "A month huh? Like you just show up for a couple hours every day? How does it work?"

"No, Sawyer, like rehab. Like, I go away, to their facility. It's four hours north of here. They take my cell phone. There are no laptops or tablets allowed. A month where I'm just their...their victim. That's how it feels. Like I just volunteered myself for some mad experiment." Her arms tighten around my middle. A *month*? No contact at all?

"So, can people call you there or visit? Like during regulated hours or something?" I ask, trying to find the right words to say, to have the most supportive reaction. I don't want a month apart. I don't want to lose her. My gut seizes in anticipation.

"No calls, but people can visit during the hours they specify on certain days," she says. I let out an audible sigh of relief.

"I'll be there every time then." I smile and kiss the top of her head. Her arms loosen their grip on my torso.

"I don't want you to visit me, Sawyer," she says, hushed but determined.

"What?" I pull back to glance down at her face. Maybe she's kidding. Not funny, but surely she's not serious. Her brown eyes glisten barely, but they're serious.

"I don't want you to visit me there. I don't know how I'll do or be. I don't want to use you as a crutch. I need to do this for me without distraction. I tried to think of a million nice ways to say this on my drive over here but...there aren't any, really. I want you, but this is something I need to dedicate to myself. I want to do it alone. I understand, I guess, if you don't agree and end this, but that's not what I want," she finishes. I'm shocked. Disappointment courses through me. I feel like I've been sucker punched. "Sawyer?" she calls out.

"I'm going to have to think about things, I guess. I'm pretty shocked to be honest...not about going to the retreat, but about you wanting to have no contact for a month. I thought you'd want my support, Pepper. It kinda feels like a slap in the face." She cringes at my words and tears flood her eyes.

"It's not like that. I *do* want you. I just have a lifetime of mess to work out from before I ever knew you. I need to do it on my own." She is pleading with her eyes. I understand what she's saying. It sounds smart. My heart doesn't agree with my brain, though. My heart feels like it's been tossed aside and left in the road like a dead animal.

"When do you leave?" I mutter, confused by my own conflicting responses.

"Tomorrow. They have a spot open for the session starting Friday." Her voice is so quiet, like she doesn't want to admit that she's planned all this already. But she has. She solidified all this before she came to see me. This wasn't a discussion between us. I had no say.

"Tomorrow?" I blurt out, flustered. There's not even time to prepare for her departure. She's just going to up and be gone tomorrow.

"Can I ask you to stay with me tonight?" she asks hesitantly. "Please, Sawyer." The need in her voice makes all my own hurt go to that forgotten place where I can't feel it. It disappears.

All I see are her caramel brown eyes pleading with me to spend the night with her.

All I hear is her voice, fragile and soft.

When she sucks her plump bottom lip between her teeth and bites it I lose whatever battle I was having with myself.

"Of course."

Her eyes crinkle at the corners. She pushes up on to her tiptoes and winds her hands around my neck. I lean down and brush my lips against hers.

Warm, soft, lush. I'm not sure I have a month of no contact in me at this point. I scoop her up into my arms and carry her to the back room. I'm going to make damned sure that the next month is unbearable for her without me.

Lying her down on one of the tattoo tables, I kiss her neck, collarbone, and the décolletage that shows from her V-neck shirt. Her hands drift to my waist, lifting my shirt, toying with the skin at my pant line, up my abdominals. I push her shirt up and taste the skin at her ribs and stomach, slowly trailing my way to her breasts. Her legs splay, begging for me to take up the space between them. I root a knee on the table between them and hover over her. Her shirt rests above her breasts. They heave with every breath she takes. Using my teeth, I pull the demi-cup down, letting her breast spill out. She groans as I drag the material down. Her hips surge up to mine as I take her nipple in my mouth and play with it. Her nails drag down my back. I repeat the process on the other breast. Pepper's entire body is shaking and she wiggles under me, trying to find relief. I grin and drop my hips just a little, letting her rub herself on me. Her expression is dazed and her body is moving on its own accord. I lick her nipple, then bite down gently before suckling. Her hips push up against me again. Oh, the wicked things I'm going to do to her. She will never be able to forget what I have planned.

"SHIT!" Clara yells, surprised. I jump off the table, leaving Pepper exposed from the waist up before realizing it. She mewls in embarrassment. Clara's face is a mixture of chagrin and pure delight. I move to stand in front of Pepper as she sits up while trying to get her breasts back into their cups.

"I, uh. Well, crap. Hi, guys," Clara finally blurts out, laughing. Pepper's face is a shade of hot pink that I've never witnessed before. I let out a deep chuckle at the complete absurdity of the situation. Pepper peeks out from behind me at Clara.

"Hi, Clara," she laughs.

"When you asked me to meet you here I didn't think it was to put on a show." Clara grins. Pepper shakes her head, smirking, and scoots off the table.

"I thought maybe we could grab a drink and talk actually. I can't be out late," Pepper says, looking up at me with wild desire. "But, uh, I had some things I wanted to chat with you about," she finishes.

"Sure! I'd love that. There's a great place across the street actually. Allie's home with Dom so I have an hour or so," Clara responds.

"Sawyer? Do you mind?" Pepper asks.

"No. No, go ahead. Your place or mine?" I ask. What's going on? Pepper out with Clara? I feel like this could either be a death sentence or a wish come true.

"Mine, I need to pack still." Pack. Right. Because after tomorrow she will be gone for thirty days. Thirty days where I can't see her. I sigh and nod at her while Clara eyes me warily.

"Okay. I'll be there."

Chapter 31

I hear the bike before I can see it. There won't be a whole lot of riding days left before the snow starts. Pepper pulls into her driveway, kills the engine, and strides towards the front door. As soon as it swings open I yank her inside and throw her against the wall. Our lips collide with force. The passion in her kiss leaves me dazed but wanting more. I palm her ass cheeks and pull her upwards. Her legs immediately wrap around my waist while her arms snake around my neck and shoulders. Using her back, she pushes her hips and ass away from the wall to grind against me. Without my lips leaving hers I move us clumsily down the hall towards her bedroom. I kick open the door and stumble us to the bed. Pulling back I fight with the button of her pants before finally getting it and tugging them down her lean legs. Panties next. She's already stripped off her shirt and bra for me. God, every little thing about her is amazing. I spread her legs and lick hard up her center. Her hips buck and she groans loudly. I repeat my movements over and over again reveling in her responsiveness.

She's about to come from my mouth between her legs so I stop to kiss and tease other parts of her luscious body instead. I do this four more times, leaving her panting, sweating, and both our bodies' blood pumping wildly from needing release. My tongue laps circles around her right nipple before taking it into my mouth and biting down on it. I play with it with my tongue while I finger Pepper's inner folds. She moans loudly when she's close and I soften to a slower stroke, moving her wetness around which is hot because she's drenched for me. She's scrunching the sheets up in her hands. I love the delirious look in her eyes. Stormy and needy. I push in slowly once before widening her legs more to drive inside with more force. Her head rolls to the side and I watch her back arch from the ripple of pleasure my thrust causes. Sliding my arms under her arched back, I pull her up to face me. We are sitting straddling each other, with our knees bent at each other's sides. Pepper bites down on my neck. I place my hands under her butt to lift it and get more movement. With her on top, sinking down on me, we both cry out from the pleasure. I want this so badly I don't have time to feel anything except her tight pussy choking my dick. I let myself get lost in the sensation and let my body instinctively take the lead. It's wild. Feral. Hot. Her teeth sink into the skin at my neck once more as our chests slide up and down against each other, slick with sweat. She comes hard and fast, screaming out nonsense. I ride the tail of her orgasm, finding my own. We stay clinging together for a few moments before either is ready to move.

I kiss the top of her head and she nuzzles up under my chin, sedated and content as we lay next to each other. My voice is gritty as I stroke her back slowly.

"I don't want you to shut me out," I admit.

She plays with the muscles on my abs, lingering in the crevices as she goes.

"I'm not, Sawyer, but, I need to do this my way." I nod into the pillow. We cling to each other in silence until each of us drifts to sleep.

* * * * *

She wakes gasping for air, startling me awake. I pull her into a tight embrace.

"Shh. You're safe. I'm right here," I whisper softly, over and over until her body relaxes limb by limb. A month is going to be a really long time. My thoughts whirl around my brain as she sleeps soundly finally. When morning comes, she'll pack and leave me. I'm all for counseling, but will it change her? Will I become obsolete suddenly? My own insecurities and fears pummel me, keeping me from finding sleep.

Chapter 32

SEND-OFFS

She softly kisses my lips and keeps our noses touching. I pray to every God I know of that this month apart, this intense therapy, doesn't break us. My chest is caving in from the idea of not seeing her for four weeks and what it could mean.

"It's only four weeks," she breathes. I try to look away from her, from the need I see, the plea in her eyes. But I can't. She doesn't say any more, but I hear her loud and clear anyway. She wants to do this on her own. She's leaving no matter what I say.

"I know."

"I'll come home better," she says, gazing into my eyes. The crisp air has her arms covered in goose bumps. I rub my hands up and down her arms to warm them. I'm not going to tell her that her words are exactly what I'm afraid of, that she'll come home different, moved on from her past...and me. I kiss her lightly again and open the door to her junky old car for her.

"You sure this thing will make the drive?" I ask, trying to lighten the mood. She rolls her eyes at me playfully.

"It's not as old as you are," she smirks. I chuckle, unable to resist.

"Har har. Be safe," I answer as she folds into the driver's seat. Her bag is in the backseat, the car's running, and she's about to drive out of my life for the next thirty days. Thirty days with no contact.

My throat constricts.

A lump forms that is impossible to swallow.

"Kiss me," she says. Her whiskey eyes are glistening ever so slightly. If she thinks I don't notice, she's wrong. Her hands shake just barely as she reaches out for my face. I cup her jaw and kiss her. Not a wild kiss. Not a greedy kiss. A kiss that silently pleads, "I love you, don't leave me." Sweet and sad. A kiss that begs, *please come back.* I feel like a foolish teenager. I should be supportive. I should do everything within my power to help her heal and be whole. But it feels like this treatment is so intense that she could very well come back and say, I'm finally at peace with myself, my life, but I'm not ready for a relationship. There are so many unknown variables that I can't predict, it makes my stomach roll. She's not given me a reason to believe anything will change, but I know that when people take a step away from everyday life to work on themselves, sometimes, when they figure it all out, they change. Sometimes, even the slightest change can snowball into an entirely different life path.

I pull my lips from hers and look at her, memorizing every minute feature on her face. The three freckles on her left cheek. The faint scar. The slight bump on her perfect nose where it broke. Her inky black lashes, the golden flecks in her eyes that sometimes change to a burnt caramel hue.

"I will miss you, Pepper." The words come out harsher than I meant. The emotions I feel are evident in my tone.

"Thirty days, Sawyer. That's all. And me too," she whispers. I pull back, shut the car door for her, and stuff my hands into my pockets. She gives a faint smile my way that doesn't reach her eyes and slowly backs out of the driveway. Possibly out of my life. I stand there watching her car become smaller and smaller until I can't see it anymore. Then I stand there some more, staring off into the distance.

My cell buzzes in my pocket bringing me back from my thoughts. I tug it out of my pocket to see who it is. A text from Beau.

"ATF @club looking for you"

I type out my response to Beau letting him know I'll be right over and hop my bike to head out. Now what? Will any of this ever truly be over? He must know Pepper's gone for a month. What could he possibly have to say to me?

* * * * *

Shadows stretch across the narrow parking lot in front of the two buildings that make up the MC. The air is turning chilly already, summer saying its goodbye each day a little more. I kill the engine and swing a leg up over the seat of the bike. I set my helmet on the seat and head inside, anxious to know what's going on.

Bentley sits at the meeting table behind the bar area. The door is slightly ajar, giving me a full view of him as he sits. His hands are clenched in fists resting on the table top. Two more steps and his head swings in my direction. Blue, stormy eyes glare into mine.

"Hi," I offer stepping through the threshold.

"Sit," Beau commands at the opposite end of the table. My brows knit together in confusion as I take a seat two chairs down from Bentley.

"Where is Carmine?" Bentley barks.

"How should I know? No one's seen him for a week or more now." I look to Beau for confirmation but he doesn't give any information away. His lips are a tight thin line, his jaw set. "What's going on?"

"Carmine Delanti is wanted for aiding and abetting Ezra Ash's escape from prison. He is the one who led Ezra to Pepper. I need to know any information that might help track him down."

"What?" I choke out. Carmine? The club's Carmine is responsible?

"Hydrant, if you know anything at all, please, tell Agent James," Beau says.

"*Know anything*? Are you serious? The woman I love was being stalked by a guy I hang out with! You think if I *knew*, I would have let him be around her? Around me!?" I bellow. The room gets eerily quiet. I feel sick. Carmine is truly a sick bastard.

"It's not that you knew, Sawyer, it's that you might know something that could help us find him *now*," Bentley says breaking the tense silence.

"He's an asshole. Treats women poorly. He always took strange phone calls that needed to be in private! I don't know. He mentioned family, I think in Baltimore, but I'm not positive. He never had pictures, or names, or stories to tell about them. They never came to see him. He just hung around like a creeper," I state dryly. If Carmine shows his face around here I am going to give him the beating of a lifetime. Rage ripples through my muscles. I want to tear him apart piece by piece.

"Does the name Delanti ring a bell to you?" Bentley asks in a clipped tone.

"Not any more than what you mentioned at the hospital."

"Torren Delanti is one of the largest gun and drug smugglers in the U.S. Carmine is his cousin. The family went to great lengths to make sure Ezra escaped from prison. They used him to tie up his own loose end. They used him to get to Pepper. The money she was in possession of exceeded five hundred thousand dollars. The USB contained information that convicted Ezra, but also implicated that Ezra was working for Delanti. He's lost the information *and* the money. I don't think I need to explain how dire this situation could end up."

"Is Pepper in danger still?" My chest feels like a vice is slowly cinching itself around my ribs.

"If we can head off Carmine before he talks to Torren, we have a shot at keeping her safe," Bentley answers.

"I saw him." I breathe angrily. "I saw Carmine leave Adventure World the night Ezra was there." I knew the bike. I ignored it as anything relevant. My hands clench into fists at my thighs.

"Hoot saw him the day before our meeting," Beau adds.

"That gives him what then, a little over a week in hiding?" Bentley asks. Beau nods.

"He was seeing Kylie." I grab my phone and open her contact entry before sliding the phone to Bentley.

"I haven't heard from her in a week either. She usually texts me at least once every week. I feel sick, I hooked them up," I admit. Bentley writes down her contact information and takes her home address from me before standing up and calling backup to check on her location immediately. All of Carmine's interest in Pepper makes sense now. His ridiculous warning to stay away from her. His constant questions about her. I want to pummel him. It would be best if the ATF find him first, though. I can't be sure I wouldn't kill him. There are too many people that depend on me for me to let rage take over.

"Sawyer, it's not your fault. You couldn't have known. I should have seen it. I should have been more attentive to who was around her." Bentley shakes his head, disgusted with himself. But it's not his job to babysit her either.

"Will you please call me when you find Kylie? I don't want to talk to her, I just want to know she's safe. We dated a while ago. She's a leech but she's not a bad person," I say. Bentley nods, shakes Beau's hand, then mine, and sees himself out, ear pressed to his phone, barking orders.

"I hope to God they find him," I mutter. Beau clamps a palm on my shoulder and squeezes.

"Me too, because if *we* find him first, things will get ugly. No one messes with my family," he grumbles. "It'll be okay." I want to believe him but I don't feel like everything's going to be okay. I need to find a way to warn Pepper. I can't even see Pepper to tell her, to warn her.

Chapter 33

TORMENT

The past five days have gutted me. I'm on edge, worried about Pepper and the Carmine situation. I'm struggling with our separation. There's always a risk when you open yourself up and show someone who you really are. You are always vulnerable. I think that must be how Pepper's felt for years now. I've buried myself in appointments at Bloodlines to keep my mind busy. Allie and I have taken more walks, bike rides, and trips to the Parlor than necessary. Anything to get me out of the house and keep me busy.

Clara tried to give me a Valium on Tuesday. I'd laughed and told her no thanks. I think I actually offended her. She really seemed to think I needed to relax. I miss seeing Pepper. Obviously. But more so I miss the random texts throughout the day. The way she might just bump my shoulder or hold my hand. I miss her smell. I didn't realize wholly just how much time we'd started spending together. The nights without Allie are now really silent and lonely. The weather even seems to be solemn. It's getting brisker and brisker out. In a couple weeks I'll have to put the bike away for the winter months. That makes my stomach drop almost as much as being without Pepper does. Tugging off my helmet, I make my way to the mailbox. I should check it considering I haven't been motivated to do so in three days. I jab my hand into the belly of the box and yank out the oversized pile one-handedly before heading up the drive and into the quiet house. Tossing the stack on the countertop I notice an envelope that doesn't look like a bill or junk mail. One with a handwritten address. The envelope is marked from near Roanoke. Pepper. I tear into it, pulling the papers free from their confinement.

"Sawyer,

I'm sure by now Bentley has come knocking at the club. I'm so ashamed and upset that my issues leaked into your life, your friends' lives. Carmine always bothered me but I couldn't pin down why. Why would I? I wouldn't have known him from anyone else in the MC. I was so naive to think that when Ezra was put in prison it was the end of our connection.

I always did wonder why he didn't care about the money. It makes sense, I guess, if it wasn't his to care about really. I'm not sure what the Delanti family thought they'd get from me, though, it's not as if the ATF would have let me, a civilian, keep the money. It was part of evidence. Maybe they knew I'd kill Ezra. Maybe I was a loose end, or he was, and either way it would pit us against each other and things would be tied up.

It keeps me up at night. Round and round my mind goes trying to figure out *why me*? I was just a good girl, who made excellent grades who fell in love with a boy. I had normal dreams, fears, hopes. My entire being was altered the day I shot Cane by accident. I might have been able to come back from being raped, but Cane would have killed Ezra anyways. Locked away in prison and still not with me. What if I had shot Ezra, if Cane hadn't walked in? Would we have run together? I'll never know. No one will. That is a cold, hard, torturous truth. I've made progress, though. Cane loved me. I don't question that and I had the opportunity to prove to him that he needn't question my love either. I keep that close to me. That ring around my neck is the ring he bought me, the ring that was supposed to be our happily ever after. I find small bits of comfort in the fact that our love was true. That our circumstances didn't break that love, not in the end.

Demons. Monsters. They live inside my skin. I'm not happy talking to the therapist. She only wants to make me relive all my worst moments. Did you know I spent an entire year not letting anyone touch me? A brush of an arm sent me spiraling into a panic attack. I felt shame. Disgust. I couldn't breathe. It's painful to go back and let myself feel that way, even if it's only to work through it.

Bentley was the one to break through to me. He saved that part of me. I'm grateful for that. If he hadn't, maybe I'd have never been at that bar the night we met. I'd have never have let you touch me. He held me at night when I was all alone in this new life here in Virginia. I knew he wanted more, he knew I didn't, but he was all I had. He risked his career for me. He kept me grounded somehow.

It feels like he did all that for you, too. No, that's not right, more like, to build me up enough to lead me to you. I don't want to be a face in the crowd anymore. A statistic. I've done that for so long. I'm tired. So exhausted from all the facades, emptiness, the cover stories. I'm ready to participate in life again. I think. I've been falling asleep by eight p.m. lately. How ridiculous is that? The therapy sessions wipe me out. Drain me of any leftover energy. I haven't even worked out since I've come here. (gasp)

Want to know a truth?

I miss you right now.

xx-Pepper"

I set the letter aside and think about the words she's written to me. My legs feel solid. Like concrete. There are things that she alluded to in the past that she outright spelled out for me in this letter. I had no idea she felt so isolated. My heart feels heavy, though. The letter leaves me hopeful, but also leaves a lot of questions in my head. I walk to the couch

and fall back into it clutching the letter to my chest.
She wrote to me.

Chapter 34

Twelve days. Twelve days of feeling up one second and below low the next. The house is spotless. My bike glistens even in the dark of night. The shop hasn't looked so good since the week we opened. My truck smells brand new again. I've exhausted all my options for cleaning. I even raked and bagged all the leaves in the yard this week. I know this thirty-day deal has to happen. Obviously it is what's best for Pepper, yet also I think it prevents me from falling victim to making past mistakes. With Clara, I didn't give her room to breathe. I never gave her the chance to come to *me*, to want me. I gave her what I wanted to give and convinced myself that it was exactly what *we both* wanted and needed. It wasn't. I can't stand to think that I was walking the same path with Pepper. Our days apart have forced me to sit back and think about not only what I want, but how I want it. It's amazing what clarity can come from a little dose of solitude.

"Sawyer,

Sometimes lying in this sterile, cold dorm room makes me crazy. I know it's temporary. I know I volunteered for this. Writing to you seems to help calm me. I'm not sure you even want to know the details that I have to share with you but I'm going to write them to you anyways.

We were talking about reality versus...well, not reality. Like movies. It got me thinking. I've had all these moments, movie moments—grenades, guns, the dramatic death of the love interest. It sucks. I want the movie moment where the girl finally gets the guy. The one where the music takes over, and they stare into each other's eyes and just know they finally have each other. You know like when Samantha Baker finally sees Jake in *Sixteen Candles* waiting outside the church for her. I want *that* movie moment. I guess that's ridiculous considering life doesn't have a soundtrack. Or, that the entire point of talking about it was that movie moments and reality don't line up. That in reality people don't just bounce back. That it takes work. That feelings have to be dealt with. SUCKS.

The ache in my chest hasn't gone away. I wanted Ezra dead. I feel no remorse for killing him. That sounds terrible I know. I know it's natural on some level to feel that way. He violated me. He killed his nephew, my first love, my first *everything*. But yet, normal people don't act on that hate. They seek justice but not revenge. They don't execute. I did. I wanted it to be over. But, it's not, is it? It never will be because I hold on to it all. I need to purge it all. Talk it out, I guess. I'm rambling. The therapist said that writing things down would be cathartic. I guess it is, but I don't think she intended me to write them down for someone else to read. Thing is, what's the point of writing it all down for myself? I already know it. I live it. Seeing the words on paper doesn't help what I already know. Maybe, though, maybe it will help you to understand me. I can hope. Can you believe there is NO DESSERT here? Like, any. At. ALL. Some bullshit about sugar, caffeine yada yada, your moods, brain function. It's CRAP.

I keep having the moments. Usually in group therapy (it's wicked boring sometimes), little snippets of memories. They shine so brightly, though. Little slivers of happiness. Group stops and the leader always asks, 'why are you smiling?' Every time my answer is the same, 'I was thinking about Sawyer.'

- - -

Truth time:

I remember thinking I wanted to make you smile the first time we met at the bar. I hadn't wanted that for anything or anyone in a long time.

xx-Pepper"

My heart feels so light. Her open candor, quick wit, and truths bleeding out on the page actually raise my spirits. Smiling to myself, I know exactly what I need to do. I set out straight away to put a plan into action.

Chapter 35

Day twenty. I've grown mildly used to my days being Pepper-free. The mailbox has never held such appeal before, though the days that there is nothing from her waiting for me are hard to swallow. My disappointment is crushing some days. It's amazing how in the span of just months someone can grow to be such a fixture in your life, no matter how small or large their presence is.

To my utter surprise, Greta stopped by earlier this week. She'd stayed for thirty minutes. It was slightly tense between us. She's really not a people-person by nature. She'd wanted to check in on me and to let me know that she'd be gone for work when Pepper came home. She'd handed me a sealed envelope and asked if she could *really* trust me to get it to Pepper. It was strange to say the least. Of course I would. I wouldn't be an asshole and open it either. I'd told her that too and she'd laughed at me and shook her head, as if I was the one being ridiculous.

The mailbox is stacked with bills when I pull the door open. Taking the stack out, I sift through it as I walk into the house. I toss all the crap on the floor at the front door, kick of my shoes, flip a light on, and tear into the letter I've been anticipating.

"Sawyer,

Confidence in myself. I'm discussing it at length. Shoot. Me. Now. Please.

I know rationally that all the things that have happened aren't my fault as a person. I know I acted on instinct. I did what I thought was right in the moment.

Fight or flight and all that shit.

Still, I harbor this secret insecurity that if anyone is close to me they'll get dragged down. That the choices I've made, the person I became after I was violated, after I pulled the trigger the first time, they are consequences for those that I let in. Bad ones. I'm going to try and see what you see, what you said you saw in me, in myself. I know that I will find that place again, the one where I wear a smile, naturally, instead of indifference. I know I'll feel joy more than sorrow and regret. I'm trying. I'm trying to get there. You deserve nothing less from someone, but I'm not doing this for you.

That wouldn't work. I have to do it for me. Holding onto resentment is like drinking poison and expecting the other person to die. Ironic really, because it's so easy to let resentment grip you. Hold you hostage and dictate your life.

It has to come from that place deep inside me that is fractured right now. I have to piece it together like a puzzle and glue it and let it set to dry. Then, then I can be. I'll be deserving of someone like you AND I'll be able to give myself. I know you're probably upset that I've let Clara visit weekly. It's strange actually. I like her company. She understands my feelings without me having to speak them out loud. It's refreshing actually. It's not a reflection of whether or not I care about you. I want you to know that. I just need to get my world straight before I let you in it all the way. You deserve that.

Truth time:

My mom died giving birth to me. It was just me and my dad until he remarried a few years later. I was so little I don't remember a time when she wasn't in our lives, my stepmom that is. I've been feeling very sad that I had to leave them behind.

That they think I'm dead. That they grieve. That guilt eats at me.

xx-Pepper

I'm stunned. Clara's been visiting her. Anger bubbles in my gut. She's *let* Clara visit. Why not me? I take deep breaths. I know there is a reason behind her choices. I'm not seeing what her plan is, but Clara wouldn't hide something bad from me. I have confidence that Pepper's doing her best. Making the best choices she knows how.

I need to let it go. I feel like a whiny child. I'm hurt. I'm dying to see her. Hold her. Kiss her. That's all it is. It's my own childish insecurities. My brain moves on to other elements she's shared.

Her mother died during birth? How awful. It sounds like she had a nice childhood, though. But on top of all the traumatic events she's been through, to have the stability of family ripped away? It's got to hurt deeply. I'm beginning to think maybe a single month isn't enough time at all for Pepper to heal the way she says she wants to. There are so many traumas. So many emotional levels to peel back, expose, and work through.

Chapter 36

Allie has jumped into the school year with both drive and enthusiasm. Her nightly homework this year is blowing my mind. I absolutely do not remember my homework being so in-depth and difficult. She's thriving, though. It's good to see. Clara brought the lawyer's paperwork for legal adoption into the shop yesterday. It'd had felt unsettling to sign my name on the affidavits attached to the packet. I know it's for my benefit. To maintain my role in Allie's life. I wasn't signing away consent since I have no legal right to her anyways. Still, though, it left me feeling down and out. I'd asked Clara about her visits with Pepper because I was curious. It was nice to hear her say that she looks well. That she's finding her way, herself. Clara wouldn't divulge anything outside of that, though. She said she didn't want to break Pepper's trust, but that I needed to trust her and Pepper both. It let me breathe easier if only for the day.

Today is day twenty-seven since Pepper's been away. I've found myself getting into this absurd routine of running home from work and checking the mail. I want more letters. I'm starting to wonder if maybe she's not going to write any more. It's strange, in today's world no one writes letters anymore. The constant access to instant contact makes mailing a letter a moot point. In the absence of her texts and, well, her physical presence, the letters she sent seem so much more poignant. She took the time to handwrite something. To address it. To stamp it and mail it. It travelled through many hands before reaching me. In a way, it seems romantic and nostalgic, even if the content isn't necessarily the most upbeat. The sound of silence is something I can't take anymore. Nobody ringing my phone now; I never thought I'd miss such a beautiful sound. There's nothing to hold but the memories we've made. I cannot wait for Pepper to come back.

I'd left the shop early to attend the MC's charity event. Dominic donated a large sum of money from his business to help get things going. We're trying to raise awareness and fund the music and arts programs in the local schools. Many of us have children in the schools and after watching the chorus disappear, then some art classes, and now that there is threat of the orchestra being cut, we'd stepped up and offered to host a community event to raise enough money to fund the programs. Clara was over the moon about it and of course sat down with a lot of the school board members and other old ladies from the club and created a fantastic event. All the proceeds from our fair day will go to the school system.

Hoot sits on a seat in the dunk tank.

He'd only agreed to do it if the tank was housed inside since the weather isn't exactly warm out. Beau is running a dart booth where you try and pop balloons. Clara has kids singing and the orchestra playing at different ends of the hall to provide music. It's all come together in the most amazing way. There are tables lined with baked goods, a bounce house just outside the door, and people are milling about in droves, dropping money at the various games and food stands. It's definitely a hit. I smile to myself, taking it all in. I watch as a little boy cranks his arm back and hurls a ball at the target. Hoot screams like a little bitch as he drops into the water. I chuckle to myself as his head emerges and he shakes off like a wet dog, scowling at the little boy.

This is good for the club. The community will see our name attached to this and hopefully be put at ease about having an *unruly* motorcycle club in its town. Carmine was found three days ago an hour south of Baltimore. Kylie had been driving; he'd told her he wanted to take her away for a vacation. Bentley had gotten through on her cell and she'd aided in delaying him from his final destination. I didn't get any more information than that but it was enough. He's trapped with Bentley and crew for questioning. That's all that matters. Pepper, for now, is safe.

"Hey stud," Clara says breathlessly while bumping my shoulder.

"Hi there." I give a return bump and a wink, which makes her cringe. Her complete aversion to winking never gets old.

"Can you bring Allie home with you tonight? I need to stay late to help clean all this up and break down everything."

"Of course." I smile down at her. This week she's sporting a pastel purple streak in her hair. I actually like it. "This went off really well. Any idea how much we raised?"

"A little over thirty thousand by the last count," she answers excitedly. "That's enough to fund all the programs we want for the next school year!" I pull her into a sideways hug and kiss the top of her head.

"That's amazing. This event was amazing, thanks for helping to pull it all together without a hitch," I say sincerely.

"Anything for a cause close to my heart. You know that. Now go round up the kid, she's going to be a total jerk tomorrow if she doesn't get some sleep."

"Aye aye, captain." I salute Clara and go on the hunt for my Alliecat.

Chapter 37

GOOD DEEDS DONE DAILY

Allie had so much sugar and excitement pumping through her that it took twice as long as normal to get the kid to just lay the hell down and go to sleep. I'd reached my critical patience-almost-extinct point by the time the house was finally quiet. Most of this had to do with the fact that when Allie had brought the mail in when we got home, there was a letter from Pepper. I'd wanted to tear into it right then, but given the tone of her other letters, I didn't think it was a good idea to read it with Allie milling about. She'd no doubt want to be able to read it and that wasn't happening.

I listen for a moment to make sure there are no last minute sounds from Allie's room. No more bathroom requests, water demands or "I can't sleep" complaints. Hearing nothing, I sit at the kitchen bar top and rip into the envelope.

"Sawyer,

I feel like my letters have been choppy and out of order. I'm sorry if they've concerned you. This whole experience has been really intense and I found it easy to just write down whatever popped into my mind.

Your voice was the only sound I heard some days. You got under my skin. You kissed my scars. You held my hand. You proved your worth. You were a friend. You were steady, just...there. You let me cry. You let me be me, even if that version of me was awful. You kissed me with passion. You held me when I needed holding.

I made myself unlovable, yet you tried. You saw beyond that. I knew I'd fall for you if I let my guard down. I didn't want to burden you with that. With me. And, maybe you wouldn't fall with me. My heart's so fractured that if it breaks one. more. time. I'm done. Ruined. That scares the ever living shit out of me.

It's not right, though. I need to prove myself to you. I need to give you a reason to want me. A real reason. I need to show you...and myself...that I'm worth loving, because I haven't, not really. I haven't let you know me. I've given you a version of myself that I thought would put you *off* me because I was put off by myself. I hope it's not too late. I want to show you kiss by kiss, smile by smile, truth by truth, that I'm worthy of you, of love. Worthy of what you've given to me by not giving up on me.

I'll be home next week. I'm nervous. I'm excited. I'm unsure how things will go. It's unsettling, actually. Clara laughed when I told her all this. Said, 'it's natural, buck up.' How did you live with her for so many years?! I love her to death but I'm not sure I could *live* with her. She and Dominic have been wonderful, though. I should get my phone back when I check out on Friday. If you're up for seeing me, text me so I know when and where.

Have you had enough truths yet?

xx-Pepper"

I immediately grab my phone from the coffee table in the living room. My thumbs fly across the screen, typing out my response to her.

"Your house. 7pm. Friday night.

PS. there are never enough truths."

My grin is enormous. It hurts my cheeks. My breathing is rapid with excitement. Two full days and I get to see her gorgeous face again. How the hell am I going to wait out forty-eight hours sanely?

Chapter 38

Friday morning rolls in the same as any other day, except today I see Pepper. It's ten a.m. I slept like crap last night. The anticipation of having her physically near me again made every muscle in my body tense up and my brain race. I groan and pull the blankets over my head, wishing for a solid hour of sleep.

Thirty minutes later I'm stalking down to the kitchen to put some coffee on for myself.

"Ughhhhhhh, suck," I grumble. I'm out of coffee. While I contemplate my options, my phone vibrates from its charging port. A new text message from Pepper five hours ago.

"Mornin' handsome"

FIVE hours ago! It was only ten thirty, who gets up at five a.m.?! I fire off a return message.

"Up with the sun, I see. Morning. Whether it's good or not is yet to be determined."

My phone vibrates again.

"Whattsamatta?"

"Outta coffee, and no sleep."

I responded first, then scoured my pantry for old coffee. I can't have really run out. I grab my phone, which is currently vibrating, and shove my bare feet into sandals before tugging on a hoodie.

"I was too excited to sleep too. Hence 5 am."

Her message puts a wide, toothy grin on my face as I climb into the truck. It's freaking freezing outside. We better not have an early winter. I hate winter. The sky is overcast and gray. There is a bitter chill in the air. If we're getting rain, I need to remember to put the bike in the garage when I get back. I type out a quick response to Pepper letting her know that I'm excited to see her too and head out in search of caffeine.

By the time I get back to the house it's nearly one p.m. and the sky is almost black with impending doom. A storm warning has been issued for our county. A freak snow storm. It's like Mother Nature's personal "fuck you" to me. I decided to pack an overnight bag and head to Pepper's house early and wait for her. I don't want the threat of snow to ruin my chances of seeing her. I'm not a hundred percent sure she will want me there before her, but I'm willing to take the gamble. My phone buzzes from the mattress.

"Call me ASAP."

Pepper. I dial her number and wait.

"Hi," she answers on the first ring. Her voice sounds calm and light. I've wanted to hear it for so long that I almost forget to respond.

"Pepper? What's up? Are you alright?" I ask concerned.

"I'm stranded on the side of the road. The car won't start. Damn thing just puttered to a stop," she grumbles.

"Where are you?" I growl. I knew that car was a piece of shit.

"Uh, 220 southbound, there's a sign for Tinker Creek," she answers.

"Is there anything near you? A store?" I ask.

"Not that I can see. I'll walk a bit, though, if you want."

"No, it's okay. I'll leave now. Should be less than an hour, hang tight."

"Okay. Hey Sawyer..." she calls.

"Yeah?"

"Sorry for being an inconvenience."

"Shut up. You are the only thing that was on my schedule for today," I flirt.

"Oh?"

"Yes, but there is a storm coming, I need to get on the road now. Stay in your car."

"Yes sir." She laughs before ending the call.

I slam my hands on the steering wheel in frustration. Of course her dilapidated car would choose to break down in a freak snowstorm. I'm going as fast as I can. The visibility is slim to none and cars are off the road every mile or so. The blizzard we're getting is worse by the second. What should have only taken me forty-five minutes has now reached fifty minutes and I'm still five miles from where I think she is. The sky is so dark that I had to turn on the headlights. It makes the thick snowflakes look like they are moving at warp speed in front of me even though I'm crawling along.

As I approach the turnoff for Tinker Creek I can't stop my heart from racing. I'm going to see her. Any second that crappy old car will appear in my line of sight and with it Pepper. I see lights flash. The old junker is tilted at a funny angle to the road. I slow to a stop ten feet from her rear bumper. The snow falls rapidly around Pepper as she steps out of the car, teeth chattering. She's not wearing a coat. She probably didn't pack one because who the hell could have predicted a freak snowstorm at this time of year? She starts walking toward the truck. I roll all the windows down and yell to her.

"Stop!"

She freezes in place, staring at me like I'm insane. Quick as I can, I hit play on the Thompson Twins' "*If You Were Here*" track in my Spotify list and crank the truck's volume full throttle. Then I exit the truck.

I mouth, movie moment, to her as I take a few steps closer. Her eyes light up, a mesmerizing smile takes over her face and she runs full tilt at me. I brace myself for impact, boots barely visible in the deepening snow. Time pauses and I feel like I'm waiting for her to kiss me for the very first time.

Her hands reach out for me as I scoop her up and pull her to my chest. My heart jackhammers through me, drilling right out of my chest and crashing into Pepper's chest. She stares at me wide-eyed as my eyes roam her face, hair, and everything else I can see. Her arms are squeezing tightly, clinging to me. I cup her rear and squeeze back. Her hands palm my cheeks, drawing my face towards hers. Cold lips meet cold lips and I'm lost in the moment completely. Nothing stays cold for long. I lick her bottom lip before drawing it out.

Heat. Firey heat.

I work my lips over hers, our tongues mingling. I'm painfully hard.

All from a kiss.

Her lips are divine. I'm not going to stop. She nips my bottom lip before smoothing it with her tongue. She plays with my lip ring, tugging on it playfully and I groan into her mouth.

She's fire.

Finally we peel back from each other.

"I'm-I'm underdressed," she stutters out.

I'm such a dick. I've got a coat on, but Pepper's in a t-shirt and jeans. I back up slowly, still carrying her, until we reach the truck. Placing Pepper in the front seat, I blast the heat and tell her to warm up while I grab her stuff out of her car.

Chapter 39

TRAPPED TRUTHS

The small fire crackles in the fireplace, putting out meager warmth that we barely feel. Pepper shivers. I tighten my arm around her shoulders a little more. The fire's down to embers, softly pulsing their red-orange glow. It pops and hisses, its orange tongues dancing. The bed and breakfast under normal conditions would be romantic I'm sure. But we're here because it became too nasty out to drive any further. We'd checked in to Bailey's, a tiny bed and breakfast along the creek and as soon as we made it to our room, the inn lost power. I don't care, though. Nothing could ruin this night for me. Pepper's snuggled into my side and the fire is at least helping keep us mildly warm. We have the down comforter from the bed pulled down around us as we sit on the floor in front of the fireplace. We pick at strawberries, melon balls, and grapes with some cheese that the owner brought up to us. We've barely talked in the last hour. Just a quiet word here or there. Soft touches, hand holding, and chaste kisses between "I missed yous" have taken up the time. It's lazy and calm and comforting just being in her presence.

"What's the biggest thing you took away from your month?" I ask.

"That life doesn't make sense. It's pretty terrifying to think about. All these random events smashing into each other, playing off each other. Changing courses of action and futures. Whatever you thought you knew flies out the window and you can't figure it out. But, what I'm trying to say is, that's all okay. It's okay to just be part of the chaos. To survive it, enjoy it even."

"That's pretty deep," I murmur into the shell of her ear. She tilts her face to mine.

"I missed you, Sawyer. I missed what we've grown to have."

"I missed you too." I lean in and place light kisses on her face and in her hair as she rests her head on my shoulder, before shifting and moving my kisses further south. A small gasp leaves her and the fire light dances on her skin. I need to feel her, all of her, now.

"Stop please," she whispers. I keep going. Her body responds to mine. She definitely doesn't want this to stop.

"Sawyer." Her voice is stern now. I halt all movements and look up to her face.

"We need to talk." I sit up and scoot back a bit from her. She's all business now and I'm terrified. "Part of my therapy is to take things slow. To build healthy relationships." She pauses, shaking her head and blowing out a breath. "What I'm trying to say is, fuck, I'm horny as hell and want to jump you *right now*, but I'm going to stick with my progress plan and say no. No sex yet. I want to date. You," she says quickly as shock registers on my face. "Only you. But, I want to date you. Properly. I want a mini- do-over. I want to do this right because I'm this close," she says timidly, holding up her thumb and index finger so they're almost touching, "to saying three little words to you. Can you understand that?" Her eyes shift, looking at the fire instead of me. As if she's scared of what my answer will be. Grabbing her hands in mine, I kiss the inside of each wrist.

"Pepper, I understand. It makes sense. I will show you what a gentleman is. I will woo you by taking you on proper dates and I will absolutely respect your therapy process and any promises you make to yourself because that's how much I care." Before the last word leaves my lips she's diving head first at me, crushing her mouth to mine. I palm her shoulders and push back, separating our lips.

"Uh..."

"Kissing isn't sex, Mr. Crown. We can kiss all we want," she smirks before her tongue darts out, running along my bottom lip. *Kissing it is, then.* I pull her close, devoted to the idea of making out with my woman, all night long.

Chapter 40

NO SEX THERAPY

Our first two days back to civilization were spent shoveling, making out like randy teens, and more shoveling. After that, Pepper shooed me out the door. We're not to spend the night together. It's too complicated given our history and attraction, so she says. I'd given her my best pout, but it seemed to do nothing to change her mind. Day three, Allie and Pepper were over and we'd had an epic snowball fight and snowman building competition followed by an ice cream sundae competition. Pepper's sundaes were starting to get outrageous. Cheesecake chunks and ice cream with M&M's sprinkled on top seemed like a bit of a stretch to me, but Allie voted it the winner. When I'd finally remembered to give Greta's letter to Pepper, it'd brought her to tears. It was only three sentences.

"I'm so proud of you. You are the lightness to my dark. I'm away for work, not sure when I'll be able to catch up with you.

Greta."

I'd tried to figure out why Pepper was so touched by her words, or lack thereof, but she told me it was girlfriend thing and I wouldn't understand. Women are mysterious creatures.

After that, real life slowly settled in. The snow melted, we all went back to work or school and the days never seem long enough to get in the things I want to do. Pepper started work with Dominic. She's liking it so far but she's also dog tired by the end of her shift. Tonight I've decided to lay it on thick for her. I want her to feel the way she makes me feel.

I have a bath drawn, candles burning, and my iPod going in the bathroom with a playlist I'd made just for Pepper. I wait in the kitchen, wine glass in hand for her. The kitchen door swings open and she drags herself in, looking beat after her first evening running Dominic's club alone. Clara had called and said that things had been slightly busier than normal and that maybe she'd need a little pampering after her day. It was the perfect catalyst for my plan.

"Evening, love," I say, holding the wine out to her, smiling. She inhales sharply, looking startled. Zoned out, I'm sure, from her day.

"Hi, Sawyer, thanks." She takes the glass, pushes up on her tiptoes, and gives me a soft kiss. I watch as she toes off her shoes, sets her purse down on the island, and sits on one stool. Pushing my hips off the counter, I prowl over to her.

"Come on, love," I say and hold out my hand to her. "Bring your wine." She shoots me a curious look but takes my hand and lets me lead her to the bathroom.

"Sawyer," she breathes. "What's all this?" Taking the wine from her and setting it on the edge of the tub, I turn back to her. The look in her eyes takes my breath away. Beautiful.

Slowly, I reach around her hips and pinch the edge of her blouse, sliding it up and over her head. Next I pull the elastic from her hair, sending it tumbling down her back in soft, black waves. She stands stone still, not taking a breath or exhaling. I keep my eyes on hers. I reach for the top button of her pants.

Working the buttons, my fingers graze her smooth skin and a soft groan leaves me.

She shakes slightly, placing a palm on the back of my hand.

"Sawyer," she pleads. I move her hand gently back to her side.

"Shh."

I make short work of the buttons, then weave my fingers through her hair, pull her close, and rest my forehead on hers.

"Hop in and relax a bit. I'll entertain myself till you're done."

Then I let her go, closing the bathroom door behind me. My jeans are uncomfortably tight in the crotch. I adjust myself and sink into the couch. This no-sex therapy business is tough on a man. Minutes later I hear her humming along to the song playing and contentment sweeps through me. I grab the remote and turn on the TV with a smile on my face.

* * * * *

Forty minutes later she appears in the living room, wrapped in a silky knee-length robe. Hair wet, face clear of makeup, she is the prettiest thing I've ever laid eyes on.

"You are gorgeous," I tell her. She blushes a faint shade of pink and makes her way to the couch next to me. I pull her closer to me, letting her snuggle into my side. We watch the late night show for an hour like this, her curled into my side, head on my shoulder. Perfect. The moment is simply perfect.

As time creeps on, I can sense her exhaustion, so I shift our bodies, weaving an arm under her knees, the other around her back, and carry her to her room. She doesn't protest in the least.

"I love this," she breathes sleepily as I walked her around the bed to her side.

"What's that?"

"Being held by you. You make me *feel* safe, and cared for and...and beautiful, I guess."

I freeze and look down at her. Dipping my head to hers, I brush my lips against her forehead and set her on the bed. I cover her up, brush a wisp of a kiss on her cheek, and say good night.

"Night," she mumbles. I flip off the lights in the house on my way out, lock the door behind me, and head home with the biggest shit-eating grin. The first bit of resistance has left the building. Mission accomplished.

Chapter 41

PROPER DATES

Our schedules are proving difficult to line up. She works most nights and I'm at the shop most days. I silently curse Dominic for his job offer. It's been weeks since she's been home and we've yet to line up a time for a proper date night.

Out of frustration, I finally pleaded with Clara to take the Monday shift at Bloodlines so that I can surprise Pepper with a daytime date. Not an easy feat. Daytime dates are hard to plan and for whatever reason feel less *magical*, as Allie would say. Still, I'm a determined bastard and today is the first proper date.

I arrive at Pepper's at eleven a.m. on the dot. I'm taking her to the Lyric. Free popcorn all day Mondays and the classic *Casablanca* seem like a good date idea for a daytime excursion.

Leaving the truck idling, I saunter up to Pepper's front door and knock three times. The door swings open and Pepper greets me with a bright smile. Taking her in from head to toe, I can't help the groan that escapes me. Her jeans look like they've been painted on, accentuating the curves of her hips and waist. A simple V-neck sweater reveals just a hint of the cleavage that I dream about burying my face in. She laughs at my groan.

"Hello there, stud."

"You look good enough to eat," is the response that leaves my mouth. I take her hand in mine and pull her gently to me before wrapping my arms around her and hugging her.

"You look pretty edible yourself," she says and smiles into my chest.

We walk to the truck pressed together. I open her door, help her up and in, and shut it gently before jogging around to my side and hopping in.

"Where are we going?" she asks curiously.

"To the Lyric."

"That old movie theatre?" Her brows arch and the corners of her eyes crinkle in delight. It's one of the sexiest things I've witnessed.

"The very one."

"Oh nice! I haven't been able to go yet. It looks so neat from the outside!" Pepper's chirpy tone brightens the entire day.

She's been so much happier since she's been back. The sadness in her eyes is lifting a little more each day. She reaches over and rests her hand on my thigh. I keep it there the entire drive, stroking the soft skin of her backhand with my thumb as she chitchats about anything and everything that happens to pop into her mind. It's almost like she's a different person. A new revised version of herself and we're learning each other all over again.

* * * * *

Awed by the original 1930s tapestries, the golden glow of the replica lanterns, and the charm of the restored lobby and auditorium, Pepper gawks at me.

"This place is incredible," she breathes as we approach the concession stand.

"Wait till you have the popcorn. It's the best-tasting popcorn in southwestern Virginia." Her nose wrinkles slightly but in good fun. "Don't worry, I'm ordering peanut M&M's for you too." I chuckle. Her face splits into an enormous grin and I can't help but pull her into my side. Her smile could make a smart man stupid. Her arm loops around my waist as mine wraps around her shoulder. The feeling of her pressed against me brings a calmness and peacefulness to me that I don't often feel and I let myself take the moment to enjoy it.

"Maybe not today, maybe not tomorrow, but soon and for the rest of your life," Pepper says dramatically as we exit the theater. I'd never seen the movie but it was pretty decent. If I'm honest, though, I'd watched Pepper's face most of the movie. She'd gasp during the dramatic parts, frown when sad, smile or get that faraway look in her eye during the romantic scenes. I was mesmerized by her expressions. I sweep her up in my arms. Laughter peels from her in a surprised burst as I swing her around before dipping her backwards and kissing her passionately. Hoots and hollers ring out around us but I don't take much notice as Pepper's lips move with mine perfectly. I stand her back on her feet and admire the sexy flush of color her skin is sporting.

"Every girl needs to be kissed like that," she says quietly while catching her breath.

"I'm only concerned with making sure *one* girl is kissed like that," I tell her. She runs a hand through her onyx hair and grins at me before taking my hand in hers and lacing our fingers together.

"How is Allie doing? I feel like I haven't seen her in ages," Pepper asks while angling her body towards mine as we drive back to her place.

"She's good. Excelling in school. Crushing on *boys*," I rattle off.

"That's normal you know," she replies.

"I know what eleven- and twelve-year-old boys think in their sick little heads." Pepper laughs a full-bodied sound, filling the cab of the truck.

"You're going to have to just get used to it."

"I refuse," I answer flippantly. This earns me another blast of laughter. A broad smile creeps over my face at the sound.

When we arrive at her house, I throw the truck in park and hustle to her side of the car to get her door for her. She takes my hand and leans into me. Her lips brush mine. The high I get when our mouths meet is ridiculous. I'm smitten and I know it shows. Her soft, exploratory kiss has me vibrating with need. A need that I'm not allowed to do anything about. Her plump lips pull away from mine and she smiles a shy smile at me. She has a grip on me so powerful that one glance from her and I would do anything she asked.

* * * * *

By four p.m. I'm home with Allie. We're sitting together at the table building a volcano for her science project. My mind keeps wandering to how Pepper's evening is going at work. I wonder if she's sporting the same dopey smile I am from our date today.

"You're doing it wrong!" Allie huffs at me. I shoot her an I'm-losing-all-patience-with-her look and stand up from the table.

"Then you are more than welcome to make it yourself," I snap.

"Sawyer!" she whines petulantly.

"Allie!" I mimic. She shoots up from her seat, stomps her foot, and crosses her arms over her chest. Her pout is perfected.

"Please help me," she states, trying to sound *not* whiny. I chuckle and look at her.

"I think make we should get dinner started and then take another crack at this. What do you feel like?"

"Steak and mashed potatoes," she answers. This kid thinks anything is possible on a whim. It kills me sometimes.

"I don't have potatoes," I answer.

"Steak and corn then."

"No corn," I answer.

"What do you have then?" she asks, exasperated.

"Hm, mac-n-cheese?" I arch an eyebrow at her.

"With steak?!" she squawks.

"No. That's disgusting. With hot dogs?" I offer up. Allie's eyes slide to mine and shoot daggers at me before realizing I was kidding. Her laughter fills the house as I move to the kitchen to make us some macaroni and cheese. I grab the box, the pot, and a wooden spoon while she cranks up the music. Lord help me if Britney Spears comes on again.

Chapter 42

END GAME

"Sawyer! XOXO"

The text message from Pepper pops onto my screen and I grin.

"?" I reply.

I continue getting the shop ready for the day. I know what she's talking about but I want to drag it out a bit. The flowers I bought should have been delivered to her door by now. The florist had walked me around the shop and asked me a million questions about Pepper as she pointed out various options. I've never dropped so much money on something that's life expectancy is less than a week. But, I know that it's well worth it. My phone dings.

"They're seriously gorgeous."

"Happy you approve."

"No like, I've never seen a bouquet so stunning."

"Again, if you're happy, I'm happy."

"Happy seems like a gross understatement."

"You can make it up to me..."

"eh hem....dare I ask?"

"Date, tomorrow night. Pick you up at 6."

I type out the message and hope that she will agree to taking a night off for me. I seriously hold my breath for what feels like an eternity. Finally the phone pings again.

"Deal."

"Dress warm."

I breathe a sigh of relief, shove my phone in my pocket, and unlock the shop doors, ready for a full, busy day of artwork.

* * * * *

Hippie Hill. Nothing in Blacksburg is more relaxing sitting down on the grass and eating while you watch life happen on College Avenue downtown. I spread the blanket out. Pepper holds the basket that I packed. She looks adorable in her puffy down vest and hat. I smooth out the wrinkles and pat the ground next to me. She hands the basket over and sits.

"What's in there anyways?" she asks, a hint of curiosity to her voice.

"Hungry?" I ask.

"Maybe?" she answers coyly. "This is a really perfect spot to enjoy people watching and the view."

"I thought you might enjoy it," I mumble as I dig through my bag to find the plates I packed. I set one in her lap and pull out another for me. Reaching into the basket, I pull out our dinner.

Her lips part as she watches me pull out each item.

"What *is* this?" she asks excitedly.

"Dessert for dinner. A dessert buffet of sorts."

Her eyes get wide and her plump lips turn up into a perfect, radiant smile.

"Really? This is all dinner?" she asks, glancing at the assortment of cheesecake, tiramisu, cookies, brownies, and pastries I'm unloading.

"Really. On one condition." I've left the fruit desserts in the basket on purpose. Her rule about no fruit in her dessert is ridiculous and I'm about to change her mind.

"A condition?" she snarks.

"Yup. You game?"

"Sure." She shrugs. I pull off my scarf.

"I'm going to feed you. You are going to be blindfolded."

She stares at me like I've lost my marbles and I can't help the laugh that bubbles up and out of me. "Them's the rules, kid."

"Fine." Her eyes narrow at me but she extends her neck just slightly, letting me know it's safe to cover her eyes. I tie my scarf around her head. Her perfect little nose and pouty, lush mouth are all you can see of her face now. I grab a little chunk of cheesecake.

"Open up." She does as she's told and parts her lips. "A little more." I watch, fascinated at the way her lips open more for me. I slide the cheesecake in between her lips. They close around my fingers and she moans in pleasure as she sucks my fingers clean.

"You like?" I chuckle.

"Mmmhmm."

I grab a chocolate-covered strawberry and raise it to her mouth as she swallows.

"Again," I command. She licks her lips and opens for me. I slide the berry halfway in.

"Bite." Her teeth tentatively bite down, drawing the berry into her mouth. "Thoughts?"

She chews and swallows. Her mouth curves up into a smile.

"It was yummy."

"Fruit and all?" I ask, close to her face. Her breathing picks up, the short puffs of air coming out like little clouds of smoke. I could lick her lips right now from this position. She leans in just barely and I pull back slightly. I grab a raspberry Danish.

"Open." She does as she's told without hesitating. Her chest rises and falls with small jerks. I slide an end into her mouth. "Bite." She does. When she swallows, I whisper into her ear.

"Was it tasty?"

"Kiss me," she breathes.

"You want a taste of me? All this dessert and it's me you want?" I say, hovering near her mouth. Her hands reach out, tracing up my arms until she cups my jaw between her hands. Her thumbs stroke back and forth on my cheeks.

"Yes. Always." She pulls me and just like that another little piece of resistance is gone. Her lips find mine and she draws my bottom lip between hers and sucks. She still tastes like strawberries and chocolate. It's sinful. I cup her head with a hand and snake the other around her waist, pulling her flush against me. I pull back and slip the blindfold off her head.

"Watch," I say, pointing down the hill across the horizon. Pinks and deep oranges light up the sky around us.

"How'd I get this lucky?" she mumbles quietly.

"I was just asking myself the same thing."

We sit in peaceful contentment watching the sun's rays fade and the shadows lengthen around us, holding hands. Nothing has ever felt so stunningly perfect. When the sky is a deep navy and Pepper is shivering next to me, I know it's time. Standing, I extend a hand to her. She smiles and takes it willingly. I pull her to her feet and draw her close to me. One hand slides to her waist, the other holds her right hand to my chest.

"What are we doing?" she asks.

"Dancing. Now, shh, don't be a moment ruiner." She laughs but says no more.

She is the most delicious thing I've ever seen. Our bodies begin to move as one as I sway her gently back and forth in the grass with me. I can feel her nipples bead tightly in the cool air as her chest pushes against mine. The thin cotton of her shirt does nothing to aid her vest in hiding her lust, need, and desire for me. Nothing has ever been so tempting in all my life as the idea of taking Pepper right here, right now. But I can't. We're dating. I'm proving to her that I can be the man she thinks I am. She thinks she's doing this to prove to me that she's who I want. How ridiculous. Yet, it feels right. Taking this slow, even after all this time. It feels justified to start fresh. To start this the *right* way.

I start to hum the tune to "*Beneath Your Beautiful*." It makes me think of her. I'm a terrible singer, though, so she'll have to wait on the words. I hum into her hair as her cheek rests on my chest. She fits. Every part of her fits with me. We move together naturally until I just can't hum any longer.

"How will I ever be good enough for you?" she whispers into the chilled air. I stop short and tilt her face to mine.

"Pepper. You already are." Her eyes glisten with unshed tears as my words sink in. She wraps her arms around me, squeezing tightly. I hold her close in silence and let her have the moment to try and accept my words.

Chapter 43

TIME SERVED

Since our picnic date, Pepper and I have been on cloud nine. Everything seems to just have fallen into place. She even sat down with Dominic and asked for at least two weeknights where she didn't have to work the late shift so we could have more time together. Clara won't stop razzing me about my permanent grin at work and Allie keeps singing that childish, nerve-grating song about me and Pepper sitting in a tree. Nothing breaks my mood, though. Not lately. Everything is just too good to bring me down. Even Beau and Hoot said I better find my badassery or they would kick me out of the MC. I know it will wear off. I know it won't be new and shiny forever but I'll be damned if I'm not going to enjoy the shit out of in the moment. I want to be able to look back and remember all the perfect little moments when times seem tough. I want to have it all sitting in my heart to ride out the bumps in the road when they come; I'm not naive, I know they will come.

Pepper stands before me in a striped, emerald-green, low-cut shirt that makes her boobs look amazing and her waist look tiny. Her dark wash, boot cut jeans and strappy gold heels make her legs look like an appetizer rather than a body part. The layer of pink lemonade lip gloss shines in the light and all I want to do is taste it. It's been months of our taking it slow. I'm about to just take her. She'd only protest for a second before giving in. I know it. I lick my lips and smile salaciously at her. I can't help it. It's as if her body was made to make all red-blooded men drool and think with their lower halves.

"Ready?" I question as she steps towards me.

"Yeah." Her voice is breathy as I reach my hand out for hers and lead her to the truck. Her eyes glitter with mischief.

"Is there something I should know about?" I ask curiously.

"Nope. I'm just happy to see you." Her reply sounds suspect to me but I can't pin down why.

"Alright then," I answer sweetly. She quirks a brow at me and smirks. She's definitely up to something. Opening her door for her, she steps in front of me and climbs up into the truck, wiggling her ass near my face as she gets in. Torture. And she knows it. She's teasing me. Our drive is filled with bad innuendos and flirtatious banter. I will explode at any moment. One over-the-top statement from her, one look of need or desire, and I'm a goner. I'm actually thankful when we arrive at the restaurant. It's the best steakhouse in three towns. I usher us in, resting my hand at the small of her back. I want to let it drift lower. I want to feel the exact spot where the small of her back turns into the top of her ass. I groan as I hold the door open for her.

"What?" she asks.

"Nothing," I answer, embarrassed that I let the sound slip out.

"Uh, huh." She smirks.

The food is to die for. I can't remember the last time I had a steak done to perfection. Salty, tender, and barely pink in the middle.

"Mmmm," I groan, "this is soooooooo good."

"Best steaks in Virginia," Pepper says between bites.

"Oh yeah?" comes my dorky reply. Pepper and I talk in spurts during dinner about nothing and everything. Favorite sports teams, worst college class ever, boxers or briefs, the economy, and why she doesn't eat seafood. It's amazing how good it can feel to get a little inside information on someone after what seems like a lifetime of getting only resistance.

"Dessert?" she asks with a grin.

"I'm stuffed." I pat my belly. "But have at it." I know better than to get in the way of my girl's dessert. She smiles a broad smile and asks the waiter for the dessert menu. It's ridiculous that something so simple makes her eyes light up so brightly.

After Pepper indulges in her favorite pastime, dessert, we make our way back to her house. She sits in the middle of the bench seat. The feel of her arm wrapped around my waist as we drive home sets my hormones on fire. I walk her to her front door and watch as her golden eyes transform from clear to dark. Her eyes, trained on my mouth, are bleeding desire.

I lick my lips and lean just slightly towards her. Taking her chin in my hand, I tip it up, bend down close, and seal my mouth to hers. Fire. Always so much passion in the slightest of contacts. My dick is throbbing with anticipation and we'd barely begun anything.

She reaches back, pushing the door open, and pulls me inside with her. Clothes rustle as we stumble through the threshold. I need this. I need her. I'm going to score tonight. It's happening.

"I wish I could tell you how much I love you, how much you mean to me." Her voice falters slightly. She nuzzles my cheek and continues down my neck, setting a fire across my skin, coals deep in my soul bursting into flames.

"Show me," I whisper and move my hands to the hem of her shirt, pulling it off. She grabs my shirt, pulling it up and over my head as I kick the door shut behind us.

Her hands move on my chest, ribs, belly, and sides as her lips move to my jaw, neck, throat, collarbone, and down. It shouldn't be this thrilling to watch. Her breasts thrust forward and her nipples remain hard, and I can't seem to get enough of the show.

Everywhere she touches and tastes, my muscles jump. She goes down further, tracing the ridges of my abs with her tongue as one hand goes to my belt buckle and tugs. I growl, fingers flexing at her neck. I haul her up, her legs wrapping around my waist, and kiss her. Without breaking our kiss I move us to the bedroom.

Trailing her tongue along the line of muscle that curves from my hip to my groin, my entire body shudders. She's branding my body. The hand at her neck disappears and she looks up wildly at suddenly being pulled up my body. I haul her up so she's straddling me. My erection between her legs sends chills through me. The warmth of her around me is torture. I want inside. There is nothing else I want or need. Her hips grind down on me. My hands come to her sides and sweep upwards. One hand goes to her breast, lifting it slightly. She breaks away from our kiss and looks down to watch me take it to my mouth.

My lips close around the nipple and suck, hard. Her hips buck in my lap, causing me to moan against her nipple. She whimpers at the sensation. I pick her up and lay her back onto the soft bedding. Looming over her, I trail a calloused hand on her from shoulder to waist and trace the edge of her panties. She shivers and I can't suppress my grin. I love knowing I have that effect on her. I run a hand over the branches of her Magnolia tattoo at her shoulder and bicep. There are so many things I'm going to do to her body.

Chapter 44

"Beautiful," I groan, looking down at her. I move to remove her panties and pause. I need permission. I need to be sure. "You want this?"

"Yes," she rasps.

"You sure? After this, there's no *just friends*—ever again," I state. My willpower is dwindling fast. For the love of all that is holy please let the answer be yes. She sits up.

"There's only one thing I need," she says, placing a hand over my heart. "The rest are just details."

Puddle of mush. I am nothing but sludge as my hands make impossibly fast work on the button and zipper of my jeans, and with one tug they're gone. Just as fast, her panties are tossed on the floor. She wraps her legs around my waist while my kisses work her ear, neck, and collarbone. She tastes fresh and clean. My fingers toy between her legs and her groans drift into my mouth as we kiss.

"I need you," I grunt. My thumb puts pressure on her clit, moving in a slow circle, and I watch as her hips buck again. So hot. I could watch her pleasure move through her all day long. Her muscles flex with every stroke inside her from my fingers. I shift my hips and she adjusts her legs around mine as I drive in. Her lips part, her neck arches, and her eyes flutter closed. My thrusts are driving us towards orgasm too quickly. I pull out. I watch with amusement as her eyes fly open.

"Don't stop!" she admonishes, panting. I smirk at her and flip her onto her belly, moving us backwards towards the edge of the bed. Resting a palm between her shoulders, the pads of my fingers trace the large tattoo.

I am going to burst. I can feel it coming on hard as I dive back into her warmth. I enter slowly, taking my time. She glances over her shoulder at me, our eyes locking as I start rolling my hips. My hips move faster, the pace frenzied. The buildup is too intense. "Sawyer!" she pants as she comes. The sound of hearing my name on her lips in that moment is pure ecstasy. Five seconds later with my legs tightly wound, I plant my face at the nape of her neck, drive deep, and groan her name.

I adjust us so we're lying side by side on the bed. She turns her head into my neck and kisses me behind the ear as I lightly trace the muscles of her back. She angles her body so the arm closest to me is bent back and angled behind her head and the other rests so her palm is over her heart. She is stunning in the pale light of the room. I blame the orgasm, but before my brain caught up with my mouth I whisper, "I love you, Pepper."

Her body stiffens in my arms as if she's shocked but then she kisses me. Her body relaxes against mine. "I love you, too," she says on a whisper. Four words. Four short words. Eleven letters have made me the happiest man alive.

After three rounds I am sated, close to drooling, and spent. We lay snuggled, her back to my front, my arm tightly wound around her. Heaven.

"Night, love," I whisper, burying my face in her hair.

"Night," she murmurs sleepily. Just like that, I physically feel the last shred of resistance dissolving between us.

I lay awake until I hear her breathing steadily. Then I find sleep.

* * * * *

I open my eyes slowly, feeling a warm, sleepy, heavy arm draped across my stomach. Her head is on my shoulder, face tucked into my neck. One arm slung across my waist and a leg wrapped around my leg. Her breathing is heavy and steady. Three in the morning. No nightmare. I close my eyes and drift back to sleep with my girl in my arms.

Chapter 45

SMOTHERING

She rolls slightly but doesn't get far before I pull her back against me. The sun is shining through the bedroom window with the promise of a beautiful day.

"Promise you'll wear out those three little words," I whisper in her ear.

"Good morning to you, too," her voice, heavy with sleep, replies.

I chuckle before showing her just how good of a morning it is.

Watching her move around the kitchen sends something warm and liquid through my belly. I tell myself it's because I can smell coffee brewing, a trigger response, really. I move to the coffee pot and pour two mugs, careful to make hers just the way she mentioned over dinner she likes it.

"How is it you remember everything?" she says, eyes wide with humor.

"You're hard to forget."

"Good answer," she answers, a tiny sliver of a smile on her lips.

"Good enough to convince you to take a bike ride today with me?"

"I promised Greta I'd meet her at the gym, but after, yeah."

"Perfect," I call from the fridge. "Pancakes or eggs?"

"French toast!" she replies. I chuckle at her idea but start pulling out all the items I'll need to make my girl French toast.

We're on our bikes. Pepper's speeding ahead of me, decked out head to toe in a leather get-up. It's still a little chilly for bike rides but we were both so ready to get back out and ride that we just bundled up. The trees blur past as I speed up to catch her. Greta had put Pepper in a funk at the gym earlier. I think mostly it's just because Pepper is starting to push Greta into talking more, about personal things. Pepper's heart is in the right place but I'm not sure Greta is the friend to try and save. She's always polite and friendly enough, but she definitely has a fortress built around her heart. She's very reserved, emotionally speaking. It's almost like she has a permanent poker face. She's always quiet, watching, surveying her surroundings. I don't mind her at all and if Pepper wants to try and dive inside that head of hers, more power to her, but I'll stay out of it.

Pepper's tail lights shine. She's pulling into the spot where I first took her. Her hair tumbles out of her helmet as she waits for me to catch up.

"Here?" I laugh.

"What? You too good for a repeat performance?" she asks. My heart leaps out of my chest with excitement. Blood rushes, making it impossible to hear anything over the sound.

"Calm down, lover boy. That's not what I had in mind, but maybe if you behave..." She crooks a finger for me to follow her up the path as I try and quell my raging hormones.

We climb the half-mile path to the flat rock that overlooks the road we just travelled. You can almost see the whole of Blacksburg from it. When we reach the landing, she sits and motions for me to join her.

"Can I ask you something?"

"Anything," I answer.

"Do you want kids? I mean, more kids?" Her question hits me out of left field. She's never mentioned anything about her wants or needs regarding having a family of her own outside of the fact that she chose a life where she *couldn't* have that.

"Absolutely. I want marriage, too though."

"Truth or lie?" she asks.

"Truth."

"The idea of living with me." Her caramel eyes bore into mine, presumably looking for any hesitation or negative feelings.

"Living with Pepper. Hmmm." I tap my chin, drawing out the moment. "The truth. I'd wake up a happy man, every single day. It wouldn't be easy. She doesn't like to share her sweets, she hogs most of the couch during movie time, and she definitely has some communication issues, but I think as a whole, the truth about living with Pepper is that it'd be...amazing." Her gaze holds mine. "Are you asking me to move in with you?"

"I'm...I'm asking if we should move in together." Her voice is quiet, reserved.

"Don't clam up on me now. This conversation is just starting to get good." I smile. She tips sideways, resting her head on my shoulder. I kiss the top of her head.

"I need smothering, I think," she mumbles. I wrap my arms around her and hold her firmly to me.

"Pepper. Will you move in with me?" I ask formally.

"Yes please."

"Yes please?" I repeat.

"Yes please, I would like to move in with you, Sawyer Crown. I want to share our lives. I want to claim you. I want everyone to know me with you and you with me," she rambles off quickly.

"Are you going all cavewoman on me?"

"Me, Pepper, you, lay down." She laughs and pushes me to my back.

"If cavewoman is going to unzip my pants, I like her." I laugh. Pepper's eyes glimmer with desire as her hands work the zipper of my jeans. I am seriously the luckiest man on the entire planet. The. Entire. Planet.

"I'll be over tomorrow with the truck to move you."

She licks the head of my dick before bursting out laughing. A belly laugh so deep and true that she doesn't continue her plight in my pants.

"Moment ruiner!" she says and giggles, crawling up my body. I pull her down on top of me and kiss her until I'm sure she's breathless.

"Pepper, you're my heart. Do you understand that?"

She closes her eyes for a moment and breathes deeply before nodding and nuzzling her face into my neck. Piece by piece I will chip away all the resistance.

Chapter 46

FAMILIES

It's family night: declared to happen once a week, no matter what, by Allie. Not just our new little unit either, but close friends and Dom and Clara, too. This is the second one we've had so far. The weather has finally warmed up enough to grill and sit outside on the patio.

Arms loaded with plastic cups for everyone, I pause outside the patio doors, just out of sight. Clara and Pepper are deep in conversation and although I know it's horrid to listen in, I want to know how Pepper's doing. She's formed a strong bond with Clara over the last few months. Maybe it's sharing the same therapist or maybe it's built from sharing some experiences. Either way, I'm listening while Dom grills and Allie dances around the backyard and Greta fends off Hoot's advances at the table.

"He said I was his *heart*, and you don't leave your heart behind. You can't live without your heart, Clara," Pepper says disbelievingly.

"He loves you. I mean it's obvious how much he cares for you, but I was hoping he didn't really love you, not like I saw when he held you that night...like your pain was his and he would do anything in the world for you, to protect you..." Clara answers.

"I know. That's what scares me. I'm destined to screw it up." Pepper's voice sounds timid and fragile.

"You can't screw up true love. Trust me. I'd know. Buck up, kid."

I push through the doors to the patio, slapping a smile on my face so the girls don't know that I've been eavesdropping. Dom announces that the food is done and everyone shuffles to the table. Taking their seats, Hoot, Dom, and I start passing around platters with various delicious foods to everyone.

Silence ensues as people chow down. The food is damn good if I dare say so. Pepper wipes her mouth on her napkin and shoots me a grin. I nod and finish what's in my mouth before speaking.

"Hey guys," I say, getting everyone's attention. All eyes stare, waiting. I glance at Pepper and she nods at me. "Pepper and I have decided to move in together," I state proudly. Dom smiles his dazzling pearly whites. Clara claps her hands together and gasps while Allie jumps up and hugs Pepper. Hoot and Greta both stare at us.

"Why ruin a good thing?" Hoot calls out, chuckling. Greta smacks him, hard.

"Congratulations," she says over Hoot's grumbling. And just like that, we're a solid thing. A family of sorts.

* * * * *

Everything from our dinner is picked up, washed, and put away. Pepper's gone upstairs to change into pajamas while I take a breather and plant my ass on the couch.

"Will you bring me a beer?" I ask, hearing her footsteps in the stairwell. She agrees. I hear the suction on the fridge door as she retrieves my drink. The bottle appears in front of me. I look back to Pepper to thank her and my eyes nearly bug out of my head.

She's wearing a tank strap nightie covered in little cherries. It clings to her chest just enough to suggest that what lives under the fabric is the stuff wet dreams were made of. I push off the couch, beer forgotten, bend at the waist, and slide my arm under her knees while my other one comes around her ribs. She reaches up and laces her arms around my neck as I pick her up. I press our foreheads together.

"Your nighties are hot," I grunt.

"You like? This old thing?" she responds playfully.

"I more than like," I answer. She juts her chin, angling her face to kiss me. It's soft. Her lips just barely graze mine. Her tongue runs over my lip ring before she pulls back and wiggles free of my hold. She heads towards the stairs, tossing me a sultry look over her shoulder. I don't need to be told twice. I follow after her, ready to play.

Chapter 47

CHANGES

Pepper's arms wrap tighter around my waist and her hands rub against my abdomen and chest as she presses the side of her face against my back. The temperature just dropped dramatically. We have another twenty minutes to go before we'd arrive home. An ominous cloud moves over the sun as we cruise down the twisty road. When the first drops start to pelt us, I pull to the side.

"Come on, let's wait it out under cover." I grab her hand and tug her towards the thick canopy of trees that will provide minimal shelter from the passing rain. Her long, black hair is drenched and rain falls down her face and drips off her lips. Those perfect lips draw me in like a magnet. Overcome by need, I grab the back of her neck, and pull her into a kiss. I step forward into her until she's pressed against a tree. My soaked shirt clings to me and it sticks to my skin as Pepper starts trying pull it up and off.

"What're you doing?" I raise a brow at her playfully.

"Passing the time?" she suggests with a predatory grin. Who am I to stop her?

I pull Pepper in close as we kiss and each press of her lips against mine feels like our very first kiss all over again. There is this electricity in the air, you can almost hear it. I can't control the jerk of my dick as she presses into me and moans.

I lose it.

Fumbling slightly with her wet jeans, I yank the zipper down and button open before peeling her jeans down her legs. She laughs as they get caught on one ankle. Lifting Pepper off of the ground, she wraps her legs around me. With her pinned there, I free myself from my wet pants and with her back pressed against the tree, I make passionate love to her in the rain, our breaths making little fog clouds as we pant into the chilled, damp air.

It's not until the rain has stopped that we hop back on the bike. The rush I get when her arms wrap tightly around my waist borders ridiculousness. Love is a simple thing, really. It's not in the gifts or the money spent. Sometimes it's not even in the *time* spent. It's something that happens in the "in between" moments. The space between minutes. The space between music notes. Love is having all the little things. The hand holding, the unwavering devotion and respect. It's the bland nights of cooking together and watching trashy TV. It's being content in all that.

It's been a little over a year since Pepper first walked into my life. I still get a heady schoolboy rush watching her twist her dripping hair up into a towel or sing under her breath while making sundaes or gather her panties around her thumbs as she poises a foot for entry. I draw near and kiss her between the shoulder blades.

"How was your day?" I ask as she stirs a pot of tomato sauce.

"It was wonderful. I'm really learning a ton from Dominic on running a business." She smiles as she turns into my arms.

"Yours?" she asks.

"It's perfect, now," I tell her before closing the distance between our faces and kissing her senseless. Her chest presses against mine, chest heaving, just as it should be.

"Uhhh guys, can you do that *not* in the kitchen?" Allie snits from the entryway. I release Pepper and scoop up my girl, causing her to squeal with laughter.

"And how was your day, Alliecat?" I ask, keeping her in my arms.

"Fine. It was actually kinda boring today. We didn't learn much," she answers.

"Oh no?! Really? I'm sure you learned something," I state with mock concern. She shakes her head at me, wide-eyed. Pepper laughs in the background. My heart swells in my chest.

"Hmm, I'm *sure* you did. If you want me to stop, you have to think of one thing you learned today," I say.

"Stop what?" Allie asks curiously. I wiggle my fingers against her ribs, moving towards her pits. She screams with laughter, begging and gasping for me to stop. She only holds out for thirty seconds before reciting some new piece of knowledge she learned today.

* * * * *

"Wake up," Allie's voice interrupts my dream. I groan. *Noooo, it was a good dream.*

"No," I mumble.

"Wake up!" she calls again with attitude. I rub the sleep from my eyes and roll toward Allie's voice before glancing at the clock. Eight fucking thirty. *Why?*

"What is it, Allie?" My voice is still thick with sleep.

"Surprise!" she yells and points to the door frame where Pepper stands, holding a tray complete with breakfast, coffee, and a *Maxim* magazine. I barely notice the tray, though; Pepper is there in bare feet, wearing a green nightie with lace on it. It's modest but sexy as fuck. Her hair is sleep-tossed and her mega-watt smile sets me on fire. My boxers incinerate themselves as I stare at her. I'll have to let her know that later, when we're alone.

"Breakfast in bed, love." She smiles from the doorway. I make some kind of grunt before I snap out of it and come to my senses. Holy mother of God.

"Wow!" I direct at Allie.

"Are you surprised?!" she squeals.

"Very. What's the special occasion?" I ask her.

"We just wanted to do something nice." She beams with pride.

"Well thank you!"

Pepper sets the tray on the bed and winks at me.

"Relax and enjoy." Then she turns to Allie. "Time to eat ours now, pretty girl." They head towards the kitchen and I look down to my tray.

I take two bites and listen to Allie's giggles floating down the hall.

"Hey!" I call.

"Yeah?" Pepper calls back.

"It's lonely in here. Come eat with me." My two favorite people carry their plates to my bedroom, hop on the bed with me, and we all eat our breakfast together. This life I've found, the one I've claimed, has sorted itself out. The wrinkles dissipate a little more each day, leaving behind a smooth, stunning surface.

Epilogue

PEPPER PHILIPS

Life is what Sawyer gives me. It's the most amazing gift to give, really. Every moment I am with him I feel alive. For so long I lived with grief and lies. Grief is a place where a person goes alone. A windowless space where you can't see a way out. I've never been good at saying out loud what really matters to me but, I'm working on that. Because if you wait for the right time, you end up running out of time. Without Sawyer there is no color, no passion, there is no fun in existing. He ignites a fire inside my soul that helps heal me.

There is a certain safety in pretending you are okay. Real pain requires actual feeling. It hurts. If you don't feel it, though, you'll never accept it, move on, and heal. It's been hard for me to face everything I've experienced. Yet, somehow I've managed, and all along Sawyer's been right next to me, supporting me.

"Mmmm," he growls in my ear as his arms tighten around me. "Love wakin' up with you." And cue the belly whoosh. It never gets old. It never goes away. He makes my stomach feel like we've hit a big bump in the road and are in mid-air. He tells me this almost every morning we wake up together. Every morning I need to hear his words. They bring a calm peace with them.

"I think you *overuse* the words 'I love you,'" I tease him.

"Maybe I should just show you," he grumbles as his hands slide up under my nightie. I have invested in a few new ones after finding out how much he likes them on me. This one is pale green with lace trim. It seems to be his favorite.

"Hop to it then." I smirk. He chuckles and then gets to it.

* * * * *

Today we are spending a day lazily hanging around the house. Allie had picked the first two movies and is now playing in her room after declaring Sawyer's movie choice boring.

His arms are wound tightly around me as I snuggle into his hard, large frame before the movie comes on. His thumb draws slow circles on my hip. The circling thumb hooks my pj pants and pulls them lower to expose more of the tattoo he recently did for me. Tiny lettering on my hip spells out "*Adapted.*" It's my own personal "*fuck you*" to the universe. I made it. I survived. I thrived. And I did it while finding happiness. No small feat. Beside the word is a small aster flower. I'd finally told him about my cousin Aster and how much I love and miss her. About how, like him, she just was. She's a constant in my life. I don't need her physically around because I've got her words inside me. In my heart and head. Her support and love lives there, deeply rooted in me. I'd finally been able to tell him everything about my life before Christiansburg and it felt so good.

Every Wednesday he comes into work to have lunch with me, declaring he needs time with his woman. Needless to say, I've been swept off my feet. My head is stuck in the clouds and I count my lucky stars for that every single day. I didn't think I'd have this. A life. A full life. Something to look forward to every day. Someone to look forward to every day. This man next to me, he didn't fix me. He allowed me the space and time I needed to fix myself. The idea of love was so embarrassing to me when we first met. I was this awkward and uncomfortable thing who was running out of places to hide. But Sawyer's love grew in me like a tumor, like a parasite bent on devouring its host. I let him devour me. I let him grow inside me and the result it has yielded is the most astonishing reward.

"Stop that." I giggle and swat at him. He captures my hand in his, twining our fingers together as we settle in to watch his movie.

After Ezra, Sawyer had stuck to me like glue for the first few weeks. I assured him I was fine but he wouldn't quit. Then, although I really thought I was fine, I started having nightmares. Sawyer was a saint. I was fine all day and a mess all night for the better part of a month. He found a trauma counselor via Clara and set up appointments for me after my return from the *retreat*. Still, every time I had a bad dream, Sawyer pulled me tightly to him and whispered in my ear that I was safe until I fell back to sleep.

Now a night devoid of nightmares happens plenty or by mostly avoiding sleep—the things that man can do with his mouth. They happen much less frequently but Sawyer's always in bed next to me, ready to distract. It's a secure feeling for me. One I lacked in the past. There are moments when I feel like the exchange of air between us is life altering. As if somehow his oxygen is more pure than mine. But that being near him, with him, allows me to share his pureness of heart. That sharing the air he breathes is all it takes to set my soul on fire.

I'd tried to meet with Greta this week at the gym but she is mysteriously out of town. Again. Now that I'm more open to sharing things about myself I notice even more how much she holds back. She's hiding something and I want to dig deep enough to find it. I want to be able to be there for her the way, albeit shallow in a way, she was for me. I'm blessed to have Sawyer and Allie but I'm also blessed to have found Dominic and Clara and Greta. The boys at Mayhem watch over me with a careful eye too, always ready to have my back if I need them. I miss Greta lately. I need to call her more often. I need to be a better friend. Here I am with all these wonderful people surrounding me and I find it hard to make time for anyone outside of my tiny bubble of bliss here at home. I'll call her tomorrow and find out when she's due home.

"Tell me a truth," he asks. I tip my head and grin at him. God, I love this man.

"You take my breath away, Sawyer. I'm just thinking about how lucky I am," I admit.

"'Bout to get luckier," he whispers. I grin and kiss him.

Allie bounds through into the living room with a shit-eating grin on her face. She leaps up onto the couch and settles between us.

"Hi," I say.

"Hi!" she chirps. Sawyer reaches into the end table drawer and places a small, velvet, square box on my partially reclined chest. Sucking in a sharp breath, I open the box slowly, trying to peek inside before it's fully opened. Allie giggles at me.

"Sawyer!" I hiss. "It's stunning!" He pulls the ring out of the box and puts it on my finger immediately. It slides on with ease. "Oh my God. Look at it sparkle!" I squeal. Tears burn my eyes. I want to run away and bury myself inside of him simultaneously. My emotions run rampant through me.

"Almost as bright as you, love." A tear slips down my cheek and he wipes it away with the pad of his thumb. Yes, sharing his life, his space, his oxygen is all I'll ever need in life.

"Will you marry us?" Allie asks, eyes full of tears. *This kid. Us.*

My heart, that mass of scarred tissue, *beats*. Really beats. Blood rushes to it, filling it, filling me. This man brought me back. I thought I was broken. Forever shattered, yet he taught me to love again. He taught me to *want* to love again. He proved that the very definition of "broken" means "able to fix." And this sweet, sweet child embraced me with open arms. How could I ever say no to them? How could I ever think of disappointing them? They've supported my every move. I can't fathom a single moment of my life, my future, without them in it.

"Is that a yes?" Sawyer asks, the tinge in his voice concerned.

"That's a *fuck* yes!" I bellow. I start to laugh, completely overwhelmed by the crushing love I feel in my chest.

"Uhh," Allie groans. "I'm really happy, but I think you're gonna kiss now and I'm going to go watch The Regular Show in my room," she rambles before scrambling off the couch.

"Hey!" I call out. She stops, pivots, and runs back to my side. I open my arms to embrace her tightly. "Thanks for asking me." I kiss the top of her head and let her go. She smiles and bounds out of the room.

"Now, it's time to get lucky." I waggle my eyebrows and straddle Sawyer, starting a trail of kisses from his jaw downward. He grins devilishly before standing us both up and stalking to the bedroom. He strips my shirt up and over my head, tossing it on the floor as the door shuts behind us.

Lucky is an understatement. What he's given me, it is more than luck. It's pure and true and tangible. It's everything I never thought I'd have and yet it's so much more than I could have conjured up. *This time* I'm going to show him just how *lucky* he makes me feel. I'm going to make him understand. And there's no time like the present.

THE END

Stay tuned for the last installment in the Bloodlines Series, Greta and Bentley's story, *Target 84*, coming next. Don't miss it, the whole gang will be back in *Target 84*.

In the meantime, try my best-selling novel, 30 Days, Absolutely FREE!

Abused by her husband. Dealing with the loss of her only sister. A suicide attempt that doesn't end in death and a husband who wants her inheritance. Elle's life is a catastrophe. But she has a list and thirty things she's determined to accomplish. Love isn't on that list but it comes crashing unexpectedly into her life.

Ryan's current lifestyle requires a lot of funds, he likes his toys. He married his wife knowing she had a hefty inheritance and is bent on securing it for himself by any means possible.

Boxing coach and personal trainer at the gym he co-owns, Colin's content with his life. Until a chance meeting with a woman eating alone at a restaurant sets his heart in motion. As secrets unveil themselves his only goal becomes holding on to what he's found.

Or if you've already read 30 Days, try one of my other highly acclaimed novels:

Divorced Delaney Peters found her soul mate at nineteen...and lost him. She's been up and down and everywhere in between since then but when hot Jake shows up on her porch one day her whole world is thrown off its axis as she struggles to give instead of lend her heart.

Delaney's School of Hard Knocks- Summer Course.

** The fall semester will offer such classes as Learning When to Shut Up, Asking for Directions, Chick Flicks 101 and The Art of Loading the Dishwasher (Lab Fee Extra)

SAVING CAROLINE

K. Larsen

After a tragic accident kills her family Caroline unexpectedly moves to Alabama in an effort to start over but her nightmares and panic attacks hinder her ability to move on.

Trick's intrigued by the new waitress working at his bar but after some strange behavior he's determined to break through her walls and help her heal if she'll let him.

About the Author

I am an avid reader, coffee drinker, and chocolate eater who loves writing. I received my B.A. from Simmons College-a while ago. I currently live in Maine, The Way Life Should Be!

I'm working on my eighth novel currently. I've published Saving Caroline, 30 Days, Committed, Tug of War, Objective, Resistance, and Dating Delaney.

I have a weird addiction to goat cheese and chocolate martinis, not together though.

I adore my dog. He is the most awesome snuggledoo in the history of dogs. Seriously.

I hate dirty dishes.

I like sarcasm and funny people.

I should probably be running right now... because of the goat cheese....and stuff.

I love hearing from you so please feel free to contact me!

http://ferrarik.wix.com/klarsen

@klarsen_author

www.facebook.com/K.LarsenAuthor

Made in the USA
Charleston, SC
30 May 2015